So now it was payb

He hovered grimly, expectantly, like a thundercloud about to burst open. "Don't tell me you're reneging?"

"Ah, no," she hedged. "Not exactly."

"You can't expect Ivy to go on paying your rent."

"Of course not—"

"And you can't expect to run a tab with Della."

"But there is my book project," she croaked feebly.

"We covered this last night. You won't be making money any time soon with a notebook full of romantic scribbles about a big-city girl wronged."

She set her chin stubbornly. "Still, you gotta admit, the plot's compelling."

He leaned over, placing one hand on the bedpost, the other on the mattress. "Very lifelike. About those dues, Mandy," Brett pressed. "Going to pay up or not?"

It was always Amanda's first impulse to decide how best to manipulate her sparring partner. But Brett was different from all the others. There was something masterful about the way he handled his affairs—handled her.

"Okay, Doc. You win."

FLIRTING WITH TROUBLE
Leandra Logan

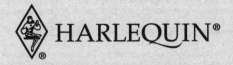

TORONTO • NEW YORK • LONDON
AMSTERDAM • PARIS • SYDNEY • HAMBURG
STOCKHOLM • ATHENS • TOKYO • MILAN • MADRID
PRAGUE • WARSAW • BUDAPEST • AUCKLAND

In Fond Memory of Marge Schoenecker

The streetlight on the corner of
Schletti and Nebraska burns a little dimmer

ISBN 0-373-75020-X

FLIRTING WITH TROUBLE

Visit us at www.eHarlequin.com

Printed in U.S.A.

ABOUT THE AUTHOR

Leandra Logan is an award-winning author of over thirty novels. A native of Minnesota, she enjoys writing stories with a midwestern flavor, full of realistic characters of all ages. She presently lives in the historic town of Stillwater with her husband and two children.

Books by Leandra Logan

HARLEQUIN AMERICAN ROMANCE

Chapter One

It was the society gala of Amanda Pierpont's dreams.

Without question, her father had made good on his promise to host her a dazzling engagement party that would be well attended and well remembered.

On this warm September Saturday evening, his Grandview-on-Hudson mansion was teeming with the nation's elite. Nearly two hundred of the Pierponts' closest acquaintances graced the spacious ballroom overlooking the river, sipping champagne and grazing on a buffet laden with exotic delicacies.

"Attention! I want your attention!" Lowell Pierpont's commanding boom brought a swift, obedient hush over the room.

Satisfied that all eyes were upon him, Lowell summoned Amanda to his side with the crook of a finger. With a toss of her long, butter-colored mane, the debutante skipped through the throng to her father's left side. Always determined to be a standout, she'd chosen a shimmering white dress for the occasion that would play well off the glitter of the room's chandeliers.

She now leaned into her father, a mere pale slash against the big man in black. "You called, Daddy?"

A small wave of knowing chuckles erupted as Amanda

fluttered long lashes at Lowell. The pair had long been at odds over the debutante's spoiled and spirited lifestyle.

Lowell busied himself lighting a cigar and bristled when she set a creamy hand on his tuxedo lapel. "I want to welcome all of you to my home," he continued. "Some have been here on other occasions, trying to squelch a story, promote a story, or just plain curry favor in general with this newspaper publisher. But no other visit, no other gathering, could possibly compare with this one."

"I second that!" Grinning, Amanda reached up to tweak his cheek. He stretched his neck out of bounds.

"Twenty-six years old and my little girl has reached a new milestone. It's been a tough road, raising her alone. Two full decades have passed since Pamela died, but I will always remember and admire *her* determined spirit. She started out as a cub reporter on the crime beat of the *New York Times* before finding a real home with me and my newspaper. No husband could have asked for a more sensational wife, no boss for a better journalist." He took a thoughtful puff on his cigar. "We all know Amanda's journalistic leanings are much fluffier than her mother's—all her goals are, in fact. But what can a man expect from a daughter with a dramatic arts degree, if not some drama?" He shrugged in feigned resignation. "Just the same, she soon will make me the happiest man on earth."

Amanda winked at the crowd with a thumbs-up signal. "I finally did it," she announced in a stage whisper.

Lowell voice rose over hers. "In three short months she will be taking a vow of maturity. Her days of jetting 'round the world teasing princes, crashing political events and hounding movie stars all in the pretense of supplying readers of the *Manhattan Monitor* with juicy tidbits finally will be over."

"Oh, Daddy. I'm not planning to die. I'm only getting married."

He glared down at her through a cloud of his own cigar smoke. "And retiring from the *Monitor*."

"I didn't realize… Surely my column would be missed…"

If her father noticed the hurt and surprise in her tone, he didn't let on. "Now it's no secret that I've long wished for a suitable son-in-law. And it's no secret that I've hit the jackpot in Trevor Sinclair. Come join us, Trev."

Amanda watched her handsome, golden haired fiancé take his cue and launch forward. Rather than joining her on the left as she expected, Trevor eased in on Lowell's right. Another painful surprise, from the other man in her life.

Lowell proceeded to clap Trevor on the back. "See? He's the perfect *right-hand* man! From here on in I'll be satisfied in knowing that one day our family newspaper will land in capable male hands. I'll pass the publisher's torch down to Trevor as my father handed it down to me and his father to him. So eat, drink and share my joy!"

Lecture over. Amanda inched by her father and tugged at Trevor's sleeve. Both men looked mildly disgruntled over the interruption.

"Trevor, some friends from my spa have just arrived. Come meet them."

"Well…" Trevor deferred to Lowell.

"Go on ahead, Trev. But that editor I've been courting from the *Boston Globe* just arrived, too. Part of your duties as my new executive assistant will be reeling in his kind."

Amanda pressed her lips together. "Oh, Daddy, Trevor can't pander to you every minute of the day."

"Your father didn't mean it like that, Amanda."

"Executive assistants assist," Lowell said. "And a party like this should serve us on a professional level as well as a personal one."

"Engagements are supposed to be fun, though." Amanda pulled Trevor over to her friends. Like the bride-

to-be, the trio of women were in their twenties and remarkably lean from their spa workouts. They quickly surrounded her with well wishes, fussing over her white,
exquisitely cut three-carat solitaire, flirting with her handsome fiancé.

Amanda was always so damn lucky, they teased. Only
the best for Amanda.

Amanda assured them she certainly had no complaints.

Three hours later, as had been their custom for years,
father and daughter stood united to see off their guests,
enduring a wave of perfumed air kisses and firm hand-
shakes.

Ultimately, Lowell glanced around the empty foyer, impatient and gruff. "Where the hell are the Sinclairs?"

Amanda rubbed her arms. Standing by the swinging front
door had chilled her. "I haven't spoken to Trevor privately
since nine o'clock."

"Well, have you seen his parents? Thought I'd offer
them a brandy before bed. The missus said something about
bringing some old snapshots of Trevor's high school foot-
ball days back in Lincoln. Seems like as good a time as
any to go over them."

Amanda rolled her eyes. "I believe I'll pass on that treat,
Dad, and go to bed."

"Sure, sure. If you run into Lydia and Ron, mention that
I'll be in my study."

"Their names are Linda and Roger."

"Make certain they know it's the main study. Somehow,
they keep getting lost here in the house. They must live in
a cracker box back in Nebraska."

"Good night, Daddy."

Amanda climbed the broad, sweeping staircase and made
the necessary journey through the second level's maze of
corridors. No sooner had she entered the private wing of
bedrooms than she heard low voices.

"There is nothing to cry about, Mom."

Trevor's desperate plea caused Amanda to pause in mid-step near a partially closed door. With a stealthy turn, she peeked inside the room that had been allotted her future in-laws, Linda and Roger Sinclair. A single lamp glowed in the far corner, casting shadows. Worn luggage was stacked by the closet. Trevor sat on the old, impressive queen-size bed while his parents paced in front of him.

"There's plenty to cry about!"

"Keep your voice down, Linda."

"Oh, Roger, as if any of those uppity people give a hang about us anyway. The hayseeds from Nebraska. That's what I heard someone calling us—someone in a server's uniform!" With an angry sniffle, Linda snatched a tissue off the nightstand. "As for the guests, they deliberately set out to make us feel like outsiders, acting shocked that *we* are Trevor's parents, discussing business concerns we know nothing about."

Anxious at long last to meet the couple who had produced his precious protégé, Lowell had flown them in for a long-weekend getaway. When Amanda had first seen them in the airport terminal yesterday, the plump and stout Linda in her tight, blue-knit, two-piece and the thin Roger in his ill-fitting suit had made quite a startling contrast to the sophisticated Trevor. And to top it off, they had been extremely quiet during the ride back. The situation had left Amanda feeling rather awkward, responsible for filling the silence with chatter.

Overall, with the party plans looming, Amanda hadn't given the elder Sinclairs much more thought. She took the time to study them now, however. Certainly this family conference was meant to be private, but the deep emotion involved was most intriguing, since it was the sort completely foreign to her own upbringing.

"Mom," Trevor implored, "keep in mind that some of the most arrogant people on the face of the earth were in that ballroom munching on seafood."

"I'd liked to have tossed the lot of them into the sea myself!" Linda scoffed, blowing her nose. "Let the alligators get 'em."

"I think it's more likely the sharks would get them in the sea, Linda."

She whirled on her husband, nearly swatting him with a flailing arm. "It wouldn't matter either way with their thick skin."

Trevor's voice grew firmer. "You had to see this coming. I went to Columbia. I've been working my way through the big newspapers. It was only a matter of time before I settled down with a society girl."

"But did you have to aim so high above our comfort level? The *Manhattan Monitor* is second in size only to the *New York Times*."

Trevor beamed. "Gee, I'm impressed you know that."

"Don't be. Lowell Pierpont is a broken record on the subject."

"Look, son. The job is one thing. We can appreciate your achievement there. But did you have to involve yourself with the boss's daughter, an heiress set to inherit millions—the entire newspaper?"

"Probably not, Dad, but it's making for a cozy arrangement."

Roger expelled a long breath. "We've tried hard to read between the lines of your most recent e-mails. All the glowing reports of your growing attachment to Lowell, the responsibilities he's feeding you. You've been climbing to the top, fast."

"They're hardly the letters of an infatuated man, however," Linda complained. "Don't be offended, but we can't help worrying that you landed your last giant promotion at least in part because of your romance."

Trevor spoke carefully. "Let's just say Lowell's come to recognize my talents a whole lot sooner because of my interest in Amanda."

The elder Sinclairs gasped, as if their worst fears had been confirmed.

"Do you ever think about Brittany Malone anymore? She is such a sweet girl."

Trevor was beginning to lose some of his polish. His head was tipping back and forth and his voice showed signs a midwestern twang similar to his parents'. "Naturally, I remember Brittany."

"Do you ever regret breaking it off with her?"

"I don't know. Seemed best when I headed for Columbia—"

"Well, she's still available. Cute, even at twenty-nine. Unlike the debutantes here tonight, *she* actually has some curves to grab on to."

Amanda ran hands over her minuscule hips in bewilderment. Did any man actually want to touch curves of cellulite?

"You can't blame us for preferring her, Trevor. We've always been able to relate to Brittany's family, could better meet them on common ground through marriage, share the grandchildren, the holidays. A family like the Pierponts will only want to shut us out at every turn."

"It doesn't have to be that way. Naturally they won't care to visit Nebraska, but you'll be welcome here anytime."

"I've never seen you crawl the way you do for that man."

"C'mon, Dad. Crawl?"

"Don't deny that when his feathers get ruffled, you're the one to smooth them."

"It's all part of the job—a job I happen to love."

"But do you love this girl Amanda?" Linda demanded. "I've yet to hear you say the words."

"I'm very fond of her."

"Trevor, answer the question properly. You owe us that much."

"We've spoken of love, of course."

"And you share the kind of love Dad and I share."

Amanda waited for his passionate outburst on the subject. Puzzled over his silence, she leaned in closer.

Trevor hung his head and took in a ragged breath. "Well, no."

Amanda was struck dumb. Her ears began ringing sharply. It was a few seconds before she realized the sound was Linda's wail.

"Four years of college and you're stupid enough to marry a girl you don't love!"

"If her father could hear you now," Roger fumed, "I bet he'd beat the tar out of you."

"I doubt that," Trevor said ruefully. "Fact is, Lowell doesn't deal in terms of love. He deals in methods of control. You've heard some of his big, blustery statements about playing matchmaker to Amanda and me. Well, he means it, literally! He didn't just encourage our romance, he initiated it. My relationship with Amanda began in his private office with my psychological profile laid out on his desk."

"The man riffled through his own personnel files to find Amanda a suitable mate?"

"It sure wasn't Cupid."

Linda gasped. "How could he do such a thing?"

"He's at the end of his rope with Amanda's world-class antics and her insipid gossip column. What he wants most is a responsible male on board, preparing to take over the reins of the newspaper, capable of supplying him with heirs."

"Does Amanda realize any of this?"

"I doubt it." Regret tinged Trevor's voice. "Amanda is spoiled, even selfish at times, but I do feel quite sorry for her, in spite of all her money. Her dad doesn't show her any love. He barely knows she exists. I guess she's settled for life's minimum, since she doesn't have a clue about real love.''

Settled for life's minimum? No concept of real love? Feeling weak, Amanda rolled back on her heels, using the wall for support. Eight months of hot and heavy dating followed by a whirlwind St. Thomas proposal and plans for a stellar wedding. Why, words of love had been exchanged between them every day. Day and night! She'd totally believed in him, in their love match. Now he was telling his parents she didn't even know the meaning of the word.

What a fool she was. He had never loved her at all. And she had never suspected it!

Roger went on. ''First she settles on her father, now she settles on you? Do two rights make a wrong, son?''

''Don't you think I'm worthy husband material?''

''Of course you are!''

''But you are making an unworthy decision,'' Linda scolded.

''I can make her reasonably happy. You'll see.''

''Watching her flit around that party like a bird, kissing everyone, I wonder if she's been reasonable even one single day of her life.''

Roger murmured in agreement. ''I wonder if she can adjust to the normalcy of home and family, properly raise *our* grandchildren! They will be ours, too, you know, not moneybag's private property.''

Amanda was astonished. The past few months had been the most purposeful of her life, with her plans secured and her father satisfied for the first time ever. Now the whole rosy picture had been shattered in a heartbeat, by the most unexpected source of all!

Not that this was her first bit of man trouble. She'd met plenty of anxious suitors on the international party circuit, but not one of them had ever breached her trust. Fact was, none of them had been given the chance to do so. Lowell had raised her to be wary of everyone, on the constant lookout for fortune hunters.

What Lowell hadn't done was warn her against himself—and the man of his choice.

Unable to handle any more, she fled down the deserted hallway. Locking herself away in her suite, she dived for her enormous bed and let the tears flow.

AMANDA AWOKE the following morning to a bright slash of sunlight against her eyes. In all the commotion she hadn't thought to pull the blinds over her breathtaking view of the river. But it appeared she'd barely moved a muscle since hitting the mattress. She was still curled in a ball atop her mauve satin comforter, wearing her glittery white gown.

Easing off the bed, she padded to her bathroom. She opened the faucet on the huge pink marble tub, added some scented bubble bath and began to strip off her clothing. Standing in front of the first sink at the double vanity, she gently cleansed her face of its smudged mask of makeup, then studied it under the row of salon lights. Her skin was unusually pink and tender, especially around the eyes. She wasn't a crier by nature and what a lucky thing. Tears were murder on the complexion.

But last night had been a special exception.

She'd been betrayed by the two men she cared for most. One was pretending to love her and other was bribing him to do it.

By now the room was full of lightly scented steam. She moved back to the tub, shut off the faucet and stepped into the warm, soothing water. Easing back in the bubbles she allowed herself to relax, to think.

She desperately needed a next move.

Should she just forget everything she had heard last night? Pop in at breakfast with a grand smile for her rogue father and a big kiss for her no-good faker of a fiancé?

Keep up appearances for the sake of the Pierpont name? Appearances were everything to Lowell and lately life with him had never been better.

For his part, Trevor would try very hard to keep her happy. Maybe she should let him try and see if he really had the guts to handle the so-called *unreasonable* Amanda Pierpont any better than her father had.

Might be fun watching both men jump through hoops to keep the newspaper and the Pierpont legacy going at full tilt. Having an inside look at their real motives would put her in the driver's seat for the whole ride. Whenever she wanted something from one man, she could play him like a violin—off the other one if necessary.

She took a breath, struggling to rein in her emotions. Was she overreacting? Being unfair, especially to her father? As it stood, she was taking everything Trevor had said at face value. Maybe he'd exaggerated Lowell's duplicity in the matchmaking scheme. Maybe they were in a meeting about business and Lowell got to singing her praises and suddenly Trevor saw a chance to date the boss's daughter. Maybe Trevor knew his parents were still crazy about that girl back home and didn't want to upset them further by admitting his tastes had changed considerably. Claiming Amanda fell into his lap might make him seem less guilty of letting down the family.

True, all this was farfetched. But Amanda's colorful imagination had served her well all her life, attracting witty friends, giving her gossip columns for the newspaper an added spark.

The small, insecure girl who'd missed out on real mothering, who still held a corner inside Amanda's heart, wanted to believe things weren't as bleak as they seemed.

She glanced over to the vanity, where a small china clock was chiming ten. She simply had to get at the truth of the matter, corner her father for a chat away from the Sinclairs. She would appeal to his business sense to draw him out. If

Trevor was lying to his own parents, it should give Lowell pause—he could just as easily lie to him, as well! Popping out of the bubbly water, she snatched a fresh monogrammed towel from the brass ring on the wall and vigorously dried herself.

Twenty minutes later Amanda was on the warpath in fresh makeup and a vividly striped Paul Smith cotton dress. Catching Lowell in private didn't prove a bit of a problem. She found him alone in his study, seated at his desk, barking into the telephone. Catching sight of her in the doorway, he nodded impatiently.

"Hang on a minute, Carl." Lowell glared at Amanda. "What the hell is going on?"

Already feeling defensive, Amanda arched a brow. "Meaning?"

"As lady of the house, you should've been up hours ago, helping me volley the Sinclair situation. If your mother were alive it would have been different."

Amanda stepped inside and firmly closed the carved wooden door behind her. "I don't need a reminder that I have no mother. Just tell me what happened."

"Trevor's parents announced quite abruptly that they were going home. Happened hours ago at breakfast. Surely you've heard of breakfast. Even if you don't eat it, you should've been around, seated opposite me at the table."

Amanda's pulse jumped. "Did they give you any explanation?"

"Some candy-ass nonsense about his job. He's a plumber, for crissake! What kind of leak needs his specific attention?" Shaking his silvered head, he spoke to Carl. "Call Jonesy on another line. I'll wait."

Amanda spoke as her father made eye contact again. "Trevor drive them to the airport?"

"Yes, yes. You'd think my driver would be good enough, but oh no."

"Maybe he *loves* them so much he felt he should do it."

The mention of love didn't appear to move him any. "Who knows? The both of 'em looked beaten, like they hadn't slept a wink. I don't know. Maybe Midwesterners get homesick fast."

"We really need to talk about a problem that could affect business."

His irritation escalated. "You can see I'm already talking to Carl—about bigger business. There's some kind of electrical short in one of the presses downtown. Too bad Sinclair isn't a mechanic rather than a plumber. Now that would have made him a most valuable cog in this family today."

Amanda marched over to his desk and placed her hands flat on its polished surface. "We need to talk now, Father."

He tipped back in his large, leather chair and regarded her mockingly. "Father, eh? How formal. Must be serious."

"It's about you and me—you and me and Trevor!"

"Then it can wait until Trevor returns."

She smiled thinly. "Maybe he won't return, after the rotten time his parents had here."

Lowell's tone was hearty. "Oh, he'll be back—and soon. I made that directive abundantly clear."

"Guess there is no order he won't follow, is there?"

"He does exactly as I tell him."

"You told him to chase me, didn't you?"

Lowell was again listening to his employee on the line. "Eh?"

She pounded the desk. "*Eh,* who, Father? Carl or me?"

"Carl, keep Jonesy on the other line a minute." Again he spoke directly to his daughter. "What is this about, Amanda? More money?"

"Excuse me?"

"Cash. C-a-s-h. It usually is."

"No. It's about love. L-o-v-e. Do we Pierponts know anything about it?"

Her plaintive cry made him shift uncomfortably in his chair and clamp a palm over the mouthpiece. "You said it was business."

"Yes! Family business!"

He became flustered. "This isn't the time for riddles."

"It isn't the time for me, you mean. Never is." Amanda began to wrench the huge diamond off her ring finger. "When your errand boy returns, tell him the wedding is off."

Lowell was flabbergasted. "I just don't get it."

"You aren't even trying to get it!"

His eyes narrowed. "Leave it to you to go crazy under some nonsensical pressure. Wreck the only sensible plans you've ever made."

"That's me. Going crazy again." She plunked the ring in his ashtray. "Care to stop me?"

Lowell was momentarily torn between his two conversations. Ultimately he removed his hand from the mouthpiece. "What's that, Carl? Okay, good. Now put us on a three-way line."

Amanda stalked to the door. "Goodbye, Father."

He didn't even seem to hear her.

Chapter Two

Retreating to her bedroom, Amanda sat at an Edwardian writing desk and buried her face in her hands. The office scenario with her father was very similar to ones played out in the past. Lowell on the phone with someone far more important than his closest blood relative, his own little girl. Everyone else always came first. Always.

It was true that he hadn't answered her direct question about whether he'd ordered Trevor to chase her. But the odds seemed unbeatable. At twenty-nine Trevor was extraordinarily young to sit at Lowell's right hand. He was still in the process of paying his dues. Made sense that marrying her was part of that debt.

Her father had finally crossed the line with this setup. But what to do about it? What she needed most right now was space to think things through without his interference. For that she needed the support of a good friend.

Sliding open the top drawer of her desk she removed a thick address book. It was little more than a keepsake these days, with everything that mattered to the Pierponts stored in a massive computer system. She began to riffle through the book's loose-leaf pages, smiling over small remembrances the names evoked.

Alpine ski trips with Lindsay Alden. London clubbing

with Paige Covert. Paris fashion shows with Madison Fuller.

The bottom line wasn't pretty, however. Her father had ingrained in her a distrust in both sexes, so like her romances, most of Amanda's female friendships were surface experiences only. It was a sad revelation to accept that most of the names in the book were mere acquaintances.

When was the last time she'd felt truly close to someone? Had a trust thing going that stood the test of time? If it was her late mother she was in deep trouble.

Her thumb stalled near the end of the book. In the W section. Ivy Waterman. There's a name she hadn't heard in a good long while. Five years, anyway, since their time together at Berkeley. They'd met freshman year in the dramatic arts program and clicked immediately. Ivy was a debutante like herself, who always had plenty of money and inventive ways to spend it. They'd been thick as thieves for several semesters, sharing an apartment and escapades too numerous to mention.

With the onset of senior year, Ivy had abruptly bailed out of their cozy lifestyle. She'd traveled abroad that summer and opted to finish her studies in Europe. Points of contact faded away, except for the obligatory Christmas card.

Amanda rarely gave her relationships serious thought, but she was assailed by a strong rush of feeling for Ivy. Their friendship had been a rare and good thing. They'd completely understood one another, trusted one another. Suddenly, Amanda missed her terribly.

She traced a manicured finger down the page, tracking Ivy's addresses over the years. About eighteen months ago she had settled in an Oregon town called Fairlane. In her last Christmas card Ivy had called it her heavenly little burg. Amanda reached for her laptop computer and logged on to the Internet and a favorite map site she often used in her work. Fairlane was a mere dot on the landscape, just outside Portland.

Perfect. Just perfect. No one would think to look for her there. And look they would. When Lowell came to realize that she wasn't coming home for dinner tonight or any night soon, he'd be frantic. After all, how could he hope to acquire a son-in-law and grandchildren without his daughter's help?

On impulse, Amanda rushed to the closet, hauled out a large piece of Coach luggage and flipped it open atop the bed. A practiced traveler, she flicked through her elaborate wardrobe and began tossing clothing in the suitcase, expertly choosing pieces that would mix and match well.

In the midst of this task she opened her small, royal-blue cell phone, called information in search of Ivy Waterman's number and allowed the operator to connect them.

"Hello?" a feminine voice croaked.

"Hey, Ivy Divey."

There was a startled intake of breath. "Amanda? Amanda Pierpont, is that really you?"

"Yes! How clever of you to realize."

"Well, no one else on earth calls me Ivy Divey."

"Oh, sweetie, I'm so glad you're home."

Ivy yawned extravagantly. "It's a sure bet, being only seventy-thirty in the a.m. here. And it's a Sunday. Fairlane, Oregon, is pretty much closed up on Sundays."

Closed up? Amanda frowned in puzzlement but let the remark slide. "It is so wonderful to hear your voice again."

"Has been quite a while."

Encouraged by Ivy's warm and familiar lilt, Amanda got right to the point. "I need you badly, Ivy. I'm in a real tight spot."

"Oh, how many times have I heard that refrain? Who is it this time? The cops? The press? I still catch your name in the society pages on occasion. Appears you're still up to all our old tricks."

Amanda thought she caught a tremor of surprise in Ivy's observation and wondered about Ivy's current circumstances. But her own problems were center stage right now.

"It's Dad. Screwing up my life. The same old story you know so well. Caring more about the family image and that damn newspaper than he does for me." Amanda marched to her dresser, yanked open her lingerie drawer, grabbed a handful of panties and tossed them in the suitcase. "I've really had it with him and need some space to relax and think." There was a sudden rap on her bedroom door. Before Amanda could stop her, a maid in a black uniform came barreling inside.

"I am busy right now, Helga."

Placing hands on ample hips, Helga glanced sharply at the bed. "You are taking a trip?"

"Never mind. Just leave me alone."

"But this is the time I clean your room, Miss Amanda. Every day I clean right now." There was a touch of consternation in the old German woman's voice. She'd been with the family a decade and though an excellent worker, she complained over any variances in her schedule—and was far too nosy.

"You'll have to come back later. Just this once."

"But Miss Amanda—"

"I am on the phone, Helga! Go."

With a disgusted huff she bustled out in a rustle of nylon.

Amanda spoke into the tiny phone again. "Great. Now that snoop has seen me packing. She'll tattle to Dad the minute he comes out of his office. I really must get out of here fast."

Ivy tsked sympathetically. "I'm assuming you want to come here."

"Please say yes, Ivy."

"By all means do. Only thing is, I won't be able to put you up in my apartment. It's a small studio above the local photographer in the business district. He lives in an adjoining apartment and has a stern rule about no pets and no guests. Says it disrupts his artistic flow or something lamebrain like that. The only accommodations I can recommend are a couple of decent motels on the highway near the edge of town.''

"That will do if necessary.''

She hesitated. "Just be prepared for a rather quiet time of it.''

"Quiet time? Studio apartment? I expected you'd still be living it up in the grand style of the Bostonian Watermans.''

"I pretty much cut loose of my legacy, Amanda. I'll explain it all when you get here. But in the meantime, whatever you do, don't mention my link to Cornerstone Jewelers to anyone.''

"Okay. Now all I need to do is to figure out how to get out of this town without a trace that my father can pick up. Used to be easy, flitting under the radar as Mandy Smythe. But airlines, trains and car rental companies are all keeping more careful records these days. My false ID from college would never be accepted anymore.''

There was the sharp intake of breath on the line that Amanda recognized as vintage Ivy.

"You have a suggestion, Ivy Divey?''

"Yes. But you're gonna hate it.''

"Tell me anyway.''

So she did.

"The bus?'' Amanda shrieked. "You can't be serious!''

"Luxury coaches, they call them now. It's about the only way left—short of hitchhiking—to travel without leaving an obvious trail.''

"I bet a trip like that will take days.''

"Several. But it'll give you a chance to unwind in peace and quiet.''

"MATTY, put that gun away!"

"But the funny lady likes it."

Amanda glared across the bus at the small boy with the big cap pistol seated beside his flustered grandmother. She'd been the "funny lady" for the better part of a week, since her luxury coach had picked up the pair in Pittsburgh. The tag was due in large part to Amanda's head gear, a pair of sunglasses and a brimmed hat large enough to conceal her hair.

One day out of Manhattan, she'd discovered her engagement had, at the very least, made the big New York papers. Scanning the society sections over a fruit cup and coffee at a chain restaurant called Denny's, she happened upon a few mentions and some color photos.

Did it increase her chances of being fingered? She didn't know. But before the bus pulled out again she dashed into a drugstore and bought a hat, huge, outdated sunglasses and a package of hair dye. She immediately donned the first two items, tucking away her blond mane as best she could. The last piece of disguise was a bit trickier. She was already a curiosity piece to the occupants of the bus with her nervous movements, but she might appear downright criminal if she went as far as to change hair color midtrip. She opted to use the color the minute she was settled into her motel.

Since that first night her cell phone had been ringing off the hook. Lowell and Trevor, over and over again, appeared on her caller ID. She was keeping her phone on only for the sake of her efficient assistant at the newspaper, Jen Berry, who was handling her column for the time being. As anticipated, only the men clogged her voice mail. Lowell sounded gruff, then annoyed, then outraged. Trevor sounded puzzled, then wounded, then scared.

The members of the dynamic duo, each handling the crisis in his own way.

"Bang-bang-bang!" Since Granny had confiscated the kid's caps, he now made do with verbal sound effects.

But it was all right. They were well into Oregon and had even passed through Portland. Fairlane was next.

It was midafternoon on Sunday when the bus pulled off the highway into Ivy's proverbial backyard.

Amanda gazed out her window. Some backyard. They'd landed at a truck stop with a convenience store and a McDonald's.

"Fairlane!" the driver announced.

Amanda gathered her purse and jacket and scooted up the aisle. "Where is the bus depot?"

The young male driver looked amused. "Isn't one. The buses pull off here on this turnabout. Most of us usually gas up at the pumps and allow our passengers time for a Big Mac." Watching Amanda's pained expression, he asked if anyone was meeting her.

"Not exactly. Not out here. I hoped to take a taxi from the depot—to a motel."

He rose and escorted her off the bus. Amanda stared into the sunny distance as he retrieved her bag from the storage compartment. There were two motels on the frontage road beyond the truck stop, surely the ones Ivy had mentioned. She'd called them decent. They looked like rambler shacks to Amanda. One was weathered cedar, the other a dirty tan stucco.

Setting the giant wheeled bag beside her, the driver pointed to the smaller cedar place on the left. "The Fairweather isn't a bad spot," he told her kindly. "I've stayed there a couple of times myself. I'm afraid you'll have to walk the rest of the way though."

"I see. Well, thank you." She pushed a folded bill into his hand.

He glanced at the fifty dollar tip with pleasure. "Thanks very much!"

His appreciation lifted her spirits. Fifty bucks didn't impress many these days. As she leaned over to grasp the handle of her giant roller case, her hat fell off and blond hair tumbled to her shoulders.

The driver's gaze turned to wonder, making her nervous. "What are you looking at?" she snapped.

He was sincerely taken aback. "Just a beautiful girl." Pocketing her tip, he politely plucked her hat from the blacktop and held it while she knotted her hair again.

"Oh. Why, thanks." She realized she had overreacted. Which, if she did it too often, could do more to blow her cover than any newspaper coverage. With a hat readjustment and a fortifying sigh, she began to plod across the blacktop along a row of parked semis.

AMANDA TACKLED the Fair-weather with a puff and a clatter. Bracing open the glass entrance door with her hip, she impatiently attempted to navigate her giant suitcase over the threshold while balancing her tote bag on her shoulder. She wasn't accustomed to sweating outside the spa and didn't care for the way her slacks and blouse now clung to her clammy skin. Even worse, she wasn't accustomed to males of any age or temperament standing by offering no assistance. After finally winning her wrestling match with her suitcase and the narrow entrance, she realized a man had stood idly behind the counter through her whole ordeal! He was a strange-looking fellow of about fifty, small and painfully thin, with a beak nose and dark, narrow-set eyes. His skin had the color and texture of brown leather.

Convinced he must be comatose, she marched up to the wooden reservations counter and hit the button of a service bell.

The little man jumped. "The bell is for when I'm away from my post," he explained patiently. "As you can see, I'm right here."

"Could've fooled me."

"Can I help you?"

"That remains to be seen, Sir Galahad."

His egg-shaped forehead wrinkled. "The name's not Galahad, it's Geller. You musta misheard somebody."

She pulled a tight smile. "Yes, that must be it."

"You lookin' for a room?"

"Very perceptive, Mr. Geller."

"You can call me Fritz. Everybody does. 'Cept my wife."

"What does she call you?"

"Nothin'. Met her maker about six years ago. Before that, she had a pet name for me that I don't care to tell you. Too personal."

Amanda tugged a tissue from her pants' pocket and dabbed her moist forehead. "About that room, Fritz—"

"How long will you be stayin'?"

Amanda gave an exasperated cry. "I don't know! Does it matter?"

He reared. "Just wonderin'." He set a short registration form on the counter with a pen and turned to snatch a key from a maze of cubbyholes. Turning back, he watched her fill in the form. "I can put you in number ten right now, Miss Smythe. It's around the back of the building, facing the parking lot. You payin' by credit card?"

She pushed the form and pen back at him. "Cash."

"You sure, little lady? It's thirty-nine dollars a night. Plus tax. We all owe Uncle Sam his due."

"Cash is my offer. And I'd like to run a tab for the time being."

"Never done that."

She shrugged. "It is a pretty progressive system, for the trendy."

"Oh, we can do it, I suppose. I'm one to keep up with trends."

"Great." Near exhaustion, Amanda snatched the key from his hand and trudged to the door to wrestle her suitcase back outside.

"Let me know if you need anything!" he called after her. "Friendly service is our motto."

The room proved a cramped eyesore. Insulated gold drapes were sagging on a bent rod, and the white bedspread showed signs of wear. Amanda tiptoed across the worn shag carpet gingerly, feeling like she'd landed in foreign and destitute territory. The closet was the size of a phone booth and the bathroom not much bigger. The latter held an ancient toilet, sink and shower stall, all tinged with rust. She'd always wondered what comprised a one-star motel. Well, now she knew.

After all the luxury suites she and Ivy had shared on the party circuit, Amanda could not believe her old friend had steered her here.

Not trusting even her luggage on the dingy shag carpet, she set the case and tote on the dresser top. She dug out her hair dye and fresh underwear, and headed for the bathroom for a shower.

An hour later, Amanda stepped into the bright sunshine of the parking lot clad in white capris, a yellow blouse knotted under her ribs and strappy gold sandals. With her hair tinted auburn and tied in a floppy topknot against the heat, she felt reasonably comfortable.

Fritz Geller was still on duty at the counter. He admired her with open appreciation, looking her up and down.

"I'd like to catch a taxi to town, Fritz."

"Sure, I s'pose you could take a cab." He scratched his small chin. "If we had a cab for the takin'. But there are only two of 'em in Fairlane and they're busy on Sundays, especially 'round this time. The ladies auxiliary always ties them up with their card parties and flower shows and the like."

"You have any other kinds of transportation?"

"Well, you could take one of the motel bicycles."

"You're kidding."

"Why, no, Miss Smythe, I ain't."

Amanda pondered grumpily. "How far is it to the center of town?"

"Not too far. Two miles or so."

"Fine. Show me your bikes."

"Would like a deposit…"

"Fritz, all I'm carrying is my room key." She patted her pants' pocket.

"The tab then?"

"Yes, the tab."

He led her back around the building to a large garage. Hoisting the wide door, he showed her three rusty eyesores. "Take your pick."

Amanda chose a girl's three-speed. "Now about air for the tires—"

He flashed a boastful smile. "Free of charge, miss. Free of charge."

"Wonderful. Can I have some?"

"Pump's over there near the lawn mower. Help yourself."

"Aren't you going to help me?"

"For that, little lady, there will be an extra charge."

"How about five bucks?"

"Why, sure. It'll go right on the tab."

Ten minutes later Amanda was swinging onto the seat and aware that Fritz was eyeing her with some hesitation.

"Something the matter?"

"It's just your choice of clothes."

"I think I look rather nice."

"Why, sure you do. But that little outfit is hardly right for bicycling. The pants are tight and the shoes all stringy. Won't be good for pedaling."

Since it had been a good fifteen years since Amanda had done any riding, she could not remember what she'd worn. But whatever it was, she didn't have it along. "Just tell me how to get to the center of town."

"You take this alley behind the garage here and turn left."

"And then?"

"Ride two miles."

"What's the name of the main street—with all the shops?"

"Main Street." With a fluid shrug, he sauntered off.

Fritz proved right about her outfit. As she pedaled along on the creaky frame her feet slid around in her sandals and her tight pants constricted her movement. But she was managing to keep her balance, which proved more important than gaining speed. The rising heat of the afternoon sun wasn't energizing her, either. Why adults deliberately bicycled was beyond her comprehension.

Up for any adventure, however, she tried to forget her discomfort by focusing on the picture-book-like terrain. Fairlane was the antithesis of bustling Manhattan, where she kept a Park Avenue apartment and spent most of her time. The streets here were wide with deep yards boasting old, well-tended homes and colorful gardens. Children played on some of these streets, contending with only the occasional car. Adults tending yards and strolling along sidewalks actually waved. Everything was so peaceful and clean.

Amanda hoped she wouldn't collapse in boredom before reaching her destination.

Despite Fritz's topnotch directions, a flagging Amanda eventually paused at a boulevard stop sign to ask a friendly couple for the shortest direct route to Main Street. They guided her left down Simpson to Geranium Parkway. A right turn there would give her a straight shot.

Simpson was set on a slight incline, so Amanda was forced to pump a little harder to keep her momentum. By the time she made Geranium, her front wheel was on the wobble. She rounded the corner, picking up speed on the sloping parkway.

She would have been all right if she hadn't allowed herself to be drawn to the second house on the right.

Images hit her fast and hard.

A grand old Victorian home of deep blue with plum trim.

A gorgeous man with jet-black hair, high on a ladder leaning over to wash a second-story window.

Shirtless. Suntanned skin over rippling muscles.

A blinding pinpoint of sunlight against a windshield.

A crash. A flight. A landing.

Half stunned, Amanda realized she was laid out flat on the cool, moist earth. She wiggled her fingers and bare legs to feel freshly cut lawn beneath her.

If the celebrity columnist were to write her own headline it would have read, Bike Meets Fender, Girl Meets Grass.

Ever so slowly she opened her eyes to the sunlit afternoon. Shadows clustered 'round overhead, bringing relief from the brilliant sunshine. Excited murmurs blended in crescendo, "Hurt" and "Help" and "Not my fault" among them. Then there was a call for a doctor from a loud, assured female voice. "Doc Handsome! Hurry! Quickly!"

"On my way, Della."

Suddenly the bobbing shadows parted and a large, dark, commanding silhouette stepped center stage. It was the same natural wonder she'd spotted on the ladder! Amanda blinked several times in amazement. Against the deep blue sky and golden sunshine, he was nothing short of celestial.

Senses spinning, Amanda opened her parched mouth to speak. "Doc Handsome?"

Her soft croak brought an unexpected round of chuckles. Amanda turned her head to discover the owner of the hearty voice was a middle-aged woman with graying blond hair. She was kneeling nearby now, her face wreathed in a gentle smile. "My name's Della, dear. As for him, he's Doc *Hanson*. Dr. Brett Hanson."

Chapter Three

"Not that Doc isn't handsome. In fact, the name Doc Handsome fits him quite nicely."

"Knock it off, Della." Brett slanted an impatient look at his landlady and made a shooing motion to everyone else. "Please! Step back!"

Sometimes the citizens of the *fairest Fairlane*—as Della Scherer called the town—made Brett claustrophobic.

"But, Doc, is she all right?"

"Doc can fix her up."

"Wonder who she is…"

"You gonna ask her who she is, Doc?"

Brett shook his head. The young woman on the ground was doomed in a way. Not only was she a stranger in town but she was a beautiful stranger who'd arrived quite dramatically. She would be subject to instant celebrity among fifteen hundred or so nosy inhabitants.

To Brett, instant celebrity was neither a plus nor a privilege.

Brett pressed fingers to her wrist to take her pulse. Understandably, it was jumpy. As she struggled to sit up, he put a hand on her shoulder. "Settle back and tell me where it hurts."

Her response was a soft moan. "My ankle. The left one."

Brett checked it for swelling. "Wiggle your toes for me. Good."

"I didn't mean to hit her, Doc."

"We all know it," Della assured Martin, whose car the cyclist had hit. "I saw the whole thing. She was eyeballin' the doc and rammed straight into you."

As Brett held his patient's face in his hands to examine her pupils, she studied him with green eyes that reminded him of exquisitely cut emeralds. "What's happening?" she murmured.

Absently, he grazed her cheeks with his thumbs. Blind-folded, he'd have sworn he was touching baby's skin. "You're up for charges of reckless driving."

Her eyes widened. "Really?"

The crowd erupted in laughter. Brett stood. "Get out of here. Everybody. Right now." Slowly the group began to disperse. Brett enjoyed having such authority. In a small town like this with one lone medical clinic, doctors were treated with great respect, obeyed far more often than the chief of police. With grim satisfaction he squatted back beside Della and his newest patient.

"What are you going to do?" Della asked under her breath.

"I don't think she's injured too badly. Let's take her over to the clinic."

Suddenly there was a burst of patter on the sidewalk, and Brett felt a pair of small arms around his waist. "Oh, Daddy, what's goin' on here?

"Is the lady hurt, Daddy? Did she fall off her bike?" The child pushed a lock of jet-black hair out of her eyes and regarded the victim with concern.

"Yes, Tess. She had an accident."

"What's her name?" Tess peeped.

"I don't know yet. But that's a good question to ask. To see if she has her wits about her," he added, giving the patient's impractical outfit a dubious inspection. If midriff blouses showing smooth tanned bellies were in fashion, they'd yet to hit Fairlane. Ditto for the loosened topknot tickling his forearm, the unique shade of a brilliant autumn leaf.

"I'm...Ama...Mandy," his new patient said.

"Mandy," Tess chirped. "That's pretty, like her gold shoes."

Shoes that should be burned from a doctor's point of view. Unsuitable for bicycling or even walking. Sexy shoes, though, made to display manicured toes like hers. The tiny nails were painted coral, a match for her perfectly shaped fingernails. All in all, she reminded Brett of one of Tess's larger lifelike dolls with her pampered body, vivid hair color and huge, expressive eyes. Her lovely features were actually in perfect balance—which was more than he could say for her riding skills!

Frustrated by his fascination for Mandy, Brett untangled Tess's arms from his waist. "Baby, go find Frank. He's in the basement washing screens. Tell him to haul this bike up on the porch and call Rochelle for me. Rochelle should meet me at the clinic to help me with a patient, okay?"

"Okay, Daddy." Planting a big kiss on his cheek, Tess started across the grass.

"You want me to bring my station wagon around front, Doc?" Della asked.

"Guess that would work better than my Corvette. Thanks, Della. Oh, and grab me a shirt and my medical bag."

Fairlane's only medical facility was a low, red-brick building located in a small industrial park. Fairlane still took to heart the tradition that Sunday was a day of rest, so the entire park was quiet. And deserted, save for Rochelle Owens's green Cutlass sitting in the clinic lot. Brett noted it with relief from the back window of Della's old Chevy wagon as Della wheeled into his designated spot. The clinic's head nurse had arrived quickly.

"We'll have that girl inside in a jiffy." Della shifted into park and shut off the engine. Climbing out of the driver's seat with a large white purse dangling on her arm, she yanked open the back door where Brett sat beside his reclining patient. "Should I run in and get a wheelchair?"

"No, just hold open the doors for me."

Brett edged out of the car then turned to scoop Mandy up in his arms. After getting a good grip on her, he made long, steady strides to the entrance. She wasn't especially heavy, surely weighing little more than a hundred pounds. But Brett suspected she could be a tremendous burden if she put her mind to it. Even now, bruised and barely conscious, she was grumbling about no good men.

Rochelle was on hand to greet them in the waiting room. She was dressed in a snug plaid blouse and beige hip-huggers that set off her lush curves. Her red hair was loose.

"Thanks for coming, Rochelle."

"I was just off to the movies. Lucky thing Frank Scherer caught me."

"Hope I didn't spoil a date."

"Forget it. I'll always come for you, Brett."

Della arched a grayish brow at the coy remark. "Yes, Rochelle, one can always count on you to be on the spot and professional with *Dr. Hanson.*"

Rochelle shifted away from Della. "What happened, *Brett?*"

"Just a little fender bender."

"She have any identification?"

Brett was taken aback by the unnecessary question. "Well, I know her name is Mandy."

"How about an insurance card?"

"All she had in her pocket was a key to the Fair-weather Motel." He struggled to control his impatience. "Look, you know I don't give a damn about such details—especially in the middle of a crisis."

"That's your trouble." Rochelle shot Della a haughty

look. "If you tended more to the business end of the clinic you could lift yourself out of that boarding house situation with the Scherers."

"He loves livin' with us! Any fool can figure out that a man driving a Corvette can settle anyplace he wants to."

Annoyed with the uncomfortable course the conversation had taken, Brett moved past the dueling ladies with his bundle. "Turn on the lights in exam room one, will you, Rochelle?"

The nurse trotted behind, flipping a switch on the wall to flood the room with fluorescent light.

"Help Mandy into a gown and get that ankle elevated. I'll be back."

Brett returned to the waiting room for a last word with Della. "You may as well go home."

"All right. You know Sunday dinner is always hectic, with old Colonel Geoff expecting homemade gravy for his spuds and Beatrice Flaherty with her heart set on the good china." She jabbed a finger toward the inner rooms. "Just keep in mind that that one is way too familiar with you."

"Oh, so you heard her tirade on the male sex."

"Not our mystery girl. Rochelle Owens."

"Della, I don't object to being called Brett—by anyone in town."

"When you're ministering to your patients, you are Doc. Employees like Rochelle should set the tone for dignity."

He gave her a tiny salute. "Yes, ma'am."

Della dug her keys back out of her boxy purse. "I'll keep dinner warm if you don't make it on time."

Brett glanced at his watch to discover it was close to 4:00 p.m. "I'll try and make it—for Tess's sake. Tomorrow is her first day of kindergarten. She might be nervous."

"That child? She'll be running circles 'round that cute little teacher. But she will want you to help her pick out her clothes and inventory her backpack for the tenth time."

Brett patted her shoulder. "Thanks for looking after the two of us so well."

"My pleasure."

"If you weren't married, I'd—"

Della pinkened in delight. "Don't start that nonsense again. I'm a forty-five-year-old heap and you're a thirty-year-old hot babe."

"Still, Frank's a lucky man."

Della took a step, then halted. "Oh, yes. If Mandy doesn't need hospital care, bring her back to the house."

Brett was startled. "She doesn't belong to us, Della."

"No, but the poor thing seems all alone. I mean, no one there on the street recognized her as anyone's friend or relative—which is rare considering the busybodies on hand. Besides, in her condition, it would be unkind to subject her to that nosy dimwit Fritz Geller and a drab room at the Fair-weather. Especially since I have a room available, after Emmaline Josten's passing."

"All right. Maybe it would be best, at least for tonight."

"And you'll get her belongings."

"Eventually." He thrust a finger at the door. "Now scat!"

Clad in a hideous cotton gown, Amanda lay back on the examination table with a sigh. She'd lost sight of Doc Handsome and didn't like it. Even though she'd spent a week-long bus ride generally cursing the whole male species, there was something quite extraordinary about her rescuer. His eyes held a gentleness, his voice a firmness, his touch an assurance.

Doc Handsome was certainly no daddy's boy like Trevor, jockeying for position by marrying the boss's daughter. Doc was master of his turf. When he snapped out orders, people obeyed. Mandy hadn't overlooked his sex appeal, either. She'd spent the entire car ride with her head against his chest. Breathing against his sweat-dampened T-shirt, she'd found his scent intoxicating. Listening to his heartbeat, she'd found its quick rhythm exhilarating.

Not bad for a girl who'd just taken a flying leap off a fender.

"We're going to do a few tests, miss."

Amanda blinked at the sound of the nurse's voice. The tall redhead took her blood pressure, then jammed a thermometer in her mouth and excused herself to prepare for an X-ray. Amanda sat up and took in the exam room. It certainly was a poor cousin to her Manhattan physician's plush suites. In place of smooth white walls boasting scenic oils were fake wood panels with posters of the human body and SpongeBob Squarepants juggling the food groups. In place of a sleek, marble-topped desk with leather chair was a low Formica counter with stool. But, she supposed, all the necessary medical equipment was on hand: blood pressure cuff, stethoscope, gooseneck lamp, tongue depressors, exam gloves, lubricant. All that was missing was *him.*

Moments later the door swung open. Doc Handsome whisked the thermometer out of her mouth and checked it. With a satisfied nod, he adjusted his stethoscope and listened to her heart.

"Still feeling dizzy?"

"A little."

"That might be because of low blood sugar or dehydration. Tell me what you've consumed today."

"Two cups of coffee and something called a strawberry freezie."

"And?"

"That's it."

"Follow my fingers." With a frown he moved them back and forth in front of her eyes. "Good." He grabbed a flashlight from the counter and flashed it in front of her pupils. "Now close your eyes and extend your arms in front of you." He tsked as her arms drifted down slightly. "Okay, now grasp my hand." He gently watched her try to squeeze his fingers with little success, then asked her to describe any other painful areas on her body. Aside from a bruised elbow, her ankle was her only complaint.

"What do you think, Doc?"

"Rochelle tells me your blood pressure is a bit low. And you rated about a C on all my tests. In simple terms, I think you're exhausted. We'll get you down to X-ray, though, for a good look." He smiled as she blanched. "Don't panic, it's just a precautionary measure. I doubt anything's broken."

"Hope I won't need a hospital stay."

"Highly unlikely. No, I intend to take you home with me."

The announcement seemed a little more personal than necessary. And it had to be bringing her blood pressure back up.

As if reading something unsettling in her expression, he added hastily, "Della's personally invited you. Wouldn't take no for an answer."

"Oh, the landlady. I liked her style."

Rochelle appeared with a wheelchair. "By the way, is there anyone in town we can call on your behalf?"

"Yes. Ivy Waterman."

Brett and Rochelle exchanged a surprised look.

"What's the matter?"

"She just doesn't seem your type," Rochelle admitted.

"What type?"

The nurse all but snickered. "Well, she's too sensible to ram into a car on a bike."

Since when was Ivy Divey sensible?

Thirty minutes later Amanda's left ankle was wrapped in an Ace bandage and she was outfitted with crutches. As she eased back into her clothing in the exam room, she could hear doctor and nurse talking in the corridor.

"I don't mind driving you home, Brett. Really."

"You were so short with her in there, I thought—"

"Sorry. Guess I was surprised—that she knows Ivy, that Della wants to take her in—without a clue to her background. You know I like looking out for you!"

Brett's voice was firm. "Ivy's business is none of ours. As for Della, she's a good judge of people and has the space—since Emmaline Josten's passing. Now let's get moving."

As Rochelle's Cutlass pulled up near the spot on the boulevard where Amanda had taken her tumble, the sun was setting on the grand old Victorian house.

"Look!" Rochelle hooted. "Somebody spread dandelions on the boulevard—like a memorial."

Amanda gulped. "It was only a spill."

"That has to be Tess's handiwork." With a chuckle Brett emerged from the back seat with crutches in hand to assist Amanda, who was seated in the front. "She's got a real thing about sharing the love through dandelions."

"Her mother teach her that?" The question was a clumsy way to find out if Brett was married, but Amanda wasn't in the habit of resisting temptation of any kind.

Brett shoved the passenger door shut with force. "Her mother is dead."

"Oh."

Rochelle lingered with the engine running, her expression hopeful. If she was waiting for an invitation inside from Brett, it wasn't to be. With a thanks and a wave, he concentrated on helping his patient up the front walk and onto the porch.

"Daddy! Daddy-daddy!" Tess flung open the front door and stood jumping up and down in the foyer. "Want to see my backpack again?"

"Sure, honey. Stand back now."

Tess backed off as Brett helped Amanda navigate the crutches over the threshold. "I am going to school tomorrow, Mandy. Afternoon kindergarten. In the afternoon!"

Della appeared in the hallway, drying her hands on a dish towel. "Finally! Frank! Come and meet Mandy."

A tall, angular man with thinning brown hair, dressed in twill pants and a yellowed T-shirt, appeared in the living room doorway to the right of the foyer. He waved the folded newspaper in his hand. "It's a pleasure." With a congenial nod, he disappeared again.

Della went on excitedly. "I take it your patient is well enough to stay on here rather than a drab hospital room."

Amanda felt unusually shy under the woman's friendly, straightforward inspection. "This is really nice of you. But I am registered at the Fair—"

"Yes, I recognized the bike. But anyone who lands on my curb gets a dose of my hospitality."

Brett rubbed his hands together. "Boy, am I hungry."

Della hooted. "Then you better get busy."

"Meaning?"

"The bike! Pack up that thing in my station wagon and get over to the Fair-weather. Collect Mandy's things. If Fritz Geller gives you any lip about a bill, tell him that clunker of his is a hazard—that he's up for a lawsuit."

"Can I at least have a snack for the road?"

"Wait, Daddy." Tess dashed into the dining room and returned with a single carrot stick. "Here you go."

Brett bleakly accepted his snack. "Keep the oven warm. I'll be right back."

"I should come along," Amanda suggested. "I'm half unpacked."

"Can't be much to it. I'll pack it best I can."

"But I really should…"

Brett touched her chin. "You need rest. Starting now."

Their gazes locked in a dueling current that made her weak knees grow slightly weaker. Stubborn by nature, Amanda tried to fight off the overwhelming desire to surrender to his will without protest. It seemed unwise to allow anyone the chance to riffle her belongings at leisure and discover her true identity. Taking a quick mental inventory of what he'd see, she decided the risk would be minimal.

"All right," she relented. "I'll settle in here." So much for her stab at an incognito arrival!

The spell between them was already broken as Della crossed between the couple to shoo Tess back to the living room, where Frank was enduring a children's program on his own.

Peering in after them, Amanda decided the scene was straight out of an old movie. Cozy home in a residential neighborhood, the smell of beef in the air. Hostess with apron. Host with yellowed undershirt. It was nothing like her existence back in New York, time spent between the formal Pierpont mansion and her impersonal upscale apartment. It was true that she'd always treated her father a lot like Tess treated hers, but Lowell had never responded in kind.

"Can I show you upstairs, Mandy?" Della returned to ask solicitously. Suddenly feeling dizzy again, Amanda leaned on her crutches.

Brett was quick to intervene, knocking the crutches out from under Amanda, scooping her up in his arms. "Good thing I was still here."

"As if you've even shown signs of leaving!" Della caught the crutches and led Brett and Amanda up the stairs. Wheeling into the first room on the left, she switched on the overhead light.

Amanda judged the decor was several notches above the Fair-weather, with peach-toned bedspread and curtains. The furniture was plain and white, but plentiful.

Brett deposited her on the bed.

"Quit hovering," Della scoffed. "She'll be here when you return."

He strode out.

Della propped Amanda's pillows then moved to the windows overlooking the front yard to lower the shades.

"You're welcome to stay as long as you like. I do happen to have a new vacancy for this room."

"Why, thank you. I'll give that some thought." The bigger question was, why hadn't Ivy given this place some thought before sending her to Fritz?

Della turned back with a broad smile. "Normally, I don't take in strangers so readily. But I liked you on first sight, Mandy. Sure, you were knocked silly. But you seemed so sweet. And the way you called Brett 'Doc Handsome.' He just melted right there on the boulevard. I've never seen him express the slightest romantic interest in anyone the entire two years he's lived here. Keeps things all bottled up, you see. Oh, he's polite to all of us, and crazy for that little girl of his. But not one single female in this town has yet to make his eyes crinkle with delight the way you did."

"Maybe it was just the bright sunlight making him squint."

"Oh, no. There was no mistaking his reaction. And I say it's about time things livened up a bit under this old roof. But don't you go telling him any of this." Della dusted her hands together for a final inspection. "Yes, you should be quite comfortable here in Emmaline's space. Our best room."

Emmaline's passing had been mentioned by Rochelle during her X-ray back at the clinic. Had she died in here? Gotten dandelion sprinkles from the kid? Amanda couldn't help but be a little spooked. "I hope Emmaline's passing wasn't too…traumatic."

"Gosh, no. Just upped and left one night around seven. That traveling salesman did propose, it's true. But I overheard the whole thing and it wasn't a proposal of marriage!" With an indignant huff, Della swooped out the door.

Amanda fell back on the bed laughing and groaning in pain all at once.

"Evenin', Doc."

"Hello, Fritz." Brett leaned into the reservations desk at the Fair-weather Motel. "I'm here about your new tenant. You know, the brunette."

"You mean, the blond."

"I wonder if we're talking about the same woman."

"Sure we are. But she got off the bus as a blond."

Brett frowned. "How do you know?"

"Saw it all through my binoculars. Sometimes I take a peek at the buses pulling in to scope for customers. She was standing by the driver and her hat flew off and yellow hair spilled out. Then she tucked her hair up in her hat and hauled her cute little butt up here to register. Next time I see her, she's a brunette."

"Interesting story."

"Bet it's just as good as the story behind my mangled bike. I seen you unloadin' it out of Della's station wagon."

Brett laid his palms on the desk. "Well, she took a nasty spill that required medical care. Della insists on putting her up at the boarding house."

"But she's officially registered here. A guest of the Fair-weather."

"*Was* a guest of the Fair-weather. I'm here to collect her belongings." Brett held up her room key.

"But we've got our own trendy deal. She's running a tab."

Brett appeared amused. "Consider it canceled here and now."

"Fine. But I want compensation for the room and bike, now damaged."

"As for the room, she hardly could have used it."

"She must've at least taken a shower. Looked real clean when she came lookin' for a taxi."

"So she actually requested a taxi and you put her on a bike instead?"

"Tough to get a taxi—"

"Knowing your bikes are ancient!"

"Ain't that old."

Brett didn't bother to hide his disgust. "C'mon, Fritz, let's have a look at the room, then figure out what you deserve."

Fritz snatched the room key from Brett and led the way outside to the rooms facing the back. Inserting the key in the loose doorknob, he tripped the lock and pushed opened the door. "Hey, she left a lamp on!"

"Probably didn't want anything to jump out at her in the dark."

"Like what?"

Brett merely chuckled and headed for the bathroom. He quickly returned with cosmetics, which he set in the open suitcase on the dresser.

"Big suitcase for such a little lady. But she wrestled it like a pro. Know what that means?"

"That you didn't help her."

Fritz's mouth pruned. "It means she travels a lot." He eased by Brett and checked out the tub and plastic curtain. "Told you! She showered."

Brett moved to the bed and started pushing things back into her overflowing tote bag. A wallet lay in sight, so he flipped it open for a look. There was no plastic, aside from an old photo ID for one Mandy Smythe.

Fritz appeared at his side. "The likeness is unmistakable. But the hair is actually a third color, someplace between blond and brunette."

"So what? Lots of women dye their hair for the sheer fun of it." If nothing else, he perceived Mandy as fun.

Also, among the clutter was a cell phone. Presumably the ringer was turned off, but he knew someone was calling because it was buzzing and vibrating like crazy. Brett rested it in his palm for a moment, sorely tempted to answer it. This could very well be his chance to fill in some of the blanks. He debated the issue as the vibration traveled clear up his arm. Mandy herself sent the same kind of tingly current through him—an odd sort of thrill he was long un-accustomed to but suddenly realized he missed.

She was all wrong for him, of course. And her stay was most likely temporary. Still, he didn't want their unique chemistry shattered so soon by jarring reality. And as she wasn't seriously hurt, she had a right to her privacy. He tossed the phone and other things into the suitcase.

He moved to the closet, where Fritz was now inspecting a bright red blouse. "Nice stuff here. Quality. Convinces me that she can afford the room fee and the cost of the bike."

Brett slapped the man's hand off the silk garment. "I didn't even see a credit card."

"She planned to pay cash, which I found mighty strange."

So did Brett, but he was determined not to show it. Protecting Mandy every step of the way was quickly becoming a habit.

"Dyed hair, cash-and-carry, all sounds fly-by-night," Fritz pressed. "Seems only fair I get what's comin' to me this very minute—out of your pocket if necessary."

Brett snorted. "Fair? You'll be damn lucky if she doesn't sue you. Handing out two bald tires on a bobby pin for a spin around town." He handed Fritz a twenty he had ready in his pocket. "Take this and call it square."

Brett went on to collect the garments from the closet, add them to the suitcase and snap it shut. Satisfied he had everything, he hauled the luggage to the door. "Part of the deal is that you keep your suspicions to yourself. I don't want to hear you crowing about hair color or credit cards—or anything!"

"What are you gonna do if I talk, take back your twenty?"

"No, Fritz, the next time you come see me at the clinic all sick and weak, I'll use your sorry ass for a pin cushion."

"Then I'll go see Doc Graham instead."

"Even worse. Jack Graham is still smarting from that worthless marsh land you sold him last spring." Energized by his slick maneuver, Brett flashed him a wink. "Have a nice night."

Chapter Four

Della Scherer must have heard her own rattletrap station wagon in the driveway. Brett entered the boarding house to find her in the dining room, setting out serving dishes heaped with steaming food to complement the traditional platter of Sunday roast beef.

"Pour the water, will you, Doc?"

Brett hadn't lifted the water pitcher from the sideboard before residents were flowing into the room. His appearance had set in motion Pied Piper magic. People ducked in and around him to reach their chairs as he deftly filled Della's red cut-glass stemware. The whole table was set with the Scherers' Sunday best. Rosebud china and the good stainless utensils were neatly arranged on an Irish lace tablecloth.

Frank Scherer sat at the head of the table. On Frank's left sat Della. Next were the other two boarders, retired army colonel Geoffery Witherspoon and librarian Beatrice Flaherty. Brett sat directly opposite Frank and to his left sat Tess. The last chair between Tess and Frank, which had been filled by Emmaline Josten, currently sat empty. Brett, as yet, hadn't given the vacancy much consideration, beyond the rumors swirling 'round Emmaline's abrupt departure with that unsuitable stranger and what the loss of her rent would mean to the Scherers. But now he couldn't help envisioning Mandy Smythe seated there, perhaps tapping those lovely fingernails on the table during one of Colonel's long-winded stories about the Korean War.

Even now, Brett could almost imagine her faint tap on his arm. Then he rallied enough to realize that real small fingers were dancing near his wrist. It proved to be Tess, watching him with shiny blue eyes.

"I saw you with Mandy's suitcases, Daddy. Does she have more pretty things? Like those gold shoes?"

He recalled some pretty racy lingerie that had been buried in the suitcase, then inventoried the table to make sure no one was homing in on what had to be his dopiest expression. Fortunately, serving up food appeared to be the priority. In fact, Beatrice was about to hand him the platter of meat and it was a welcome distraction. He chose a small slice of beef for Tess and two larger ones for himself. "I'd say Mandy has some very nice things," he finally replied.

Tess clapped her hands. "I can't wait to see!"

"Now, Tess." Brett set the platter in the center of the table, aware that everyone had perked up to monitor his parenting skills. Their interest was understandable. Savvy beyond her years, Tess was a handful to all of them—and a rare Fairlane resident who wasn't particularly intimidated by his revered status. "It's important that you respect Mandy's privacy. That means not making yourself at home in her room when she's out."

Tess's small face furrowed as it always did when she was looking for some loophole. "What about when she's in, Daddy?"

"Then you can visit her, of course. Just be sure to knock before you enter."

"Hear, hear," Colonel rumbled. "Ladies learn to knock."

Tess gave the old gentleman a charming smile. "Oh, Colonel Geoff, I did knock. You just didn't hear me."

"We won't speak of it anymore." Colonel took a jerky sip of water.

"All I can say is, you sure got a lot of freckles." Tess giggled innocently, triggering sly titters 'round the table.

"Mind your manners," Brett interceded.

Tess lifted her chin to scan the table. "I would like some fruit. Please."

Frank stood up to spoon a blend of grapes and berries onto the child's plate. "Sure do miss Emmaline on the assembly line between us, Tess."

Tess nodded. "She used to cut my meat. In nice neat squares."

"So how is your newest boarder doing, Della?" Beatrice asked.

"Last time I checked she was snoozing comfortably."

"Not anymore," Colonel observed with a smile, gesturing to the arched doorway leading to the foyer.

Heads jerked to where Mandy Smythe stood, leaning on crutches, dressed in white satin tap pants and top, half covered by a hot pink kimono.

Brett popped to his feet. "We weren't expecting to hear from you until tomorrow."

"Guess all I needed was a short nap."

"As your doctor, I have to disagree."

She tapped across the hardwood floor with the aid of her crutches. "Lighten up. I'm not used to being cooped up all by myself in a little room. And I like to stay up late. Enjoy the nightlife."

"Isn't much nightlife around here," Beatrice complained, her cheery round face clouding. "Unless you fancy a trip to the drugstore."

"In any case, I'm feeling much better."

Brett moved to her rescue, covertly tying the sash of her robe snugly before guiding her to Emmaline's old seat. Della went to the sideboard to get another place setting.

Tess gave Mandy's hip an affectionate pat as she sank

into the chair beside her. There was a silence then as everyone eyed the oddly dressed newcomer.

She self-consciously raked fingers through her hair. ''I probably should have changed my clothes. I only intended to sneak into the kitchen for some juice. But then I heard you all having fun.''

''It's perfectly all right,'' Frank assured her. ''I mean, you've been through so much today. Feel free to relax.''

The silence returned.

''Well, don't stop talking on my account!'' Mandy said.

''We were talking all about you, Mandy,'' Tess announced. ''About how I want to come to your room. About Daddy getting your suitcases.''

Mandy glanced at Brett. ''I saw them in the foyer. Thanks.''

''I was just going to tell everybody how you should cut my meat instead of Emmaline.''

''In nice neat squares,'' Frank added.

''So you're the star of this house, little one,'' Mandy observed.

''Yes,'' Tess was quick to confirm.

Mandy sighed. ''Well, I usually get top billing wherever I go.''

By now Della had not only equipped her with silverware but had also scooped generous helpings of steaming food onto her plate.

Mandy gave her plate a wary look. ''I'm not accustomed to eating this much.''

''That's obvious, by your waistline,'' Brett said. ''But you're bound to be weak and need to build up.''

''Well, if it's doctor's orders, I better obey.''

That settled, Della glanced down at Tess. ''Shall I cut your meat just this time?''

''No, Mandy can do it.''

She reached over to oblige.

Tess was right on her. "Remember that I'm going to school tomorrow? Afternoon kindergarten."

"Fun stuff, kid." Mandy settled back in her chair and took a large forkful of mashed potatoes to her mouth. "Wow, this is delicious!" For a brief intense spell she seemed to slip into her own ravenous zone, jamming food into her mouth.

"I got a list of supplies in the mail. Crayons, glue. Oh, I love to glue things."

"These rolls are superb. May I have another?" Mandy asked.

Della was surprised but extremely pleased. "Certainly."

"You must see my backpack, Mandy," Tess persisted.

"Think I'll try one with butter. Pass me that butter dish."

Tess carefully lifted the cut-glass dish holding the margarine stick before Brett could intercept it. "I'll be happy to see your suitcase, too, Mandy. Very happy."

Brett was sure the distracted young woman hadn't heard a word uttered since the fork hit her lips. "Tess," he said, "Mandy knows your teacher."

Tess tugged on the pink sleeve of Mandy's kimono. "Daddy says you know my teacher!"

Cheeks ballooned with green beans, Mandy stared blankly at Brett.

"I'm talking about Ivy, of course."

She swallowed with a choking sound. "Ivy!"

"Miss Waterman," Tess corrected. "I can't call her Ivy at school. I have to call her Miss Waterman."

"You didn't know she's Fairlane's kindergarten teacher?" Della demanded.

"Well." Mandy expelled a slow breath. "I guess I assumed she'd be teaching older kids. That's it, you see. Kindergartners are so…small." Smiling, she helped herself to some pickles off a relish tray.

"Then you two haven't kept in constant contact?"

"There's been a bit of a gap. We're old college pals—

roommates. Seemed high time we reconnected. So I decided to drop in on her.''

By bus. Toting a case of designer clothing. With newly colored hair. Brett's frown deepened as she lifted her water glass to her mouth with a movement as jerky as Colonel Geoff's had been in the spotlight.

"Speaking of Ivy," Frank intervened, "she called a while back asking after you. Heard your leg fell off. Naturally, I set her straight about the sprain, told her you were safely tucked in for the night. She was busy with lesson plans anyway and will drop 'round tomorrow morning.''

"What's your profession, Mandy?" Beatrice asked.

"I'm a writer," she replied before clamping her mouth shut for the first time since sitting down.

Brett couldn't help but feel she regretted speaking. "What sort of writing?" he asked.

"Why, ah, fiction.''

"You sure?''

Her vivid green eyes narrowed at Brett. "I'm not sure what to say about it, as I am just starting a novel. In fact," she said with growing confidence, "that's why I've come to your little town. I want peace and quiet to concentrate.''

"So the place you're from isn't quiet?''

She appeared to hesitate again. "New York City.''

"All this is so exciting!" Beatrice enthused. "I've never known a serious writer before. Certainly no one published. I am well read as Fairlane's head librarian, Mandy. I adore tending to the town's books. You must come and give a book talk.''

"She hasn't published anything yet," Brett objected.

"I have written things," she rebutted with pride. "I respect my own work.''

"So you must do something else to make a living," he pressed.

"Well, sure," she said. "I have quite a history of making a living doing other things. Office work, even a little teaching, like Ivy. But writing is my main passion," she said with more force. "I am determined to give this book my best shot or die trying."

"She must have a wealth of angst behind her already, Doc," Beatrice said. "From New York City, where good writers surely know how to suffer, with all that crime and smog and traffic and strong little coffees. Good as published, I say."

"What's your book about?" Della asked.

"It's... It's about a very misunderstood big-city girl. People have cheated her, lied to her. But she is determined to rise above it all."

"Gripping stuff," Brett teased.

"Surely you'll throw in a bit of the old s-e-x," Beatrice chittered.

"Miss Flaherty!" Brett chastised.

"Oh, relax. Tess dashed off two minutes ago. No doubt to get that backpack of hers."

Brett sighed in relief, then with humor tried to make up for pouncing on the librarian. "Still, we must be concerned about Colonel's delicate ears."

The old man snapped to attention. "I am not delicate. I just don't care to have my freckles discussed in mixed company."

"Perhaps it's best to call freckles beauty spots in a romantic novel," Della declared. "What do you think, Mandy?"

"I think I agree. May I please have some more potatoes and gravy?"

"Hey, Mandy Smythe, snap out of it!"

Amanda opened her eyes to find Ivy Waterman standing beside her bed with a breakfast tray laden with food. Her old friend's black hair was clipped shorter than Mandy remembered, but her stunning smile was the same.

"Ivy Divey! What time is it?"

"Six o'clock."

Amanda struggled to sit up. "In the morning?"

"Turnabout is fair play. You roused me last week with a wakeup call. Now I'm returning the favor." Ivy set the tray on Amanda's lap and leaned over the bed to give her a huge hug. "It has been too long, hon. But leave it to you to arrive in town with a bang."

"My entrance was hardly the incognito one I'd planned, crashing on that bike. I must've looked a fool, laid out on the grass."

Ivy stood beside the bed with hands on hips and a smirk. "Yes, calling for Doc Handsome."

"I can't believe I said that out loud." Amanda rubbed her temples.

"Your every word and action has been recorded for posterity."

Amanda shifted on the bed and winced a little.

"How are the bruises?"

"Not bad. Even the leg feels decent." She flipped the covers aside to reveal her Ace-bandaged ankle. "The doc says I'll be light on my feet again in a week."

Ivy glanced around the pretty room. "As usual, you seem to have come in for a cozy landing."

"No thanks to you. Why didn't you tell me about this place—in the first place?"

"I didn't hear about Emmaline Josten's passing until after we spoke. But even if I had, I would have hesitated in hooking you up here."

"Why?"

"Because this is a quiet household, where people take naps and strolls after meals, watch a little television until bedtime. Somehow it didn't seem a fit for you."

"It is pretty tame. Ended up playing a card game called Old Maid for a couple hours last night after dinner."

Ivy jabbed a finger at her with glee. "*You* played a children's card game?"

"Brett and Colonel Geoff did, too. Apparently the game is a favorite of Tess's. It's all a lark to her, of course. She has no idea what it feels like to actually worry about ending up an old maid in real life!"

"Hold on to that thought." Ivy put a finger to her lips then scooted across the room to close the door firmly and set the lock.

Amanda gave her the thumbs-up. "Good idea. Passing along gossip appears to be an Olympic sport here in Fairlane."

Ivy returned to the bed, sitting gingerly on the mattress close to the tray. "As if you should complain, penning that gossip column for the *Manhattan Monitor*."

"It's celebrity news," Amanda corrected crisply. "So you've seen my column then?"

"The bookstores in Portland carry the *Monitor*, so yes, I've managed to keep up." Ivy picked up one of the two steaming coffee mugs on the tray. "You may as well eat while it's warm."

"Oh, no. Della Scherer lured me into temptation last night with a feast. I can't bear to think of the calories. Toast and coffee are all I deserve today."

"Della will expect a clean plate, so I better help you out. Go ahead and rant while I eat. You're expecting to be an old maid now?"

"Could be at the rate I'm going." Amanda watched her old friend tear into some scrambled eggs.

"So the trouble with your dad has something to do with your love life."

Amanda nodded, then sipped her coffee. "Dad finally crossed the line of decency by setting me up with a husband."

Ivy wasn't particularly shocked. "He's always been a tyrant making power plays. Like my own father."

"Yes. We've both learned how best to deal with that

kind of relationship. Gleaning perks while settling for the harsher realities.''

Ivy's eyes twinkled. ''Getting at least some satisfaction by staging attention-grabbing antics.''

''Do you remember the time we impersonated Swiss dignitaries to crash that garden party at Liz Taylor's?''

''Our accents were awful!'' Ivy doubled over with laughter. ''Your father had to fly to California to bail us out of jail!''

''He didn't *have* to come himself, he could've sent a lawyer. Truth was, he wanted to meet Liz and hoped to do so by offering an apology on our behalf. In the end they became great friends.''

''Remember the time we got lost in Italy and my father had to organize a search party to comb the countryside?''

''Found us just as we were getting cozy with those adorable vintners. Your father got some very choice cases of wine out of that one.'' Amanda grew pensive. ''You know, even when we tried our best to cause them static, they always seemed to walk away winners.''

Ivy shrugged. ''Just the same, I guess it's no mystery why at age twenty-six, Lowell would want you out of circulation permanently, be anxious to help the cause with some matchmaking.''

''I understand that he longs for a son-in-law, descendants. But tricking me to get those things is unforgivable. Why, it appears he scavenged his own personnel files for just the right prototype male to lure me in.''

''And his selection…''

''Was on target! Trevor Sinclair is everything I've always been attracted to, sinfully handsome, conversant in all social situations, a snappy dresser thoughtful enough to complement my clothes. The months of our affair were blissful. And just as important, a sort of euphoria even set in over my relationship with Dad. Finally, he and I agreed on a man—my future. It felt so good to be getting Dad's attention the easy way for a change. A fairy tale ending seemed a certainty—until I learned that together the two of them set me up like a clay pigeon.''

Ivy appeared puzzled. ''You dated this Trevor for months, clicked with him. So what if your father found him first? Why make it an issue?''

''Because Trevor never was sincere about me. I happened by his parents' guest room after our engagement party and could tell something big was going down. Since I was being discussed, I felt I had a right to listen.''

''Of course!''

''It was clear they didn't like me much.''

''Any man with guts would have defended you.''

''He did defend our marriage plans, all right. Laid out the terms like a lucrative business deal!''

''No wonder your father likes him so much. So how did his parents respond?''

''Badly. They want him to marry for love.''

''And his reaction to that?''

''Trevor claimed that wasn't necessary, for him or me. That city folk like the Pierponts don't know what real love is. He went on to argue his best case for a marriage of convenience with a lot of perks. The Sinclairs couldn't understand. And even though they weren't sold on me, I had to admire them for their feelings.''

''What happened next? You charge in to bust his game?''

She smiled faintly. ''For a change I was totally speechless. And there was nothing to gain. Trevor would have only tried to smooth things over with more lies.''

''Might have been fun to watch him squirm, though.''

''I needed time to absorb the shock, so I slept on it. In the morning I decided to get Dad's version, see if it jibed with Trevor's. But all Dad cared about was a crisis at the newspaper. He stopped a phone call long enough to chew me out for oversleeping and allowing the Sinclairs to get away. When he wouldn't listen to my concerns, again for the millionth time, I snapped. I dropped my engagement ring in his ashtray and called off the whole thing. Then I called you and hopped a bus.''

"So neither man has the real picture.''

"No. Judging by their voice mails, they've taken a united stand, decided I'm simply pulling one of my attention-grabbing stunts. They're more annoyed than worried.''

Ivy grew thoughtful. "We all say crazy things not meant for public consumption. Do you think it's possible that Trevor was telling his parents what he thought they wanted to hear because he feels guilty about straying so far from his roots?''

"That occurred to me, too.''

"Was it wise to break off the engagement before you were sure of his motives?''

"I had a lot of time to think on the bus. Any man who could say those things to his parents for any reason is not the man for me. I'm anxious to move forward without him. What worries me most now is that Trevor's type might be the best I can ever expect in a husband.'' She shook her head. "Maybe a marriage of convenience would be good enough. It might be okay, if I accept the terms up front, with eyes wide open.''

"C'mon, you know urgency,'' Ivy challenged coyly. "New Year's Eve of ninety-eight, London, estate of Earl Downs, that con artist cum bullfighter...''

Amanda laughed. "Forbidden passion naturally feels urgent. No husband could hope to be a turn-on like Pedro, making love to me on a stone bridge while the fraud squad searched the grounds for him. Knowing that at any moment we might be discovered.''

"I'm afraid I still don't have the experience to guide you,'' Ivy admitted.

"All I know for sure is that I'm suddenly very confused about what love is. I thought I had it down this time. Everything fell into place like never before. Being tricked has been painful and humbling. I don't even know if I loved Trevor in the right way because I don't know for sure what it's supposed to feel like." She fluttered her fingers helplessly. "Maybe it was all just an infatuation. Maybe I'll grow into the old maid who never was able to tell the difference!"

Ivy seemed surprised by the depth of Amanda's concerns. "You just need time to mend. As you've noticed, there's plenty of time for things here in Fairlane."

"And this is a place you've settled in? On purpose?" Amanda was bewildered. "I simply can't get over it, finding you in this one-horse town, teaching children. And what's up with you not wanting me to reveal your background to anyone? You aren't in hiding, too, are you?"

"Not really." Ivy glanced at her watch. "Still, it's a long story that will have to wait."

"Give me something to go on."

Ivy raked her fingers through her short hair. "I'm sort of on the outs with the Waterman clan, so there never was a reason to mention them. I don't have their wealth behind me anymore and wouldn't want people to think I do."

This was enough to temporarily satisfy Amanda. "Just like the old days, we're backing each other up."

"Right."

They shook crooked right pinkies to seal the deal, the way they had in college. Ivy stood as if to leave, then a thought seemed to occur to her.

"What have you told people about your situation so far?"

"I told them I went to college with you. That I am here for some peace, in which to write a novel."

"Oh, no! A novel?"

"Well, under the influence of painkillers, mind you, I blurted out that I'm a writer. Then I realized that admitting to being a celebrity columnist would only arouse unwanted interest. So I improvised with the first red herring I could think of.''

''Guess we'll just have to work with it.''

''What's wrong now?''

''For starters, Beatrice must've went nuts.''

''She was pleased.''

''Yes. She adores books. Did you claim to be published?''

''No.''

''At least that's something. She'd have marched right to the card catalog to look you up.''

''So no harm done.''

''No? After working with Beatrice a whole summer, I know she is a wannabe author who is too scared to give it a shot. Kids of all ages come to her for writing tips, help with their work. She lives vicariously through local budding writers. So no doubt she'll be keeping a close eye on your progress, anxious to be involved.''

''But I'm not really planning to write a book.''

''Not so fast. What is it supposed to be about?''

Amanda lifted her chin. ''A big-city girl who's been cheated and lied to.''

''Ah, autobiographical. Shouldn't be too hard to come up with a rough draft to throw people off the scent.''

Amanda balked. ''It's only an idea. A darn good one, but nothing more. I hoped to take a break—from everything! Relax.''

''And feel sorry for yourself, no doubt.''

''Well, sure. I've been cheated and lied to.''

''Well, unfortunately, you've made your own trouble with this cover story. You'll simply have to make an attempt to live up to it to divert suspicion.''

''I will be laid up for a while. I suppose I could jot down some notes.''

''Bring any paper?''

''Well, no.''

"I'll get you supplies." Ivy brushed some toast crumbs from her blouse onto the tray. "I suppose you wouldn't want to go back to the motel after your bandage comes off."

"No, Ivy. That place is awful." Watching Ivy bite her lip, she added, "I promise to be good."

Ivy sighed indulgently. "So, have you discussed rent with the Scherers?"

"Not yet."

"I hear their going rate is two hundred bucks a week."

"Fine. Naturally, Dad would be able to trace any checks or credit cards, but I have some hundreds concealed in the lining of my tote bag."

"How do you intend to explain your ability to flash hundreds all over Fairlane?"

"Must one explain flashing hundreds?"

"In a town this size? You betcha." Ivy grew thoughtful. "Did you happen to give the impression that you have a great job to support you while you're writing?"

"Well, no."

"Then people will wonder how a starving artist came into so much cash."

"Oops."

"We'll have to work around the problem." Ivy went to collect the tote bag leaning against the dresser. "Give me four bills for starters. I'll write Della a check for your first week and get you change for the rest, so you'll have expense money."

Amanda dug out the bills and handed them over. Ivy stuffed them into her pocket and lifted the breakfast tray off the bed. "I'll have a talk with Della right now. Settle up."

"But we haven't even talked about Brett."

"What about him?"

"Is he as irresistible as I think he is? Or is it a doctor-crush thing going on in my rattled noggin?"

"Half the town has a crush on the doc," Ivy admitted. "Every functioning female, even a gay man or two. In medical terms, you might call it an epidemic."

"Where do you stand?"

Ivy replied with reluctance. "Been there, done that."

"You dated Brett?"

"A few times shortly after I hit town."

"And?"

"He's a tough man to know, Amanda. Quiet and polite. It was a bad mix at the time, as I was very vulnerable, trying to reinvent myself. He'd only been in town himself for about six months and I sensed he was doing the same." She shrugged. "Both on guard, we didn't make any connection."

"How do things stand between the two of you now?"

"We're great friends. Brett's fine, as long as he doesn't feel his shell is being cracked.

Amanda sighed dreamily. "Can't imagine him ever jumping through one of Dad's hoops."

Ivy balanced the tray with one hand and put a hand on the doorknob. "Surely you can't in your wildest dreams envision yourself with Brett. He enjoys being planted here, feeding off the familiar. You love roaming the world, feeding off the unexpected."

"I'm just indulging in a little harmless fantasy. In a way I'd be his perfect match, being too self-absorbed to care about his inner turmoil. He couldn't possibly ever view me as a threat."

Ivy was in the process of swinging open the door during Amanda's announcement. Both girls gasped. On the threshold stood Doc Handsome himself.

Chapter Five

"Good morning, ladies." Brett entered the bedroom. Dressed in a pale blue Oxford shirt and navy slacks, his black hair damp and combed, he looked cool and professional. His expression was wary, however.

"Thanks for rescuing my friend yesterday," Ivy said.

He smiled thinly at Ivy. "Just when we thought you dropped out of the sky with no past, Mandy Smythe bounces onto our boulevard. Makes a man wonder if there's more to you than meets the eye."

Brushing past a gaping Ivy, Brett approached the bed and took Amanda's bandaged ankle in his hand. "Looks good, only minor swelling. You'll be able to scoot around on crutches—as long as you don't overdo it."

"That's great."

"If you'd like to shower now, we can wrap your foot in a bag."

She slanted him what she hoped was a crafty smile. "I usually take bubble baths."

"Oh." His expression betrayed interest, then a measure of restraint. "In that case, you can still use the bag. First sit on the edge of the tub, then swing over— Maybe I should show you. I have a minute or two to spare."

Amanda gazed into his deep blue eyes, imagining him participating in one of her luxuriant soaks. For a change she had trouble finding her voice. "No thanks. I can manage on my own."

He patted her hand in a dismissive gesture. "Okay. Be sure to let Della know your plans, though, in case you end up in an awkward position."

Worse than this one? Amanda glanced back to Ivy to find her shaking in a silent chuckle. She was glad her old friend was showing some sense of humor about the situation, because sparks were going to be zinging through this old house. Amanda might not know diddly about love, but she was an expert on infatuation.

Brett rose and stood by the bed. "So how long are you planning to stay with us, Mandy?"

"I'm not sure," she said. "A while. Why?"

"Well, Della would never say anything, being proud and hospitable, but we boarders are in the habit of helping with chores."

"Chores?"

"You've heard of them, of course."

Yes, and that was about all. Staff hired by her father had always seen to her every whim.

"Like my washing the windows yesterday," he prompted.

"That kind of chore is way too dangerous."

"Not really—"

"I mean to girls like me." She aimed a finger at him. "If you'd have kept grounded with your shirt on, I wouldn't have been distracted enough to fall."

He looked both mildly shocked and greatly amused. "We'll make it easier on you. No climbing. And by all means, keep *your* shirt on. Especially for Colonel's sake. His old ticker isn't what it used to be." Brett glanced at his watch. "Guess we're good for now."

If he was hoping to part on a savvy note, he was to be disappointed. He hadn't taken three steps before Tess appeared in the doorway. She was dressed in a light green jumper and white T-shirt. A pink helmet tucked under her arm, her cherubic face was set indignantly.

"Hey, you girls locked me out before!"

Ivy calmly tapped Tess's nose. "No, dear, I locked us in. And you know you are supposed to call me Miss Waterman on school days."

"I will. At school." With that she barreled past Ivy and Brett and bounced atop the bed, narrowly missing Amanda's bad ankle. "Hi, Mandy. When you ride your bike you should wear a helmet. Like this." Tess plunked it on her own head and tightened the strap under her chin. "Then you won't jiggle your marbles if you fall."

"Jiggle my marbles?"

"That's what Della said you did. When you called Daddy handsome instead of Hanson."

Amanda laughed, enchanted with the rambunctious child who reminded her very much of herself at that age. There was something else familiar about Tess that tickled at the fringes of Amanda's mind, but she couldn't put a finger on it.

Brett rubbed the back of his neck. He looked increasingly uncomfortable. "It must be almost time for school, Tess."

Tess laughed gaily. "Oh, Daddy, you silly."

"What?"

"Kindergarten is in the afternoon," Ivy reminded him. "But I do have a morning class of preschoolers and should head over there myself." With a flutter of fingers, Ivy departed.

Tess grinned after her. "Whew! She didn't unpack your suitcase. I want to help with that, Mandy." Peeling off her helmet, she let it roll across the floor in favor of the suitcase by the dresser.

Brett appeared flustered. "I can take her away, Mandy."

"No, that's all right. Help her wheel the case over here, will you? And bring me some hangers from the closet?"

Brett obliged, then lingered to watch Amanda lay open

the belongings he'd repacked last night. "Hope I didn't upset things too much."

She extracted her cell phone. Like a child caught with something forbidden, she held it in her hand for an uncertain moment, then shoved it under the covers. "A little pressing will fix things."

"Hey, look at this!" Tess picked up a blue gel-filled mask and pressed it to her eyes. "Halloween is coming. Maybe I can wear this. You think so?"

"It has no eyeholes," Amanda protested.

Brett shook his head. "I really must get to the office."

"You should go, Daddy. This is girl stuff." She pointed to her chest. "*My* turn to be locked on the inside."

"Yeah, Daddy," Amanda chirped with a wink.

Brett beat a hasty retreat downstairs. He entered the kitchen just in time to see Ivy tearing a check from her checkbook.

Della took the draft most reluctantly. "I feel funny taking money from you, Ivy, on your salary. Would it help if I gave Mandy a discount?"

Ivy regarded the landlady fondly. "Not on your life. I happen to know Emmaline was paying you twenty dollars a week extra for that room because it's a corner one with extra windows. So Mandy is already getting a bargain. And I feel I should warn you," she said on a lower note, "she may not be quite as helpful 'round the house as Emmaline was."

"She's got a bum ankle!"

"Even after it mends, she may not—" Ivy jumped as Brett cleared his throat.

"Go on, Ivy," he invited her.

"It's nothing."

Brett addressed Della. "I was just telling Mandy the score. Anybody who lives here is part of the family and shares the load. It's true she can't run around with a dust rag or mop just yet, but she can...polish something."

Della hooted with laughter. ''Most chores take two good feet. But if it'll satisfy your thirst for justice, I'll put her on to polishing Colonel's medals.''

''Never mind.'' Pivoting on his heel, Brett grabbed his medical bag off the counter. ''Sure you don't mind seeing Tess to school?''

''I'm looking forward to the daily stroll.''

''At least it'll give you a baby-sitting break afternoons.''

''I never mind looking after her. And you've been very generous in paying me for my trouble. So where is she now?''

''In Mandy's room, helping her unpack.''

''Convenient. Then she'll know exactly where things are stowed for a second and third opinion later on.''

Brett knew better than to take offense. Della's observation about his darling daughter's bold curiosity was delivered with gentle amusement and one hundred percent true.

''You go on, Doc. I've got both girls well in hand.''

He paused with a sudden afterthought. ''Do me a favor and keep a lookout, in case she tries to get into that old bathtub.''

''A voluntary bath doesn't sound like our Tess.''

''Uh, no. I mean Mandy.'' Disconcerted by the misunderstanding, he blushed and zipped out the screen door.

BRETT DROVE ON TO THE clinic with thoughts of Mandy. Hearing the small snatch of conversation between Mandy and Ivy had startled him. Mandy felt their attraction just as he did! He wasn't going to make a fool of himself over it, however. Well, not again. He'd been clumsy in trying to convince Della that Mandy should be treated like the rest of the boarders. And then there'd been the damn bath misunderstanding. He'd handled that situation like a dopey schoolboy. Okay, so Mandy was smart, pretty and fun. He knew from experience those qualities weren't always enough. It paid to be cautious.

The clinic's staff parking lot was well occupied when he swung his Corvette into his reserved spot. In fact, when he entered through the rear service door he quickly discovered he was the last to arrive. Everyone was huddled together in his small private office—his partner Jack Graham, nurses Rochelle Owens and Kaitlyn Miner, and nurse's aide Sarah Draper—murmuring among themselves.

Plainly, this was to be a day for the unexpected.

"Is this some kind of mutiny?" he asked cheerily, wheeling inside. The room fell into a startled silence, faces frozen in stifled smiles.

"Good morning, Brett," Jack said. The blond physician was in the rear of the crowd, but quite visible as he was a head taller than the rest. "We were just debating whether some music was in order for the occasion, a little humming of 'Pomp and Circumstance,' maybe. But, never mind. Let the man through, girls."

Bodies parted, allowing Brett a path. There on his desk sat the object of their amusement, a plastic toy black stallion, upon which was seated a chrome knight.

"Knight in shining armor. Very clever."

Jack beamed. "We have no right to give out Nobels or Pulitzers, but when a fella is a hero, something should be done. And it's come to our attention that you rescued one damsel in distress yesterday, right in your own front yard."

Applause broke out. As it died away a familiar slap-and-shuffle could be heard out in the hallway: size nine moccasins hitting the tiles. It was sure to be Charlotte Evenson, office manager and character of the clinic. Age seventy, five foot six, two hundred pounds, pale yellow hair stiff with spray, huge earrings that dangled like tree ornaments. Like everyone else, she wore white, but unlike the others, it didn't make her appear especially professional.

The remarkably solid woman now filled the doorway. "It's eight-thirty on the dial," she boomed without preamble. "Patients are waiting."

She stood back smugly, allowing the nursing staff to scatter.

"They were just having a little fun, Charlotte."

"Don't I know it," she hooted. "Who do you think got Alan Nash to open his toy store at the crack of dawn for that pony! Fun is fun and now it's time for business." With another slap and shuffle of shoe, she was gone.

Brett moved to the coffeemaker on a file cabinet, poured himself a mug and sat at his desk. "To think I dashed over here to hide out for a few minutes before opening, to decompress."

"Well, blame me. It was all my idea." Jack Graham slid a thigh over the front edge of the desk and picked up the horse and rider. "Pretty clever gift though, eh?"

"Not as clever as the time in med school when we put that skeleton in your bed."

"Agreed. I'll just have to keep at it until I pay you back in full for that prank."

Brett laughed. "How was I supposed to know your kid sister was in town?"

"Or that she's always been especially frightened of horror movie theatrics? She still complains about you, even though she's married and living in Washington."

"Well, I've had my share of bad luck with women all my life."

Brett watched Jack sober a bit in sympathy. The bond they'd formed at UCLA had been the best kind, built not only on chemistry but on respect and trust. It hadn't seemed to bother Jack too much that Brett had always been ahead of him in class rank, had a girl who adored him.

In any case, Jack seemed quite satisfied with life these days, settled back in his hometown. With the help of his innate sense of humor, he'd come to terms with his average looks and relatively uncomplicated personal life. And he was more than happy to share his family practice with a widowed pal who needed a fresh start. It was a bonus that they made each other feel young and crazy again.

If Brett could change anything about Jack it would be his nosiness. But then again, the small town was nosy by nature. He watched in amusement as Jack shrugged, trying not to sound too eager for precious info.

"This new girl does sound real cute. Mandy. Even her name is fun."

"Turns out she's a friend of Ivy's."

"Yeah. Not a bad reference."

"Oh, I don't know. I've always felt Ivy's a confusion, singing karaoke at the Blue Parrot Lounge on Saturday night, then trotting over to church the next morning to sing with the choir."

"The bigger confusion is her nerve. She actually thinks she has a singing voice."

"If possible, this Mandy is even wackier. Can you imagine riding a bicycle in tight pants and high gold sandals? Then crashing into a car just for a look at my bare chest?"

"I've never seen much in your chest. A bit too much hair, a little too lean, if you ask me."

"You aren't taking me seriously."

"No, I'm not."

"That's not all that's odd. She has a case full of fancy clothes and apparently no money, as Ivy's paying her rent. She claims to be a master at odd jobs, in town to write her first novel. But if she has a degree like Ivy, why doesn't she have a career she could have been using to save up for this writing sabbatical?"

Jack clapped him on the back. "I suggest you nose around for answers. Give her the third degree."

The phone on the desk rang sharply. "Internal line," Brett noted. "Must be Charlotte. You answer it."

"No way, it's your office."

With a frown Brett picked it up. He held it out so Charlotte's voice boomed through the room. "When the blazes are you men starting? Mrs. Tremble is out here with a case of hemorrhoids so bad it makes her butt twitch on the chair. Willy Sacks Junior is back with some nasty acne—and he's missing first hour English as we speak!'' Her voice drifted slightly. ''Open a textbook, Willy. High school's been in session a week. You must have homework.''

Brett gingerly hung up. ''All that, shouted out in a public forum. It's so unprofessional.''

Jack stood. ''Breaches every patient's right to privacy.''

''Somehow, we've got to shatter her illusion that she runs this place.''

''The sooner the better.''

Brett thrust a finger at the door. ''You go out there and lay down the law. Once and for all!''

Jack stepped back with a swish of his lab coat. ''Me! All by myself?''

Brett regarded him pityingly. ''It is your responsibility, Jacky boy. After all, she is your grandmother.''

''I PUT MY UNDIE PANTS in the top drawer,'' Tess announced. ''But I don't think I can reach your top drawer, Mandy.''

Amanda was using the closet door frame as a lean-to, hanging up garments delivered her by Tess. Now the child was seated on the bed, distracted by the contents of the suitcase. ''Forget the dresser. We aren't finished hanging clothes.''

''I'm tired of hangers.'' Tess began to paw through Amanda's lingerie. ''I don't see any Winnie the Pooh or Cinderella pants. You've only got funny ones.'' Tess held up a pair of black lacy ones and peeked through them.

Amanda hopped toward the bed on her good leg. ''Those are very expensive and very fragile.''

''What's fragile?''

''You might rip them. Careful!''

Tess ignored the warning and hung the panties on her

head, drooped over her eyes. "Beatrice wears a hat with a black lace veil to church sometimes. When somebody gets married or dies."

Amanda snatched the panties away and ruffled the child's soft dark hair. "Oh, yeah?"

"My mommy died. But not here. A long time ago."

"So did mine."

"Really? You got no mommy?

"Nope. I lost her when I was a little girl like you."

"You have a Della to love you?"

"I only wish."

"I love Daddy and Della. And lots of other people. Frank lets me help in the garden and Beatrice reads to me and Colonel Geoff takes me for constitutionals. Those are walks."

"You do have a lot of friends in this house."

"And out of this house. Ivy sits with me and Dr. Jack tickles me."

"Who's Dr. Jack?"

"He works with Daddy at the clinic. He's got a cool grandma named Charlotte who gives me lots of suckers. But she yells a lot." She lowered her voice. "Daddy thinks girls should talk soft. And not dig holes in the backyard."

"You dig some holes, little one?"

Tess's round face beamed. "I like to dig holes."

Suddenly there was a mild buzzing sound under her covers.

To Amanda's chagrin, she realized it was her cell phone, which she'd stashed away from Brett's prying eyes. She sat on the bed.

Apparently, Tess not only dug holes against her father's wishes, she was also quite capable of raising her voice. "Eek! There's bees under there!"

"Relax, kid. It's only my phone."

"A bee stung me in the garden. It hurt bad."

"No bees in here. Ignore the sound and it will go away."

Tess frantically jumped into Amanda's lap. Amanda flicked back the covers to expose the compact blue instrument. "See? It's all right."

"Answer it, answer it. Make the noise stop."

As Tess pressed palms against her ears, Amanda realized the spunky child was truly frightened. She pushed the talk button to stop the noise. At that moment, her door swung open and Della charged in.

The landlady breathlessly surveyed the picture of Tess huddled up against her new tenant. "What's bringing down my house?"

Amanda muffled the phone against a pillow. "Just a little misunderstanding over b-e-e—"

"Bees!" Tess hopped off the bed and into Della's arms.

"It was just my phone, Tess. Sorry it scared you."

Tess was insulted. "I don't get scared of phones. Just bees."

Della made a clucking sound and whisked the child out the door with the promise of grape juice. Tess paused at the doorway, well on the way to recovery. "We'll finish your undies later."

"Don't you go telling the kids at school about my undie veil," Amanda called after her. "Everybody will want one." Left alone, she lifted the phone from the pillow. She hoped it was her assistant Jen Berry checking in. No such luck. It was her father's bellowing voice. She calmly hit the off button.

Chapter Six

"Daddy!" Tess dashed across the boarding house kitchen to her father's open arms.

He leaned over to gather her close. "You're usually waiting for me on the front porch swing! To tell me about your day."

"I was right here all the time."

He clicked his tongue in regret. "But on your first day of school…"

"It's okay. I saved my knapsack for you."

"Which can wait now until after dinner," Della piped up.

Brett glanced at his landlady at the stove stirring something in a pot, then at the table, where his patient was intent on some kind of project. There were no set rules at the boarding house for dinner on weekdays. Residents were free to use the kitchen to prepare their own fare anytime between the hours of five and seven. But unless Brett called, it was understood that he would be home at half past six to eat with Tess, and the table was always set for the occasion.

But not today.

It seemed the new boarder was shaking everything up, even his dinner routine!

From the shelter of his arms Tess called out. "See, Mandy, I told you he'd come home to eat with me."

"Was there any doubt?" Brett demanded.

Mandy twisted in her chair to look at them head-on. "Well, not really."

Tess stomped her tennis shoe. "But you said—"

"Okay, okay!" Mandy's face swiftly drew color. "I *might* have mentioned that she *could* be disappointed. Guess I was thinking out loud."

"My daddy always does what he says. He's the best one in the whole world."

"Maybe not the best," Brett denied. Then speaking to Mandy, he added, "But Tess can count on me and I don't want that questioned."

"Yeah," Tess chimed in, "you think too loud."

"I probably should've kept my mouth shut. It's just that my father could never be counted on, so..." Amanda shrugged.

Tess nodded proudly. "Daddy always comes home for dinner. Unless somebody's head falls off. Then I eat with Della."

Amanda smiled. "Heads roll often?"

"That's our family code for an inescapable medical emergency."

"Oh."

"Just a little joke in this household."

"I see."

But judging by her baffled expression, she didn't see. How odd was her life? Apparently she couldn't count on her own father and was unaccustomed to the kind of in-house slang shared by the average family.

Della had kept out of the exchange until now, as she brought over place settings. She set them on the opposite end of the huge oblong table. "We're giving Mandy a wide berth here," she explained.

"So I noticed. What are you doing?" Brett approached

the table. Loosening his tie in an unconscious motion, he surveyed her project. Glass pieces were set out in front of her on a white sheet of paper, along with glue, cotton swabs, tweezers and a magnifying glass.

"She's performing surgery on our statue of the Unknown Pilgrim."

"Frank's prized possession? How did that get broken?" He slipped into a chair and eyed his daughter.

"I didn't do it," Tess asserted with spunk. "I couldn't, all the way from kindergarten."

"Did it myself while dusting," Della confessed. "Was nearly in tears to think what Frank would say when he returned from his appointment in Portland. Then Mandy saved my skin by offering to mend the ugly thing."

Mandy used the magnifying glass to examine a couple of slivers of ceramic on the sheet of paper. "Well, it won't be like new, but it will be presentable."

Brett marveled at her confidence and precision. "This kind of mending is an art form. What an intriguing talent."

She spoke in a distracted tone, picking up one sliver with the tweezers. "It's hardly a passion. I developed a knack for it out of necessity. My father has some very attractive pieces and I was a very rambunctious child."

He stared off into space. "Yes, I can picture you a feisty kid without much stretch."

She pinched her lips together, as if perhaps she'd said too much.

Tess climbed onto a chair beside Mandy's and tipped her black head close to Mandy's auburn one. "Guess what, Daddy? Mandy doesn't have a mommy, either."

"Sorry to hear that."

Mandy concentrated on applying a trace of glue onto the chosen sliver and applied it to the pointed hat. "She died years ago. I'm well over it."

Brett very much doubted it, judging by her droopy lower lip.

"Guess we move on from losses best we can," he said simply, pulling his daughter back from the delicate surgery.

"Chili's ready," Della announced. "Come on." She delivered four steaming bowls of the tomato-beef concoction to the table.

Mandy gave her bowl and the landlady a wan smile. "No thanks, Della."

Della frowned. "You haven't eaten much at all today. An apple, some peanuts."

"I'm not accustomed to eating so much so often."

With a shrug, Della settled down with the Hansons to eat.

Crumbling crackers into his chili, Brett asked about kindergarten. Tess couldn't resist popping up to retrieve her knapsack from the counter. Dragging it back to the table, she unzipped it and began to riffle through its contents. "I painted a picture of you, Daddy." She held it up. Brett was a flesh-colored stick man with a swirl of black hair, wearing red-dotted boxers, a white jacket and a cord around his neck that had to be a stethoscope.

"I would've painted your pants but we ran out of time."

"Maybe you can still paint me some."

"No. It's art. Ivy said it's done."

"Good old Ivy."

Della tapped a blunt nail on the table. "Miss Waterman was only teasing. You paint some britches on your daddy after dinner and we'll hang that piece on the fridge."

Tess nodded in agreement. Another grope inside the sack brought a flower made of colorful construction paper. "For you, Della."

"Thank you, dear." Della held the flower to her nose and sniffed.

"It won't smell pretty," the child warned. "Only like paste." Again the hand dipped into the sack. This time she produced a steno notebook, which she slapped on the table.

"This is for you, Mandy. Ivy says you can write your book inside."

Mandy wrinkled her nose. "Good old Ivy."

"Appears you were busy all afternoon, baby," Brett declared.

"Ivy even played the piano, so we could sing songs."

Brett glanced at the goofy picture of himself with wry amusement. Ivy certainly had a creative sense of humor. Wishing to strike back a little, he said, "Did you know, Mandy, that Ivy's quite a karaoke aficionado?"

Mandy responded with true interest. "No! Really? No…"

"Most Saturday nights at the Blue Parrot Lounge. Makes a real f-o-o-l out of herself. I'll take you over there one day soon."

Mandy glanced at the patronizing gift of a notebook, then at Brett. "I'd like that very much."

"You'd like my chili if you'd give it a chance," Della mumbled. "It's quite unique, a little sweet, a little hot."

A sudden urge to give Mandy some heat came over Brett. He hadn't played games with a woman in quite some time. In fact, it almost felt like an out-of-body experience as he scooped up a spoonful of chili from the extra untouched bowl and carried it to the end of the table where Mandy sat among the ceramic ruins.

Waiting until she set down her tweezers, he gently touched her face. "C'mon, now, do it for Della."

Mandy's eyes met his. To his delight, she opened her mouth and allowed him to spoon-feed her.

Tess giggled. "Feed her more, Daddy."

Tess's voice broke the thread of energy between them. "Never mind," Mandy said brightly, moving down the table to her reserved chair, which happened to be directly opposite Brett's.

"You know what they say," he murmured. "If you can't stand the heat, get out of the kitchen."

Her green eyes now flickered with unexpected fire. "That goes for both sexes. And all kinds of heat, too."

The only adult who seemed completely smug after that was Della.

Brett generally went to bed when the other boarders did, around eleven-thirty. There wasn't much to keep him awake, aside from television or the odd emergency. Parenting and work were his only two passions and both required early morning wakeup calls. Tonight was exceptionally warm for September, so he'd kept his window open an inch to enjoy the fresh air.

Stretched out on his mattress, dressed in cotton lounge pants, he tried to settle into the safe, quieting comfort zone that always led to sleep. The occasional car could be heard outside along Geranium Parkway, the odd bark of a dog. All to the background of the rhythmic creak-creak-creak of the porch swing below.

No one ever sat on that swing at this hour. So it had to be her.

Mandy had mentioned she was the nocturnal kind, active well into the night. Not that her habits would be tested here in Fairlane, where things were buttoned up by ten o'clock during the week.

Creak-creak-creak.

He struggled to banish the image of her seated down there by herself, dressed in that little satin sleep set, swinging gently in the breeze, legs propped up on the seat. At least that bum ankle should be propped up. Perhaps as her physician, he should make quite sure it was.

In record time, Brett was standing in front of the swing with a bottle of beer in each hand.

"Oh, Doc! You startled me."

"Just thought you'd like a little company."

"Sure." She took the bottle he handed her, but her first sip was very tentative, as if beer was something new.

Brett noted with some satisfaction that she was just as

he'd envisioned, stretched out on the long swing, dressed in her white satin tap pants and top. She was wearing her hot pink coverup, too, but it lay open, serving, in his opinion, as an enticement rather than a concealment.

"C'mon, pull up a plank." As she struggled to right herself, he swiftly moved in to stop her.

"You're fine. I'll just sit beside you." He dipped onto the seat and adjusted her feet on his thighs. "There. Perfect."

They swung gently in the warm stillness, sipping beer. Brett glanced at her profile in the wan glow of the porch light the Scherers kept on all night. He'd never seen her without makeup before. Though a bit faded without color, she was still a beautiful woman.

She continued to stare at the starry sky even as she spoke. "What are you thinking, Doc?"

"That this swing could use some oil."

She glanced at him then. "Hope the squeaking didn't wake you."

"Well, I did find myself counting the squeaks. And it wasn't proving as soothing as counting sheep might."

"Think the whole house is bothered?"

"No. I'm the only one who sleeps with a window open at this time of year."

She turned back to the starry sky, so he did, too. There were so many things about her that intrigued him. If he could just get her talking, he might begin to satisfy his curiosity. But only begin to, as a woman like Mandy Smythe was bound to be a lifelong mystery to mankind.

"When I first picked you up off the boulevard, I didn't think we had a thing in common," he said.

Mandy laughed softly. "And what on earth do you now believe we have in common?"

"Well, for starters, we both find Ivy a bit of a pain at times."

Her laughter grew deeper, sexier. "Sending you home a portrait in polka-dot boxers was pretty sneaky."

"As was your gift of a steno notebook. Are you really writing a book?"

"I am! I just don't like to be pushed."

"You and Ivy were close back in college?"

"Very close. Losing contact with her was a loss and a mistake."

"Bet you were surprised to find her in a dinky town like this one," he remarked casually.

"Yes! I—" She stopped cold.

"What?"

"Nothing."

"Something, surely."

"Ivy probably fits in just fine. I can only speak for myself when I say the small-town experience is a new one."

"Pretty obviously so."

"Really?"

"Gave yourself away the minute you rode into town in tight pants and golden high heels!"

"I get it. The old fish-out-of-water giveaway."

"Right. Though a mermaid flapping her tail in the wrong pond sounds nicer."

She grew defensive. "I do have good reasons for being here, Brett."

"I'm sure you do."

"The book is going to happen."

"Right."

"Even if there is more to the story, I'm only a threat to myself."

"Now, there, you are wrong."

She turned to him with a searching look that made his heart skip.

"You know what I mean. The little sparks flying between us."

"As if it's all my fault, Chili Man. Touching my face that way…"

"What way? This way? He reached over and tenderly stroked her cheek as he had in the kitchen.

Kissing her suddenly seemed the most natural thing in the world.

Brett took her empty bottle and his own and set them on the porch. Leaning back, he drew her close and pressed his mouth to hers.

She responded eagerly, softening against him.

Heat rose quickly between them. Soon they were flat out on the long swing with Mandy on top. It had been so long since Brett had felt this sort of sexual charge from a woman. Cupping her face, he kissed her urgently, thoroughly, absorbing her taste, her scent. He thought he'd go mad as she writhed on top of him, soft skin and slippery satin rubbing against his rough chest hairs.

It was with supreme regret that he caught her hand as it began to slip into the elastic band of his lounge pants. She was surprised by his gesture, naturally, as he was in full erection. Ever so gently, he eased them both into a seated position.

Breathing heavily, he tried to explain. "This isn't right."

"Don't you want me?"

"Oh, yes."

"Then it is right. For both of us."

Brett's biggest regrets in life were made on emotional highs like this one. He'd learned to be more cautious. "I didn't expect a kiss to lead so far so fast. I'm not ready. Sorry."

She flung a hand in the air. "It's like this town moves in slow in motion!"

"Which is something I like about this town. What's your hurry, anyway? Don't you intend to stay awhile?"

She sighed in resignation. "I do intend to stay, Brett.

There is nowhere on earth where I'm truly wanted or needed at the moment.''

"Then be patient. A more practical place and time will happen along.''

"Gotta warn you, I'm not very practical."

"So I've noticed.''

Urging her head to his chest, he stroked her soft mane with a shaky hand. "This is nice too, right? Sitting here talking, swinging?''

"Decompressing so you can stand without my crutches.''

"So, have you begun to make any solid plans, since this morning?''

Lazily, she gazed up at him. "Not really. I rested, unpacked. Fixed a statue. Thought that was enough.''

"I've been thinking a lot about you all day. It's clear you don't have the money to support yourself, with Ivy paying your freight.''

"I will manage.''

"How? Certainly you can't expect Ivy to support you for any length of time on her meager salary.''

"Ivy insisted on writing that check to Della.''

"I'm sure she did, as a temporary fix for an old friend.''

"Brett, can't you please just butt out?''

"No. I meant it when I said everyone pulls their own weight around here.'' He tapped her nose. "I'm only telling you now so you don't fall flat on your face. And leave me in a huff.''

"Why do I think you have an answer to my so-called problem?''

"As it happens, we—meaning my partner Jack Graham and I—do have an opening at the clinic, for a receptionist.''

She sat up straight and pressed a finger to her chest. "You want *me* to work at the clinic?''

"Is the job beneath you?'' He fumed as she thought it over. "Honey, you aren't going to make a dime lying around here all day, scribbling in a steno notebook! I dug through your wallet for an insurance card back at the motel, so I know you have no credit card or real cash. You're just going to have to do something. At worst, I could absorb your medical treatment, but the Scherers are a different story."

"Okay, okay. Message received. Loud and clear."

"So you'll take the job?"

"Do I have a choice?"

Brett grew anxious. "That sounds like a yes. Is it a yes?"

"Settle down. I'll give it a shot."

"We'll all benefit," he assured her happily. "And it'll be nice having you around the office. If you like, I can tell you about the staff right now."

Her green eyes glazed over with disinterest. "It's gotta be past your bedtime, Doc."

He exhaled. "Actually, it is. You need your rest, too."

"You go along. I'll be up in a few minutes."

Brett kept the door ajar once he reached his bedroom so he could hear Mandy's crutches thumping down the hallway. Once satisfied that she navigated her way safely upstairs, he closed his door tight and picked up the telephone. He paused, noting that it was well after midnight, then dialed anyway.

"Hey, Jack. Sorry—"

"Brett! It's okay. I'm still up reading."

"About Mandy."

"Don't tell me you already found the chance to talk to her."

"The opportunity came along…rather unexpectedly. And it went like a dream. She is coming to the office with me first thing tomorrow, set to start her training as admissions clerk. If all goes well, we'll finally be rid of Charlotte's true confessions tactics at the front desk."

"Excellent job."

"Now it's your turn to act. To explain it all to her before we arrive."

"Run it all by me again, the logic I'm to use."

"Charlotte heard Rochelle complaining about the medical services given to Mandy on Sunday without proof of insurance or payment. And she heard me say that it's likely Mandy can't afford to pay the clinic at all. So it's a simple case of telling Charlotte that poor Mandy intends to work off her bill and generate some income. Underneath her bluster Charlotte's all mushy, has a broken-wing fixation. How can she resist a woman wearing an Ace bandage who is flat broke?"

"You go ahead and make the call, Brett," Jack urged. "You're all warmed up on the subject. Charlotte's always awake till one, watching the soaps she taped."

"No, partner. I found the perfect pigeon. The rest is up to you."

Jack groaned. "All this time, we've felt that nothing short of dynamite would blast Charlotte out of the office cockpit. And all our small overtures to possible receptionists have sent women running for cover. Are you sure this is a good idea?"

"We have to keep trying, Jack. Patients have always been horrified by the way Charlotte bandies about their ailments and doles out her old wives' tale remedies to the entire waiting room. But the younger generation is about to riot over it. Mandy's appearance is pure luck. She doesn't know a thing about Charlotte or her hold on the office—the town. She'll dive in without a qualm."

"But will it be worth our while? This Mandy is just visiting."

"She claims to be staying put for the time being. I don't see her flying off anytime soon."

"I suppose even if she does decide to leave abruptly, we'll have wrenched the reins out of Charlotte's hands. It won't be so impossible anymore to ease in another new receptionist.''

''Sure,'' Brett agreed. But he hoped it wouldn't come to that. Not anytime soon.

Chapter Seven

"Look! She's got the Halloween thing on her face!"

Lying flat on her back in bed, lost in the zone between sleep and awareness, Amanda made out the voice belonging to Tess.

"Remember it, Daddy?"

Brett was here, too? His deep, masculine chuckle confirmed it. His proximity sent a series of quick, sharp, electrical currents down Amanda's spine as she remembered last night's intimacy.

"That's not a Halloween mask, Tess," he was now chiding gently. "It's a sleep mask of some kind."

"What's that mean? It makes you go to sleep like the apple in Sleeping Beauty?"

"Well, no." He sounded stymied. "Guess you could say it helps a person relax by keeping the eyes in darkness."

"You should touch it. It's all squishy."

There was slight dip on the mattress and Amanda felt pressure on her right cheekbone. A small finger perhaps?

"See, Daddy? Squishy."

Reaching up, Amanda awkwardly undid the mask and pulled it off her face. "Hello?" she croaked, slowly opening her eyes.

Tess's nose lovingly grazed her cheek. "Hi, Sleeping Beauty."

"Yes, good morning, Mandy!" Brett chimed in.

"What time…"

"It's 6:00 a.m."

"Again?"

"Comes every morning right about now."

Tess took hold of the mask and held it up to her own face. "Frank likes the Lone Ranger. But his mask has holes. Can I show this to Frank?"

"Do you mind, Mandy?" Brett asked.

"Go ahead." Amanda waved Tess off with a jerky motion. She was in the habit of awakening slowly, privately. True, she had made an exception yesterday for Ivy, but she hadn't seen her in several years. Even her snoopy maid Helga would never barge in this way uninvited.

Rising on her elbows, she struggled to sit up. "Do you want something special, Brett?"

"I figured you'd want a heads up," he explained. "To perhaps use the bathroom before Beatrice."

Amanda rubbed her face. "Why would I want to do that?"

"She has quite a routine with her makeup. And you wouldn't want to be late for your first day of work."

"You expect me to start right away?"

Brett looked perplexed. "Naturally."

She absorbed the news in discontent. "Like today?"

"Like yes. We had a firm agreement last night."

They had a lot of things last night. A beer. A nuzzle. She had been so into him she would have promised him just about anything. And apparently had.

So now it was payback time. He hovered like a thundercloud about to burst open. "Don't tell me you're reneging."

"Ah, no." She hedged. "I mean, not exactly."

"You can't expect Ivy to go on paying your rent."

"Of course not—"

"And you can't expect to run a tab with Della."

"But there is my book project," she croaked feebly.

"We covered this ground last night. You won't be making money anytime soon with a steno notebook full of romantic scribbles about a big-city girl wronged."

She set her chin stubbornly. "Still, you gotta admit, the plot is a compelling one."

He leaned over, placing one hand on a bedpost, the other on the mattress. "Very lifelike. Still, we must all pay our dues one way or the other."

The Pierponts hired people to pay their dues for them whenever possible. There were the accountants who personally wrote out checks for all the bills. There were the representatives who walked dogs, bought groceries, made appointments—even kept them whenever feasible.

Working at an entry-level clerk's job when she had a few thousand dollars in her suitcase seemed especially ludicrous now, at this jaw-jarring hour of the morning. But the reality was clear. Staying hidden from the world was going to take some real effort. All it would take would be one Fairlane resident getting too nosy about her situation, taking the trouble to put the pieces together.

"About those dues, Mandy," Brett pressed. "Going to pay up or not?"

"You always so concerned about everyone doing their fair share?"

"Yes. Stay here long enough and you'll find duty to community contagious."

Amanda gazed into Brett's dark blue eyes. It was always her first impulse to decide how best to manipulate her sparring partner, seize the upper hand. But Brett was different than all the others, challenging her to be good, responding to her coy tactics with strength and wisdom. There was something quite masterful about the way he handled his affairs—handled her.

"Okay, Doc. You win."

Quite amazingly, all traces of thunder vanished from his

face. Suddenly he was bright and sunny, positively adorable. "That's my girl!" With a tap to her nose, he was
gone.

His girl. With a burst of colorful imagining, Amanda
tipped her head back on her pillows and imagined just what
it would be like to be Doc Handsome's girl for real.

"THE DOC was a hundred percent correct, Mandy. Confidentiality is the hallmark of the Fairlane Clinic." Charlotte
Evenson made the announcement with as much dignity as
a woman with pale yellow hair puffed up like a honeycomb
and three-inch triangles bearing the likeness of Elvis dangling from each ear could muster. "Nary a symptom or
cure ever leaves this building via my lips or anyone else's.
Call that the first order of business of my training session."
Her wrinkled face held a slightly bewildered expression as
she shuffled some papers on the long admitting counter.
"You'll have to forgive me. I didn't expect to be training
in a new girl—didn't even know we needed one."

"Perhaps you don't need one," Amanda suggested.

"But we do. We really do." The magnanimous judgment
was made by an attractive blond man in a lab coat, thumbing through a stack of pink phone messages. "You must
be Mandy Smythe."

She nodded. "And you're Dr. Graham?"

"Jack Graham. Pleased to meet you." He extended his
hand. Amanda, leaning on one crutch, shook it with her
free hand.

"He's my oldest grandson." Charlotte aimed a careless
thumb at Jack but was openly pleased and proud of the
link. "All I hear from this doc and the other one is that I
work too hard. That I should delegate more, take more va-
cations."

"Take your first vacation. *Any* vacation." Brett appeared
through an inner door with a grin, dressed in a lab coat

identical to Jack's. "Cape Cod, for instance, is lovely this time of year."

"Cape Cod?" Charlotte blasted. "Are you crazy?"

"The leaves are beginning to turn about now," Jack put in. "Red, yellow, gold."

Charlotte rolled her eyes. "Here we go again, hoist sweet old Charlotte out of her dream job to ride around looking at stuff she can watch on the Travel Channel from the comfort of her easy chair with a stiff whiskey."

Jack shook his head. "The whole of New England is nature's wonderland this time of year. You can't fully appreciate it on a dinky television screen."

"I'm not about to shirk my duty to flit across country to watch leaves change color when there's patients here to tend!" Charlotte slapped her moccasins across the tiled floor, heading for the coffeemaker. "This place would fall apart without my constant attention. Need I remind you boys that I was working here with Dr. Stanley Hickcock long before you two were anybody's good idea?" She glanced at Amanda and jabbed a pudgy finger at Jack. "Doc Hickcock delivered that boy right here in this very clinic. I was manning this very counter at the time—by myself quite efficiently—when my daughter Emily tumbled through the door in hard labor. I left my post to cut the cord and give Jack a smack on the rump. Satisfied his wail was hearty and healthy, I was back out here to tend to business."

The last proclamation was mouthed quite distinctly by both Jack and Brett, causing Amanda to emit a small giggle, which she quickly disguised behind a cough.

"Thirty-five years of faithful service and they still can't accept that I'm a one-woman show," Charlotte whined. "No offense to you, Mandy. Jack explained your situation to me. Pitiful drifter friend of Ivy's, leaning on that teacher for room and board. With a bum ankle besides—"

"Now, Charlotte," Jack objected, "I didn't put it quite like that."

"Well, maybe I'm adding my own special zing to the story, but the upshot is the same."

"My grandmother has a tendency to exaggerate her upshot," Jack insisted. "At every opportunity."

"It's just that I have my routine, my ways, my system."

"So teach them to Mandy."

"Nobody's ever lasted long," Charlotte cautioned her. "Been a while since anybody tried."

Amanda glanced to Brett, then to Jack. Neither one of them would meet her eyes. At best, this situation was fishy.

MEANWHILE, Tess was entering her new friend Mandy's room to return the sleep mask. It had been good fun, showing it to Frank, wearing it herself, putting it on her dolly. Sleep masks were great fun. Next time she painted Daddy in kindergarten, she was going to paint one on him.

Mandy's little phone was buzzing again! From within the dresser this time. Top drawer. But Mandy said not to be afraid. It wasn't bees. She could make it stop like Mandy did the last time.

Tess stood on tiptoe, opened the drawer and rooted through the heap of undies. Curling her fingers around the phone, she took it out for a closer look. Mandy would want her to stop the buzz. It might scare somebody else. Tess pushed the square button Mandy did, only to hear a gruff voice calling out. She couldn't resist holding the phone up to her ear.

"Anyone there? Answer me!"

"I'm here, mister."

"Finally! Who are you?"

"Mandy's very good friend."

"Oh, really. Mandy, is it?"

"That's her name, isn't it?"

"Well, yes. Her mother called her that."

"Her mommy died."

"I know. This is her father. Lowell."

"That's a funny name."

"How impertinent."

"What's that mean?"

"Never mind. What's your name?"

"I can't tell."

"Why not?"

"My daddy says never tell strangers your name."

"I want to speak to my daughter. Immediately."

"She's not home."

"Where is she?"

"With my daddy."

"What's your daddy's name?"

"Mandy calls him Doc Handsome."

"This is ridiculous. You tell her I called. Tell her to call me back."

"I can't."

"Why not?"

"Because I'm not s'posed to be in her room alone. I'm not s'posed to be touching her stuff."

"Oh, for Pete's sake."

"I gotta go now. Here comes Colonel Geoff from his constitutional. If he sees me in here he'll tell on me."

"Why would he do that?"

"Because I peeked at his freckles and now he's mad. Bye-bye, Lowell."

AMANDA WASN'T a receptionist, she was a mole. Despite Brett's promise of front counter work, Charlotte had delegated her to paper pushing. She'd spent the entire morning in the cramped windowless file room behind the admittance counter, filing stacks upon stacks of forms into cabinets of patient files. The most thrilling part of the process was rolling back and forth between the cabinets on a stool with her bandaged ankle in the air.

This wasn't a job for a bright incognito reporter on the lam. And she was determined to complain. Big time.

A glance at her watch confirmed it was nearly eleven-thirty. She rolled to the doorway where she had a plain view of Charlotte's solid uniformed back seated at the counter. "Shouldn't I be tackling something else? I thought I was hired to deal with the public."

Charlotte swiveled on her stool to confront her. "First off, your outfit isn't what we in the trade call appropriate."

Really? Amanda glanced down at her aqua Armani pant suit. It had been good enough to interview Brad Pitt at the Cannes Film Festival last year! "I'm afraid I don't have a white nylon ensemble with silver buttons yet."

Charlotte didn't seem to notice her mild sarcasm. "You wouldn't, of course. This sort of outfit is bought at a special store carrying uniform supplies. The docs provide a clothing allowance for all the staff."

"I see. So if I had the uniform—"

"The docs tend to wait a spell before investing in whites for a new girl. If and when your time comes, know that nobody but me wears silver buttons. I put them on special, as my own personal stamp."

"This filing gig isn't working out. I can't learn about the clinic tucked away in this box."

Charlotte stiffened. "There are many facets to my job. And you really are helping. That is the sort of paperwork I generally do on Saturday afternoons—when we're closed."

"Well, it's very dull."

"Is it? You haven't looked bored, hunched over, working at a snail's pace."

"It's your system," Amanda lamented. "You have patients separated by doctor. I have to check both sets of files to find them. Roll back and forth on this stool. Back and forth."

Charlotte rose from her seat and, with a tug of white

nylon, stalked over. "Naturally, I have them memorized. And if you last more than a week, you will, too." She jabbed a finger on the sheet of paper in Amanda's hand. "In the meantime, look here in the corner at these color codes. A green dot means Doc Graham."

"Green speck you mean."

"You'll either see green or orange. Orange being for Doc Handsome."

Amanda pinkened. "So even you heard about that Handsome thing."

"Yeah and ain't you cute." The twinkle in her eye suggested she truly meant it. "Maybe you can pick up the pace if you use the color codes."

"You should've told me the codes in the first place," she retorted softly to Charlotte's broad backside.

Charlotte apparently had excellent hearing because she pivoted on her heel with a tight smile. "Anybody with clerical experience—" Checking herself, Charlotte smiled. "Never mind, dear. It's so important to the boys that we make this work. I'll whip you into shape no matter what the discomfort or cost."

Was this charade truly worth the agony? When Amanda did work on her column for the *Manhattan Monitor,* it was sporadic and in the field. When she did come in for a landing at the newspaper, she was accustomed to tossing her filing in a basket on her desk and watching it disappear like magic into the hands of an underling.

She scowled at the cabinets. So this was what the underling did with her filing.

"Watch and learn," Charlotte was chortling for the umpteenth time today. "That's what I tell anyone they foist on me. Watch and learn."

But for how long? Amanda fought the desire to rev up her stool, bonk the woman's hideous honeycomb with a file and charge home to pack.

The doctors and staff kept the lunch situation simple.

They shut down the office between noon and one fifteen, assigning one employee to man the phones during that time span with a bag lunch, and to page a doctor in an emergency. Even the doctors participated in this rotation. Today was Brett's turn to eat in.

The moment Charlotte left to freshen up, Brett cornered Amanda behind the counter, speaking quietly. "How goes the battle?"

She struggled to keep her voice low, too. "Can't believe the way you abandoned me all morning, after dumping me in this awful job."

He winced. "I've been too busy to pop out for a look. I suppose Charlotte's gave you the 'watch and learn' spiel."

"Oh, yeah."

"It's nothing serious. Merely her attempt to appear the expert."

"Oh, c'mon, Brett, it's a complete dodge. So far all I'm doing is the roll and file."

His mouth twitched with amusement. "Sounds like some kind of dance."

"Well, you be the judge. I roll back and forth on my little stool filing papers in an isolated room with no chance to watch and learn anything."

Brett looked genuinely surprised. And irritated. "But Jack told her— That's not what we want. Any high school girl could come do that much."

Amanda grew indignant. "Hey, hang on a minute. It takes some brain power and concentration."

"I'm not trying to insult you. What I mean to say is that we want you in the receptionist seat, dealing with the patients alongside Charlotte."

"Her main excuses are that I'm not dressed for it and I have a bum ankle."

"The ankle will be like new, on schedule, by week's end. As for the uniform, if we place an order today, it should arrive by week's end."

"If you really think—"

Brett hushed her as employees began to appear from all parts of the office, boisterously gathering in the waiting room. He spoke in a clearer voice. "They rotate between the sandwich shop, pizza place and fast-food joints, if you'd like to tag along."

Rochelle was paying the most attention and paused at the door to speak with strained cheer. "Do come eat with us, Mandy. We're going for pizza today, and to have a look at Kaitlyn's family reunion photos."

"I don't think so."

"C'mon, it'll give you a chance to get to know all of us, as you know Brett."

Ha! It was easy enough to see through the redheaded nurse who had treated her so coolly on Sunday. Rochelle didn't want her company. She was merely trying to put a wedge between Brett and Amanda. Silly, as Amanda and Brett already lived under the same roof. But Amanda understood the infatuated nurse's mind-set. Seeing them together at work was much harder than imagining them together at Della's with a houseful of tenants.

"I think I'll stay here with Doc Hanson," Amanda insisted as Rochelle stood her ground. "My ankle is bothering me a little today."

This claim stumped the nurse and she had no choice but to tromp out after the others.

Brett expressed immediate concern. "I thought the ankle was fine!"

"It is," she assured him. "I just don't feel like…pizza."

"Rochelle hasn't been the kindest to you, I know. But she will warm up in a genuine way with time."

"Don't count on it. She only sees me as unwelcome competition."

Brett's dark brows arched boyishly. "For what?"

"As if you didn't know." Amanda patted his cheek. "Wipe that smug grin off your face."

''Why should I, with two women sizing me up?''

''If it were only two! Ivy tells me half the town is interested in you.''

Brett touched her face. ''Ivy tends to see everything larger than life. Just like you.''

''Don't knock our style. We make life…interesting.''

Brett worked his hand across her ear and behind her neck with a massaging motion. ''Kissing you at work would break a whole lotta rules.''

''But you're the boss, aren't you?''

With a wolfish look he hoisted her onto the counter and kissed her hungrily. They were both breathing heavily when he finally pulled back.

She felt a tad disappointed. ''Is that all I get, you tease?''

''Mandy, this is no time to get carried away.''

She kept her arms wrapped snugly around his shoulders. ''One more time can't hurt.''

With a soft growl he gave her a quick lip smack. She hung on tightly even as he tried to disengage himself.

''I shouldn't have started this.''

She rubbed her nose against his. ''True.''

''Anybody could walk in here at any moment.''

''True.''

''So it's time to be good.''

''False.''

Brett lifted his eyes to the ceiling. ''I believe you're out of control.''

Amanda grinned. ''And getting to the most eligible bachelor in town.''

''Oh, maybe not the most eligible. There's Jack and Colonel Geoff to consider.''

''Well, stand proud anyway. You're in the top three.''

Brett adjusted his lab coat as if trying to reestablish his role, then busily opened the brown sack and examined its contents. ''Now let's see what Della's packed today. Ah, wouldn't you know it, a meal for two. Cartons of milk, chicken sandwiches, coleslaw, pretzels.''

As Brett began to set things out on the counter, Amanda spoke up in protest. "Can we please get out from behind this blockade?''

"We really need to be stationed here to mind the store.''

Amanda scanned the waiting room. "How about out there?''

Brett followed her gaze. "Where?''

"At the kiddie table. It's not all that small and it's by a real window, bathed in genuine sunshine.''

Brett was dubious but lifted her off the counter and handed her the crutches.

Once they were settled in on stout, purple plastic chairs, Brett began to spread out their feast on the matching table. "You can move those Legos into that box on the floor if you like.''

"The what?''

"Those blocks in front of you.''

"Oh.'' She held up two and locked them together. "How ingenious.''

Brett shook his head, helping her push them into the box. "First you discover Old Maid. Now it seems you've never had Legos of your own.''

"I've never even heard of them.''

"The average kid has at least one set. I'm all the more convinced you've had a deprived childhood.''

"Never thought so at the time. But lately I've had my share of doubts about a lot of things.''

"Tell me more.''

She flashed him a smile. "All in time.''

His brows narrowed. "I think you like teasing me, making me wonder.''

"As if you should talk. The people around town claim you're one cagey and illusive character.'' She reached out and gave his crisp collar a tug. "A real hermit when you slip out of that magic lab coat."

"It's true I'm a man who enjoys his space and privacy. But when the timing is right, the person is right, I figure the barriers will just drop away naturally. Wouldn't you agree?"

There was no mistaking the insinuation that they were at this very moment tugging at the barriers between them. She met his gaze with what she hoped was an understanding glance. "The last thing—the very last thing—I expected to find on this trip was a guy. I don't believe I even need a guy right now."

"I don't need a woman, either. And as you've probably heard through the grapevine, I haven't even been shopping."

"So we've stumbled into this situation..."

His smile widened. "This very nice situation."

"By sheer accident."

"Sheer accidental luck."

Her heart tripped as he watched her intently, affectionately. She was so accustomed to relating to men on a surface level of play or suspicion. But this man meant business in a new and deeper way. What a joyful bonus to know his interest in her had absolutely nothing to do with her reckless reputation or her rich legacy. He liked the girl. Plain and simple.

"I want to explore what we feel here, Mandy. I want to take you places and show you things." He reached out and squeezed her hand. "I'm hoping that you'll stay on here for a long, long time."

She smiled, but it felt faint. "I do intend to stay. I've told you so. But it seems only fair to admit that I am really confused right now. About a lot of things."

"That's okay. I'm torn between pomposity and terror myself on a daily basis."

"I suppose that can't be helped, you being worshiped at work, then worked over on the home front."

He laughed out loud. "My hours of terror are restricted to the middle of the night, when I can't sleep."

"Maybe you should try sleeping in this regal lab of yours. As a matter of fact, I can just imagine you in nothing but the lab coat."

He reared in feigned shock. "Enough of that. Eat your lunch."

"Yes, Doctor." Amanda meekly sank her teeth into a sandwich piled high with chicken and lettuce. "Hmm, another Della triumph."

"You haven't even tried her coleslaw yet. It's famous."

"How famous?"

"Very. Clear out to the county line."

As they enjoyed their meal, Mandy mulled Brett's wish for her to stay on indefinitely. Could she possibly find contentment here in this slow and simple setting? A hectic life in the fast lane hadn't brought her any lasting happiness. Nor had the fruitless chase for her father's love. It was high time she explore her own heart and desires, away from the pressures of wealth and family. Discover if this detour was meant to be a permanent stop.

Chapter Eight

Near the end of the day, Ivy Waterman appeared at the clinic.

Charlotte made a show of checking her appointment book, flipping a day ahead and back. "I don't see you in here, Ivy. You still having trouble with your sinuses?"

"No, Charlotte—"

"Drop-ins are frowned upon, you know."

"I am here to see Mandy, of course!"

Charlotte plainly hadn't seen that coming. And being trumped on her turf was something she never took graciously. "For her, you most certainly don't need an appointment." With that, she shuffled off.

Hearing the welcome voice, Amanda had rolled her stool to the file room doorway in time to catch the whole scene. Now she stood with arms spread wide. "Tell me you've come to take me away from this filing cell!"

"That's what they have you doing?" Ivy glanced around the empty waiting room. "At least it must be quitting time."

Brett appeared then. Ivy wiggled her fingers at him. "Hi, Mr. Polka-Dot Shorts."

Brett smiled thinly. "The painting was very amusing."

"Tess has an active muse. It's only my job to encourage it."

"So, do you have an appointment?"

"You people are appointment crazy! I'm here to whisk your file clerk away for some fun, unless you intend to keep her trapped here all night."

He appeared offended. "No. I intended to take her over to the Frock Shop and have her measured for some uniforms."

Ivy glanced at Amanda. "Do you think you'll need them? That you'll be staying that long?"

"She will!" Brett blurted with unusual passion. When the pair stared him down, he added, "The office can use the extra uniforms in any case. And they should be ordered today, so they arrive by week's end."

"I'll take Mandy to the shop myself," Ivy said, moving behind the counter to retrieve the crutches leaning against the wall.

Brett frowned. "When will you bring her home?"

"Does she have a curfew?"

He reddened. "I mean for Della's sake. With dinner and things."

Ivy looked unconvinced. "Well, you can tell *Della* not to wait dinner for her, because I'm taking her back to my place for something."

Wistfully, Brett watched them leave.

Ivy settled Amanda into the front passenger seat of her white Saturn and was soon steering them out of the parking lot.

Amanda could not suppress an impish grin. "Brett has gotta be the cutest guy alive. Not just hot, but genuinely adorable. The way he's so confident one minute, then all fumbling the next."

Ivy's expression grew wary as she braked for a stoplight. "You break his heart and Della will track you down and break your back."

"I can't help it if we have something between us. I didn't invent chemistry."

"No, but you've always been very good at shaking the average test tube full of hormones until it's frothing with love potion number nine."

Five minutes later they were rolling along Main Street. Ivy took a right down a narrow opening and a left into an alley behind the quaint storefronts. She pulled into the space allotted for the Frock Shop. She removed Amanda's crutches from the back seat and, with care, assisted her passenger.

Laughter greeted them as they eased through the back service door.

The shop was rather narrow and jammed with racks of clothing and the occasional shelf of accessories. Back To School banners hung in the front windows facing the sidewalk.

A woman in her early thirties was at the cash register, speaking on the telephone. She was trim and petite, dressed in a navy dress with white piping.

"That's the owner, Natalie Quincy," Ivy murmured.

"Yes, I understand," Natalie was telling her caller. "The usual baggy medium-priced range are— Okay, leave it to me." Natalie hung up and gave the pair her full attention. "Hello, Ivy. And you must be Mandy."

Ivy nodded. "Why do I believe that was Charlotte on the phone?"

"No, it was Doc Hanson."

Ivy placed a hand on her hip. "Wanted to enforce Charlotte's archaic policy, I suppose."

Natalie looked bewildered. "No, just the opposite. He wants Mandy to have the updated cotton style being worn over at the dental office. I'll just go into my storage room and get some samples and a tape measure. Feel free to have a look around."

"Woo, somebody's acting wild and crazy," Amanda gloated.

Ivy frowned. ''Remember your promise not to shake things up?''

''Hey, blame the doc for this one.''

''Well, he's acting weird because of you.''

The prospect didn't trouble Amanda in the least. She hobbled over to a circular rack, checking garments and prices. ''This blouse is only twenty dollars, this one seventeen!''

''Would you want to pay more for either one?'' Ivy whispered.

''I wouldn't buy them at all,'' Amanda muttered. Then she took a look at Ivy's pale blue shift with regret. ''Oh, gee, you shop here now, don't you?''

''Yes,'' Ivy admitted defensively. ''The clothes are comfortable, fit into my budget. I can hardly teach at the school wearing gold lamé, can I?''

Natalie reappeared. She held up two white uniforms made of crisp fabric and styled in flattering lines.

Amanda inspected them with approval. ''These are a cut above the clinic uniform. Way above.''

Natalie looked rueful. ''Rumor has it Charlotte's had that place locked into white polyester blends since the Nixon administration.''

''This sort of change will make her flip.''

Natalie ignored the disgruntled Ivy in favor of the customer. ''Both styles come with pastel collar and pocket accents.''

''How about in green?''

''Hmm, Doc Hanson's favorite color.'' Natalie beamed. ''I think you're going to bring some fresh air to that office, Mandy.''

''Oh, sure,'' Ivy retorted. ''We'll just see what explodes when fresh air collides with one hot windbag from the Nixon administration.''

Trips to the drugstore and supermarket followed, where Amanda stocked up on cosmetics and energy bars respectively. Then it was on to the Blink and Click Photography Studio building where Ivy rented her second-floor apartment.

It was with a weary eye that Amanda stood in the alcove that gave access to the building's second level. The staircase was mighty steep.

"I'll understand if you want to come back when you're better," Ivy said.

"No way. We need to scream and laugh and I'm totally convinced the only truly private place for it is up those steps."

"Good." Ivy looked pleased. "Start whenever you're ready. I'll be right behind you."

Amanda took the narrow steps slowly, with a thump of crutch and a slide of shoe. Out of the corner of her eye she knew a solicitous Ivy was grasping the rail with one hand, keeping the other in midair for a catch.

They were halfway up when they were startled by a sudden flash from below.

They froze and turned to discover a man with a camera standing in the small foyer below. He was short and lean, and sported a brown goatee. "Splendid shot, ladies! Thank you so very much."

Ivy stomped a foot. "Dammit, Oliver! We might have been frightened enough to lose our balance."

"Sorry, I couldn't resist the setting. The two of you grappling with those stairs. You represent friendship in all its guts and glory. Trust, weariness, tension. A perfect reflection of life's dim and drab overall struggle. Rest assured, I used black-and-white film for the necessary noir."

A most reluctant Ivy made introductions. "Oliver Pratt, this is my college friend Mandy Smythe."

"I went to Berkeley myself, Mandy Smythe, for about a month back in 1993. A little before your time, I know."

"If you don't mind, Oliver, we'll continue our struggle."

"I might have bent my rules to allow *her* to stay here,"

Oliver remarked. "But it would have been tough for her to navigate with crutches."

"She wouldn't be on crutches if I'd been able to bring her directly here," Ivy countered. "Wouldn't have even laid eyes on that junky motel bike."

Oliver swiftly grew incensed. "You should have asked me before you told her no."

"You've always made your 'no guest' policy more than clear, Oliver."

"Don't mind her, Mandy," he said with a self-righteous sniff. "She's been cranky ever since I asked her to pose nude. Don't see what all the fuss was about."

"That is because you've never seen me nude," Ivy shot back slyly. The women laughed gleefully and a trumped Oliver disappeared through the door of his studio.

Ivy's apartment reminded Amanda of their Berkeley digs. Neat square rooms furnished with a mishmash of furniture, offering front views of Main Street and back views of an alley. With a sigh she parked on a worn floral sofa. "Drink! Drink! Please, Ivy."

"How about some iced tea?"

"Perfect. Make the first one a virgin. Then maybe we can work our way into adding jiggers of vodka."

"Not a chance. You still have to climb back down the stairs tonight."

Amanda accepted the tall, cool glass Ivy offered her and took a long sip. "Mmm, just the way your mother's personal chef used to brew it."

"It's the same tea from that little shop in Chinatown. There are some luxuries I still can't resist." Ivy settled back in a nearby armchair.

"So, Ivy, it's time to explain yourself. How on earth did you end up at the ends of the earth?"

"Where to begin?" she asked airily, kicking off her shoes. "After I went to Europe and got my degree, I eventually moved back to Boston. For a time I worked for Cornerstone Jewelers in customer service. It was difficult, dealing with the complaints of the rich and spoiled all day. But my folks were so happy to have me neatly placed in the fold, set to climb the Cornerstone ladder to an executive position. Like you, I was accepted for a change and sort of liked the feeling.''

"So what went wrong?"

"Family tranquillity never lasts, does it? Trouble began to brew when I hooked up with an artist named Nathan."

"Your family loves art."

"Not the kind of mass-produced watercolors sold at art fairs. That's Nathan's specialty. Anyway, he brought me here once on a short getaway. For several days I scouted things out while he painted the local scenery. Then we returned to Boston and I put Fairlane out of my mind. Our relationship began to wind down after that and, three months later, Nathan disappeared. I was disappointed when he just vanished, but I knew all along that he was unpredictable and moody. Certainly not husband material. Unfortunately his disappearance was in sync with that of a few Waterman jewelry pieces, heirlooms given me by Grandma Ruth herself. My family blamed me for the losses, said some terrible things about my life choices and about me personally."

Her lovely face pinched, Ivy continued. "It was clear they cared more about the missing heirlooms than my feelings. I had a mini breakdown over it. My shrink suggested I take a time-out in a new environment to try and discover exactly who I was beyond the Waterman legacy. I remembered Fairlane and decided to give it a try. Drove into town one day about eighteen months ago with a car full of belongings and a vague story about needing a fresh start away from the bustle. Spent the summer getting acquainted with the citizens by working at the public library with Beatrice Flaherty. By the time autumn rolled around, I was rested and confident and hooked on Fairlane. I applied for a teaching job at the school and got it.''

"You're really happy here?" Amanda pressed.

"Very much so. I feel safe, cared about. And I'm doing a job that brings me complete satisfaction."

"But everything is so quiet, so small."

"I do dash into Portland a couple of times a month to shop well, eat exotic and take in a show. But after a day or two of it, my heart and my wallet are ready to return home. I am living on my teaching salary these days."

"So you're completely cut off from your inheritance?"

"Well, if Dad died, I imagine I'd get my share. But my allowance was cut off the minute that jewelry vanished. Shortly thereafter, my little branch was chopped from the family tree."

"I can see why you haven't been anxious to spill that story to your friends here in Fairlane. You'd have people stirring up old pain."

"And bartering for a few of the watercolors that Nathan sold locally. All in all, I suspect it would spoil my school-teacher image for good. Not that I've ever lied about anything, but I've kept my story simple. Gave my name, place of birth and college credentials. Hinted that I'm estranged from my relatives and don't care to discuss them. I've never gotten close enough to anyone to suffer the third degree. And I quickly learned that most people would rather talk about themselves given the chance. It's simply a matter of turning the conversation in their direction."

"With Brett an exception to that rule."

"He's a model of restraint."

"I find Brett's restraint very sexy."

"You'd find his reading of a thermometer very sexy!"

Amanda tipped her head back on the sofa cushions. "Yeah... But he's wonderful in so many ways that have nothing to do with sex."

"And you've noticed?"

"I have," she insisted. "For instance, he's marvelous with Tess. He never uses his career as an excuse to short-change her the way Lowell has with me. And he makes it his business to look out for everyone in his range. His moves are so matter-of-fact, too, like he knows the proper thing to do and just does it without fanfare. It's all so gallant."

"Now there's a word we've never used before."

"Never knew the meaning of it before. Doubt I was ever ready to appreciate it before. Before Trevor, I mean. This relationship we're building seems so remarkably real and honest."

"Not totally honest. Brett needs to be told exactly who you are and what you are running from. To decide if he wants to love an heiress."

"I know. But telling him now would spoil everything. Other people would find out, then the press would get wind of it and my father would swoop in for the kill. I'm not ready for that, Ivy. I can't fight Lowell, yet. And I'm not sure I want to risk losing my whole legacy until I know exactly what I want."

"Understandable, as you have just been burned very badly. But in the meantime, Brett sinks deeper and deeper into your quicksand."

She made a half attempt to look meek. "I'll be as gentle with him as I can."

BRETT'S PULSE JUMPED at the thump of crutches along the upstairs hall of the boarding house. Finally, Mandy was home. He was cuddled with Tess on her pink gingham comforter, reading bedtime stories. Casting an eye at the Mother Goose clock on the night-stand, he realized it was almost nine o'clock. Tess had taken full advantage of his distracted state, pulling out book after book for perusal.

"So, Daddy," the child prodded.

"Huh?"

"What happened to the frog stuck under the lily pad?" She jabbed the open book. "Here in the story."

"You know, I think I hear Mandy right outside."

"She's home?" Tess squealed. "Mandy! Come here!"

That was exactly what Brett had hoped for. Somehow, he couldn't bring himself to call out. Visions of her kisses, her lingerie and her big-city savvy were bound to be enough to crack his voice in need and desperation.

"Hey, you two."

She stood in the doorway, leaning hard on her crutches. Brett recalled how good her hair smelled back at the office, how much he enjoyed kissing her.

"So I finally get a look at your bedroom, Tess. Seems only fair, as you've gotten such a good look at mine."

Brett watched her scan the pale pink walls, the white dressers, the huge yellow toy chest. Her eyes eventually rested on Tess's dollhouse.

She touched it delicately. Did she have any clue as to its value? That it was a Leon Hecker original? Next to his Corvette, it was the most pricy thing the Hansons owned.

"You like my dollhouse, Mandy?" Tess asked.

"Yes. I— I have one just like it."

She seemed to regret that admission, pursing her lips. But Brett had already figured she came from money, even if she didn't have any now. But to be fair, he didn't relish telling Mandy that Tess had earned the money for the dollhouse herself. So they both had their secrets.

"Want to stay? We're reading a very good book," Tess said temptingly.

"Well…" She glanced at Brett, as if seeking his permission to intrude.

"C'mon," he invited her. "The frog's just gotten stuck under the lily pad."

Tess's eyes danced under black silken bangs. "And Daddy's going to read him out of there."

"Sounds very intriguing." She sat on the edge of the bed, beside Tess, easing her crutches to the floor.

"Get the uniforms ordered, Mandy?" he asked.

"Two. They'll be here by Friday."

"The newer style?"

"Yes."

"Excellent."

Mandy eyed him expectantly. "Wonder if Charlotte will be able to handle the new look?"

"Jack and I vowed that we're finished with the old polyester tents. You, uh, just happen to be the first person to need a uniform." Sensing she was about to protest the unlikelihood of the claim, he began to read about the frog.

By story's end, the frog was atop a lily pad and Tess was snoozing between the adults. Carefully, Brett eased off the bed and rounded the footboard to grab the crutches from the floor and help Mandy to her feet. Quietly they made an exit.

Closing Tess's door behind them, Brett took Mandy's arm. "That was nice."

Her eyes glimmered with mischief. "We're not finished. I'm on a bedroom tour and yours is next."

He thought about the other boarders who took too much pleasure in minding his business. How they'd involve themselves if they suspected he and Mandy were getting serious. Still, it couldn't hurt to give her a quick peck.

He led her to his door to find it was locked. "Della does that whenever my medical bag is in here," he murmured with some disgust. "She's afraid somebody's going to come looking for drugs one day." He fished into his pants' pockets for his key ring, all the while gazing down at Mandy leaning against the door frame. She stretched to give him a kiss.

"Want me to check your pockets for you?"

"And run of the risk of forgetting all about my keys? No way."

They shared a soft chuckle, only to be interrupted by the sound of footsteps. It was Beatrice, presumably on her way from the bathroom, dressed in a robe, carrying a toiletry caddy.

"Glad to see you're back safe, Mandy," she said with a curious smile. "Not that the town isn't entirely safe. I mean, what with your crutches and all, you might have fallen. So what did you make of Ivy's place?"

"Very nice—"

"Her landlord is such a nut, taking pictures whenever he likes. I think a person should have the right to say no to a shutterbug. Don't you?"

"Oliver was a bit much—"

"And how is that book coming along? Most exciting."

"I've been too busy so far to make any progress."

Beatrice beamed understandingly. "There's always hope for tomorrow."

"And we'll see you tomorrow, Beatrice," Brett intoned.

The librarian finally moved on, disappearing through her own door. Brett swiftly slid home his key and they pushed inside.

He flicked on the wall switch. The bedroom was neat and masculine, done in tans and browns. Bookshelves crammed with medical journals lined one wall, a desk with computer dominated another. His bed, king-size with a carved wooden headboard, took up most of the space.

He watched Mandy tour the room, pause to admire the burl headboard.

"I think I'll sit on the bed. Take the weight off my poor ailing leg." The crutches hit the floor as she hit the mattress.

"You aren't really ailing." He scooped up her crutches, leaned them against his dresser and sat on the bed beside her.

"Hey. A little more bedside manner, please."

His eyes narrowed. "It could have been much worse, a

major fracture that would have kept you in a cast for months.''

''In any case, it's all your fault, parading around in low slung jeans and no shirt.'' Even as she spoke, she was unbuttoning his shirt. ''Gives a girl ideas she can't easily erase.''

''Now, Mandy, I thought you only wanted a tour.''

''I lied.'' Kneeling on the mattress she pushed him flat on his back.

Brett closed his eyes, aware of her hands pushing aside his shirt, skimming his hair-dusted chest. His pulse pounded in his ears as he tracked her tongue flicking his nipples, her fingers loosening his pants.

The rest happened too fast for rational thought. He began reaching inside her clothes, touching her satin skin. They rolled and tussled, explored intimate places.

''You have any condoms?'' she asked.

He did. In the bottom drawer of his dresser under some old shirts. He bolted up to get one. Easing back on the bed he gave a shudder as she sheathed him. Then gave another shudder as she hooked her hips over his and took him inside her. Locking onto his mouth she began to rock him with feverish intensity.

Their climax was a quick explosion.

''I just couldn't wait anymore,'' she confessed softly, rolling off him.

He raised up on an elbow, touched her damp brow. ''I meant to plan our first time a little better than that.''

She smiled coyly. ''But it was fun.''

''Yeah.'' He curved an arm around her and fell back on the pillows. ''Let's just rest here a minute. I want to hold you…''

''Doc? Doc! You in there?''

Brett's eyes popped open. ''Yes, Della?''

''Didn't you hear your phone ring?''

He hadn't. But it was obvious why. He kept the ringer on low so it wouldn't startle him too much in the middle of the night. And on this particular night, Mandy was curled up on the phone side of the bed, snoring softly, even now. Apparently, it took a lot to wake her up.

"What is it, Della?" The query proved enough to wake his beauty. He put a gentle hand over her mouth just long enough to whisper, "Please keep quiet."

Accepting her nod of sleepy bewilderment, he jumped to his feet, zipped up his pants and moved to the door to open it a crack.

"You sleeping already?"

He raked a hand through his hair. "Just dozed off, I guess. Anything the matter?"

"Jeremy Tyson just phoned. Seems Kiley believes she's in labor."

"Again?" He rubbed his eyes.

"It's likely to be false, of course. Should I put them on to Rochelle?"

"No, Kiley's just a frightened child herself and Rochelle doesn't have the patience. I'll take a run over there."

"Thanks, Doc."

"You happen to have their address? All those units in their complex look alike, especially after dark."

"There's a red car in the drive and the white lawn furniture I gave them. Oh, and the porch light will be on."

"Guess that will have to do," he said rather reluctantly.

"By the way, have you seen Mandy?"

"Why?"

"Well, I thought I heard her crutches on the stairs a while back, so I heated up an extra cup of cocoa—"

"Ah, the old, 'here's a cup of cocoa, now tell me all the town scoop you heard today' trick."

Della laughed. "Very funny. I'm only trying to make her feel welcome. And it was my custom to bring Emmaline a cup to that room most every night. I miss the company."

"Mandy is back." He saw no recourse but to admit it. "Looked in on us while I read to Tess."

"But I knocked on her door and got no answer."

He gave her a gentle nudge away from the doorway. "Della, I really must get dressed, go see about Kiley."

Della put a hand to her heart. "Oh! Yes. Pardon me."

"Try the porch swing for Mandy. She likes the night air." Making sure Della took the stairs, Brett slipped back into his bedroom. Mandy was reclining, just as he'd left her. "C'mon! C'mon! You've got to get back to your room before Della returns—before anybody sees you."

"What is your problem, Brett?"

"This is just the sort of juicy situation that would get tongues wagging."

"No one could know anything for sure."

"Della, for one, knows I was in bed. I look…rumpled."

"Is there real harm in admitting I rumpled you?"

He stared at her in disbelief. "How crazy is this? Acting like a couple of horny kids on spring break!"

"Is it so outrageous for them to see you fall for some-one?"

"Someone I hardly know, yes! This town is full of available women who bring me flowers and food, who complain that in two years time they can't get past first base with me. Now suddenly I go nuts for a kook in gold shoes and tight pants who hits a car while clocking my assets. This scenario couldn't be crazier from the Fairlane point of view."

"We've done nothing wrong. I haven't even lured you near wrong yet."

"Still, they'd gleefully hash it to bits. Doc and the new stranger, whooping it up." He grabbed her crutches and handed them to her one by one as she struggled off the bed.

"You care too much what they think. You're a good doctor and they all know it."

He was flabbergasted. "You still don't see it do you?

It's *Tess* I'm looking out for. She'll hear the whispers about us. Demand to know why I had the new lady in my bedroom at night with the door closed. If you don't mind, I'd rather keep her world uncomplicated as long as possible.''

Her eyes went dewy. ''Are you the best father in the world or what?''

He was startled by the turnabout and fumbled for words. ''That's the nicest thing anyone's said to me in a long time.'' He gave her a quick kiss and left.

Chapter Nine

By week's end Amanda had decided that Brett had miraculous powers far beyond medical science. With his own special sweet talk, he'd convinced her to stick with file-room duty until she was back on both feet again and in full uniform.

She got her first taste of freedom on Friday. About eleven, the UPS man delivered her uniforms. Then about twelve-thirty, Brett ushered her to an examination room and ceremoniously removed her Ace bandage. Leaning back on the table, she stretched her mended leg in the air and rotated her foot.

"That feels like heaven."

"Why not take a test drive?" Brett grasped her ribcage and eased her to her feet. "Put weight on it slowly. Take a few cautious steps."

She stood on her own power, then moved forward with one bare foot and a shod one. "You know, I don't have my other shoe along. Thought you were planning to remove the bandage tomorrow—at the house."

"I was. Originally. As it is, we can dig up something for you to wear home. A pair of shoes belonging to someone else on staff."

"Hope you know I'm now officially done with the file room."

"Thanks for being a sport about it all week."

"I mean, I've got my footing and my uniform. I'm not even finishing out the afternoon in there."

"Look, that's okay."

"It is? Who's going to tell Charlotte?"

"Jack and I are going to speak to her this afternoon about your move up front."

"Whew. Wouldn't mind being miles off for that."

He grinned. "You could be blocks off."

"What is all this about, Doc?"

"I have a favor to ask." He paused, looking a trifle shy. "You don't have to do it."

"What!"

"Della phoned to say she's got a leaky kitchen pipe. She was supposed to take Tess to the dentist at two and it's left us in a jam."

"Which problem am I more qualified to solve?"

"Della would be thrilled to discover you could manage the plumbing. But we're hoping you can spring Tess out of school early and drive her over to the dental office."

Amanda was struck speechless by the very idea. He was trying to entrust his precious child to her. A month ago she wouldn't have appreciated or even understood the gravity of the act. But she was growing in perspective due to his influence.

With an uncertain look, Brett went on. "I could ask someone else, but Tess likes you so much, longs to know you better. And you could use the fresh air and exercise. Seems like a good match on such a nice autumn afternoon."

She struggled to find her voice. "If you want my help, sure."

"You can even borrow my Corvette if you like."

"Wow! This just keeps getting better and better."

"Know how to drive a stick?"

She smiled playfully, touched his chin. ''As a matter of fact, I do.''

Brett caught her hand and nipped her fingertips. A hard, short rap on the door, however, put a quick stop to it.

Rochelle entered. ''Oh! I didn't realize you were in here, Mandy. Foot better?''

''I haven't felt this good in a long while.''

Rochelle dismissed her and focused on Brett. ''About that call I took from Della.''

''All fixed. Mandy is going to pick up Tess at the school.''

''Oh!'' Rochelle was shaken. ''But usually I am the one to fill in.''

As if in appeasement, Brett dipped his head to hers. ''I want you here. Jack and I intend to have The Chat with Charlotte and need you to watch the counter.''

''I see.'' The redhead nodded slowly and soberly, as if in consultation on the fate of a burn victim.

''Surely you'd like to see that archaic uniform policy change for your own benefit,'' Amanda said, joining in.

Rochelle eyed her coolly. ''You're a little new to worry about our policies.'' With that, she whirled out the door, shutting it behind her with a smack.

Amanda made a face at the door. ''You know, Brett, it would serve her right if you kept her in polyester.''

He laughed out loud.

THE MOMENT AMANDA made eye contact with Tess from the doorway of the kindergarten room, the child snapped into action. She abandoned her puzzle project and scooted up to Ivy's desk. Digging into the pocket of her purple bib overalls, she produced a small, folded sheet of paper. ''I forgot to give you this.''

Ivy took it with a puzzled look. ''What is it?''

Tess puffed up her little chest. ''A note from Daddy.''

With a raised brow, Ivy opened the paper. "The dentist, eh?"

Tess nodded.

Amanda entered the room. "Della can't make it. Has a leaky pipe. So Brett sent me over in his shiny red Vette."

Suddenly Tess's blue eyes grew huge. "Hey, Mandy, where's your crutches?"

She beamed. "I'm cured."

"That'll be the day," Ivy mumbled. She instructed Tess to collect her backpack and to put the puzzle back in place on the shelf. Then she ushered her old pal out the door.

"Aren't these shoes hideous?" Amanda complained, lifting one white Oxford in the air. "Rochelle lent them to me in a deliberate attempt to make me look like a frump."

Ignoring her friend's playfulness, Ivy glanced up and down the quiet corridor to make sure all classroom doors were closed. "He's actually trusting you with his kid now?" she quietly vented.

Amanda wiggled her artistically shaped brows. "He seemed most concerned that I know how to handle a stick. Zoom, zoom, zoom."

"Very funny."

"I am teasing, of course. Tess is his world. And I am very flattered that he has so much faith in me."

Ivy sighed. "It's plain to everyone that the child adores you, too."

"Strange, I've never found kids very appealing as a group. All that yelling and running. But I do like Tess. The secret must be that they're more attractive singly, versus in a pack."

Ivy groaned with exasperation. "Hon, kids in general are a huge responsibility. A child like Tess, with above-average intelligence and nerve, is especially high maintenance."

"She reminds me of myself, you know, full of spunk and verve. I can't help but wonder how I would have turned out if I'd had an attentive father like Brett and a house full of loving boarders supporting me.''

Ivy pressed her lips together briefly as if stifling her temper. ''I was so hoping this wouldn't turn into a little family threesome deal so fast.''

''What do you mean?''

Ivy poked her friend's chest. ''All three of you know how tough it is to suffer the loss of a woman, you with your mother, Brett and Tess with Brett's wife Sarita. For Brett's part, it has to be at least part of the reason he is being so cautious about getting involved again.''

''What's your point?''

''Brett is allowing you to become attached to his child. He is expecting you to take the responsibility seriously.''

''I can get her to the appointment on time, if that's what you mean.''

''That's only part of it.''

''I'm not going to hurt them, Ivy. If that's what *you* really mean.''

''That is the gist of it.'' Ivy gazed back through the window in her classroom door. ''I wish I had more time to explain further. But I don't. Children are wrestling. And other things. I gotta go.''

Tess charged out then, with her backpack strapped onto her back like a rocket. ''Oh, wow, are we gonna have fun or what!''

''Responsible fun,'' Amanda replied, grasping the child's hand. ''If there is such a thing.''

IT WAS NEARLY SEVEN o'clock before Brett spotted his sleek Corvette pulling into the Scherers' driveway. Relief and irritation swelled inside him in equal amounts as he shot up from the porch swing.

Mandy and Tess exited the car with giggles, carrying sacks. Together they crossed the grass to the front walk. Mandy wore tight slacks and a blouse he'd never seen before, sunglasses perched on her nose and a floppy hat on her head. She was swinging a fabric purse. Now that she could walk on her own, she was making a show of it with a most provocative sway. Tess, dressed in much the same manner right down to the specs, was imitating her walk.

He descended the porch steps, hands on hips. "You're late!"

Mandy eyed him over her sunglasses. "For what?"

"Tess's dental appointment ended three hours ago. I called and checked."

Mandy still seemed perplexed. "The appointment went fine."

Brett clenched his fists at his sides. "But where have you been since?"

"I needed new shoes."

"That couldn't have taken very long."

"It didn't," Tess confirmed happily. "After we got sandals we got ice cream and a hamburger and clothes and sunglasses. Oh, and Mandy got a speeding ticket!"

"You what?" Brett's voice thundered.

"I did not get a ticket," she replied blithely. "I have a superb driving record. There's no cop on earth I can't talk out of a ticket."

"How fast were you going?"

"Not very fast. Just seven miles over the limit, on County 6 near the dental office."

"Ah." He was momentarily distracted. "There is always a speed trap there. I should've warned you. Just the same—"

"Do you know that red cars are pulled over more than any other color car? So in a way, you're calling attention to yourself."

"Something you'd know nothing about."

"Well…" She twirled her purse.

"Just the same," he repeated, "you should have called, Mandy. I've been very worried."

Her face fell. "Oh. I didn't realize."

"So, Daddy, do you like my new shoes?"

He felt his expression tightening further as he inspected the little red nails jammed inside the open-toed sandals. "Exactly where did you have your nails done?" he asked.

"At Lindy's Salon," Mandy replied.

"The hair place?" He frowned again as Tess grew nervous. Then he reached out for her. Tess tried to wiggle away but there was no use. Off came her hat and short dark curls sprang free.

"Tess Hanson!" He knew his tone was harsh, but this, of all things.

"Don't be mad, Daddy," she begged in a frightened squeak. "I love my hair short."

"*You aren't that little girl anymore*. We have an agreement."

Tears welled in the child's eyes. "It's for fun. Mandy likes fun—not like you!"

"Della is waiting inside for you," he said tightly. "With dinner."

"I already ate great stuff!" With that she tore past him with her packages and dashed up the porch steps and into the house.

Stiffly, Brett hovered over Mandy. She shuffled her sandal in a crack in the sidewalk.

"What's the matter with you, Brett?"

"You went too far, that's all."

"But it's the haircut that's really set you off. Why?"

He was stunned. "How can you ask me that after this stunt?"

"Your anger seems way out of line and I think—"

"What you think doesn't matter! This is between Tess and me."

"Well, excuse me for trying to be a friend to that sweet little girl!"

"Real friends know when to back off." Shoving his hands in his pockets, he charged down the walk toward the street.

THE BOARDING HOUSE'S living room was like the scene of a wake that evening. Amanda sat glumly in an overstuffed chair while tenants skittered around her. Everyone knew of her adventure with Tess and no one approved any more than Brett did.

She couldn't help but complain to no one in particular. "Two perfectly fine feet and nowhere to take them—on a Friday night!"

"Perhaps this would be a chance to get started on that novel of yours," Beatrice suggested kindly. "It would be an awful shame if you were to abandon that project just because you're working at the clinic."

Amanda was in no mood to pretend that she was a budding novelist. She was tired and edgy and annoyed that Brett was being such a big baby over a small beauty makeover for his kid. All she wanted was to be left to stew.

But when she gazed over at Beatrice, situated on the sofa in her usual evening outfit of lavender lounge pajamas, Amanda felt a rush of sympathy for the plump librarian who feared taking risks, who settled for living through others. She offered a polite reply with her last reserve of patience. "I don't know if I have the ambition for the project anymore."

"But you traveled all this way and you haven't even tried," Beatrice objected. "I've been so looking forward to watching you make the creative journey. Told all the library patrons about you."

Amanda had a sudden inspiration. "Ivy tells me you're interested in writing yourself."

"Me? Well, I've done some poetry, a few short stories." She waved a hand. "Nothing like a novel."

"Maybe we could work on a story together."

"Oh, no. Not really." She paused shyly. "You mean it?"

"Sure, why not?"

Beatrice beamed. "How exciting. I'll go get pens, paper." She popped up off the sofa. "Must locate a dictionary, too. I just bought a new one with all sorts of new words. You're going to love it." With that she trotted out of the living room.

Della looked up over her magazine. "That was very nice of you, Mandy."

"Not at all. I can use a friend right now."

"You have plenty of friends under this roof."

"Then why is everyone scowling at me tonight? Frank and Colonel Geoff can't even bear to be in the same room with me."

"Because we're so protective of Doc."

"Care to explain just what I've done that's so wrong?"

"Don't you think it's a little extraordinary to keep a child you barely know out for an extra three hours? To solicit her a haircut? Have her nails painted?"

"Listen, Della, nobody ever gave a damn about me at any age. I thought I was doing the kid—and the doc—a real favor."

Della sighed. "You're naiveté is incredible, but still, I know in my heart you're sincere."

"So will you stop frowning at me over the tops of your reading glasses?"

With sudden realization, Della whisked the wire rims off her nose. "I don't need these for reading. I'm only forty-five. No, these specs are strictly for threading needles." She leaned forward. "And if you're serious about wanting friends, you won't ask me where my needle is!"

Beatrice appeared in the doorway minutes later with armloads of office supplies. There was a new sparkle in her eye and a confident lilt in her tone. "If you don't mind,

Della, we'll just take over the dining room table for the remainder of the evening.''

Della smiled broadly. "That is perfectly fine.''

"On the condition that we will clear up after ourselves, naturally.''

"Naturally.''

A satisfied Beatrice marched off. When Amanda was slow on the uptake, Della whispered, "C'mon, Svengali, get cracking.''

"Me and my big mouth.''

"But it's a wonderful cause. In all my life I've never seen Beatrice so excited. She never moves from the sofa after seven unless she needs a Pepsi or a book.''

"Yes, I know. Didn't expect her to *move* on my little polite idea so fast, either.''

"Oh, c'mon, the last thing I need around here is a windbag full of unfulfilled ideas.''

"All right.'' Amanda slowly rose from her chair. "I guess it'll take my mind off my problems.''

"Brett is bound to come around,'' Della consoled, slipping her glasses back on.

"Tonight?''

"He won't be moving as fast as Beatrice on this one I'm afraid.''

"Care to tell me why?''

"No.'' With a faint, dismissive smile, Della glanced down at her magazine and Amanda knew the conversation was over.

TESS HAD BEEN IN the kitchen having a glass of milk with Frank when Beatrice had come in to look for pencils in the junk drawer. She said that she and Mandy were going to write a book together. A real book with no pictures. In the dining room, if it was all right with Della.

After giving Frank a good-night kiss, Tess scooted up the stairs on her own. She would color some pictures for their book tomorrow. In kindergarten. With Ivy's markers and crayons.

Marching by Mandy's room, she remembered that Frank had changed a light bulb in her closet a little while ago. Tess couldn't help but wonder if that old light bulb was working right. Maybe she should make sure. Mandy was so sad because Daddy yelled at her. She might be scared if her closet was all dark inside.

She would go inside and make sure everything was A-OK.

The overhead light winked on brightly. So did the closet light. Tess touched a finger to her mouth. Oh, my, Mandy had a lot of shoes on her closet floor. She'd bought four new pairs today. It would be fun to try on all the open-toed ones to watch her red toenails wiggle. Tess dropped to her knees in front of the shoes and began to rummage through them.

The buzz was a little louder tonight than usual. Tess followed the sound to the bed. Mandy's phone was lying on the floor under the bed, attached to a wire plugged into the wall. Gingerly, she picked up the instrument, wire and all, pushed the same button as the last time, and held it to her ear. "Hello?"

"Hello. Is this the little girl?"

"Who is this?"

"This is Lowell."

"Yes, this is the little girl."

"What's the matter? You sound funny, sniffling."

"I had to cry a little bit. Daddy yelled at me and Mandy."

"Oh, so she is in trouble again. Might have figured."

"Just a little trouble. Daddy never stays mad."

"Lucky him."

"You stay mad, Lowell?"

"Sometimes I do."

"That's mean. Daddies are supposed to be huggy and happy to their little girls."

"I'm a great dad."

"You sound mean."

"I'm not. Really…"

"I heard Daddy tell Della that Mandy was a depraved little girl. Whatever that means."

"What? Oh, maybe you mean deprived."

"I don't know what that means, either. But my daddy said so and he knows everything."

"Mandy says that about me, too. Or used to."

"Little girls need lots of love."

"I bet your daddy said that, too."

"Colonel Geoff said that."

"Oh, yes, the one with the freckles."

Tess giggled.

"May I please speak to Mandy?"

"She's writing a book."

"A book?"

"Yes, and I am going to color pictures for it."

"I see."

"What was your name again?"

"I didn't tell you my name, remember, Lowell?"

"Yes, yes. I suppose I forgot."

"What's the book about?"

Tess paused, her face scrunched in thought. "It's about the big city. And a poor girl."

"Do you live in the big city?"

"I don't know."

"Are there very tall buildings near you?"

"No."

"Are there many cars driving around?"

"How many is many?"

"Oh, never mind."

"Okay. Bye."

"Wait! I didn't mean—"

Tess cut him off in mid-sentence with a jab to the off button. She placed the phone back under the bed and returned to the closet. The buzz soon started up again but she ignored it. Lowell wasn't half as much fun as her shoe game.

Chapter Ten

Amanda showed up at the Blink and Click Photography Studio on Saturday morning around ten. Oliver Pratt was just opening for business and let her inside through the shop entrance. Unlike her first encounter with Ivy's landlord, when he had been hiding behind a camera at the foot of the apartment stairs, Amanda was close enough to get a good look at him. His face had a milky tinge and his goatee needed a trim. Skintight black pants and a faded red T-shirt revealed a compact but wiry body.

"What a nice surprise to see you again so soon," he greeted her slyly. "Free of your bonds."

"Have you seen Ivy yet this morning?"

"It's her habit to hit the Laundromat down the street at this time. She's due back soon. Why not wait here with me?" He moved to turn the Closed sign hanging from the door to read Open.

"Tough night?" she asked as he stifled a yawn.

"Very restless. Ivy's invitation to imagine her nude was most distracting. Especially when I invited you into the picture."

Amanda knew many men like Oliver back in Manhattan. Egotistical artists with a petty streak and a wicked sense of humor, who experimented in any number of activities.

"Somehow, Oliver, I have trouble believing that fantasy would hold your interest long."

"Don't listen to town gossip about my orientation. Fact is, I'm equally friendly to both camps."

Amanda strolled around the studio, taking in the framed shots adorning the walls. Oliver liked variety in his work, as well. He was adept at portraits, action shots, still life. A vase of fire-and-ice roses took on amazing fragile life through his lens.

"You really are a puzzle," he said suddenly, tapping a finger to his mouth.

"How so?" Amanda turned on her heel with grace, as she'd done on Parisian runways more than once on a lark for the fashion industry's hottest designers. Confronted with this social scorpion every bit as out of place as she, she felt it necessary to exert sophisticated nerve.

"It's the hair for starters. Auburn isn't your shade. You seem more suited to being a blonde."

"I've colored my hair a rainbow of shades over time."

"Well, ditch the dark hues. Do nothing for you."

"Thanks for the tip." Lifting her chin a bit higher, she coolly turned away from him. Fact was, she couldn't agree more with his observation. The minute she could return to her natural blond shade, she would.

"Ivy's never had a visitor before." There was a noticeable challenge in his tone.

"Your no-guest policy hardly encourages it."

"Or maybe this place is just too damn boring to encourage out-of-towners."

"But you're here, Oliver. A full-fledged resident, living the slow-and-easy Fairlane life."

"True." He'd moved to the counter that held the cash register and was thumbing through an appointment book. She folded her arms and sauntered over.

"So what gives?"

"I was born here, dear. Naturally I couldn't wait to break

away to seek my fortune—and so I did at age eighteen. But eventually, after studying with the best photographers, snapping just about everyone and everything, I found myself back here where I started. Guess you could say I simply got bored.'' He shrugged. ''Thirty-nine years old and I've seen it all. Doesn't it break your little heart?''

''Still, I see you better suited to Soho.''

''Ah, but I didn't inherit a building there. Granny Pratt left me this place four years ago. I admit I returned for her funeral with the intention of selling her assets and jetting off again. But I was tired and decided to rest. Then days turned into weeks, weeks into months. Mind you, I'm always primed to leave again, given the right incentive.'' He lifted a brow invitingly.

''Don't look to me for encouragement.''

''But we could have such fun together.'' He reached over the counter and clasped his hands to her cheeks. ''You have exquisite bone structure. I could never weary of photographing you.''

''Bet that's a tired line around town.''

He appeared injured. ''It works more often than you might imagine. Even when I'm less sincere.''

Oliver's intrusiveness was throwing Amanda an unexpected curve. She sought to sever their lively connection. ''If I ever need a tour guide for a trip around the world, I'll keep you in mind.''

''I suspect you've already been around the world, maybe twice.''

''Knowing where Soho is hardly means anything.''

''No. But I know you went to school in California and word is you now reside in New York City.''

''So?''

He smiled at her distress. ''Look, don't try and kid a kidder. You've got that certain high-end quality and something else quite familiar that I can't put my finger on.'' He touched her face again. "The bone structure, I think. You can't disguise bone structure."

Despite her bravado, Amanda's pulse gave a nervous jump. The very idea of being unmasked by this vain know-it-all upset her. Insightful worldly people like Pratt weren't supposed to be nestled in peaceful boring towns like Fairlane. They belonged in the hardened city with their own kind.

"Hello, hello!" Ivy bounced through the door with her laundry basket. A sharp look to Oliver had him removing his hand from Amanda's face.

"We were just getting acquainted," Oliver said, stepping behind his cash register.

"I know you weren't expecting me..." Amanda began.

"It's fine," Ivy assured her. "Care to come up for some coffee?"

"I thought maybe we could go for a nice long walk." She lifted her freshly mended ankle. "I've missed zipping around."

"You're on. Let me drop off this laundry upstairs."

When they left, Oliver was on hand to open his shop door for them with a flourish. "Hope to see you again soon," he intoned. "Like tonight, for instance. At the Blue Parrot Lounge, where Ivy does a mean karaoke rendition of 'I'm Too Sexy For My Hat.'"

"I don't!" With a huff of disgust, Ivy pushed Amanda outside.

Amanda was accustomed to walking in Manhattan on sidewalks teeming with people who had their own agendas and avoided eye contact. But as the women made their way along Main Street, they were assailed by cheery greetings and short attempts at conversation. By the time they reached Fairlane's modest central park, they'd heard several jokes, answered inquiries about Amanda's leg and learned some very intriguing gossip about people Amanda had yet to meet.

They settled on a green-painted bench near the park's fountain with ice cream cones purchased from a nearby vendor. "So is it true that Donald Price's dog was found eight hundred miles away?" Amanda asked her friend.

"Absolutely," Ivy said. "I heard it first over at the Laundromat, from the principal of the high school, a very reliable source and brother to Donald."

"Wow."

They slouched side-by-side on the slatted seat, legs outstretched on the grass, and licked their peppermint ice cream. Teenagers threw Frisbees and balls to one another, kids played on some swings, adults sat on the scattered benches enjoying the sunshine.

"So what's new at the house?" Ivy asked.

"Oh, not much really," Amanda said in mild sarcasm. "I kept Tess out too late yesterday, which made Brett burn."

"It was his idea to give you the responsibility. Did he think you'd taken off for good?"

"He especially didn't care for the fact that I had the kid's toenails painted and her hair cut and curled."

Ivy's mouth dropped open. "You did all that on your own?"

Amanda was startled by her friend's dismay. "It was my idea to get the pedicure—to celebrate losing my bandage. But it was Tess who insisted on the hairstyle."

"Adults don't automatically do what children tell them to!"

"Really? Adults always obeyed me at that age—probably you, too."

"Well, yes. Hired help obeyed us. Speaking as a wizened schoolteacher now, I know full well it's never a good idea."

"Even so, he overreacted. Then he stalked off without trying to talk it over."

"He does go overboard about Tess on occasion. I suppose being a single parent makes him unreasonably nervous.''

''He seemed out of line even under those circumstances.''

''So how do things stand between you today?''

''Nowhere. I set my travel alarm for eight, hoping to run into him in the kitchen. But he was already sailing out the back door with one of Della's brown sack lunches and his medical bag.''

''He'll cool off. Eventually.''

''I suppose you really disapprove of my staying there now.''

Ivy bit her lip as she always did when suppressing a retort. ''It's your life.''

''Yeah, but it's your town. Really haven't meant to stir up any trouble.'' Amanda turned to toss the remainder of her cone in a trash bin. ''But I do think I've done something right for a change.''

''What?''

''Beatrice was pushing me about starting my book project and I dragged her into it.''

''No kidding.''

''You told me she's shown an interest in writing herself, so I thought, Why not make her take some action on a dream for a change? She dove right into the idea. We spent last night outlining some scenarios for our 'city girl done wrong' premise.''

Ivy was pleased. ''Way to go. Though you realize that if it amounts to anything, you'll have to share the credit with Bea.''

''I have no interest in being a novelist. I hope to tutor her along until she can fly on her own.''

''Who'd have thought one of your skimpy cover stories would ever turn into a good deed?''

''Hey, I've been trying to do all sorts of good deeds during my stay in Fairlane. Working hard at the clinic, trying to understand Brett, win his trust. It isn't my fault that some of my attempts have backfired.''

''It is too bad he doesn't have a better sense of humor about it all.''

Amanda stared off into the bright blue sky. ''Yes. It would do him a world of good to relax, be more impulsive.''

''If things get too chilly at the boarding house, I suppose you'll have to consider leaving, for everyone's sake. You could probably move into my place for a while. Oliver seemed prepared to bend his no-guest rule.''

''Hope it doesn't come to that. He's too much like that cinematographer we met in Spain our sophomore year. Kissing up to everyone, all the while trying to prey on their weaknesses. And he took pictures of everything, too, like Oliver Pratt.''

Ivy scowled. ''Did Oliver prey upon you?''

''Let's say he was aggressively nosing into my space, looking for an opening.''

''How exactly?''

Amanda struggled to explain. ''Oh, hinting that I was more than met the eye. I would make a better blonde, looked familiar.''

''Oh, damn.''

''Has he given you any trouble that way?''

''Not much. His extra upstairs apartment had sat empty for quite a while before I came along. Apparently he was a bit of a freak in his youth and while his talents as a photographer were immediately appreciated when he came back to Fairlane, no one actually wanted to live under the same roof with him.''

''Then he can't afford to antagonize you.''

''Nor you. I will put a quick stop to it.''

''No, Ivy. Anything you say will only encourage him.''

She pondered that. ''Guess you're right. But keep me updated on his moves.''

Amanda beamed like a kindergartner. "Yes, Miss Waterman."

"What is a teacher to do with a sassy girl like you?"

"Take her to the Blue Parrot Lounge for a fun-filled night of karaoke?"

"WHAT ON EARTH are you doing, Doc?"

Brett frowned when he realized Della had followed him into the living room that evening. "I am bending my knees. I am sitting in this chair." With that he dropped into a favored recliner and grabbed the folded newspaper off the end table. "Now I am going to read this paper in peace and quiet."

"It's Saturday night! Time for fun!"

Brett sighed. "Give me a break. The clinic was nuts today. The Carter girl fell out of a tree and broke her collarbone. Old man Sims cut his finger trying to sharpen his lawnmower blade—"

"I thought his son was taking care of his grass. Not the son with the lisp, but the other one who commutes to Portland."

"Della! The issue didn't come up." Brett rubbed his forehead. "On top of everything else, half of Scout Troop 780 got into some bad weeds on a hike this morning that caused their skin to burn. Calming their mothers proved tougher than treating the boys."

"Didn't you have any help?"

"Sarah Draper. But she is only a twenty-one-year-old nurse's aide. She knows the textbook drill but handling wild mothers is something nobody can prepare you for."

"Does sound unusually rough for the weekend stint."

"It was. Now all I want to do is sit here in a semiconscious state." Brett snapped open the paper on his lap and gazed down at the headline concerning the president's latest tax proposal.

"But you usually go over to the Blue Parrot on Saturdays."

"I go about once a month."

"So you're due. And didn't you speak to Mandy about going over there to see Ivy yodel her heart out?"

"I haven't spoken to Mandy since last night. Since she brought Tess home with that awful haircut."

"Don't you think you may have been a little hard on Mandy?"

When he replied, his voice was hard. "She was supposed to take Tess to the dentist. Back and forth. Easy. It meant so much to me to try and draw her a little closer into our circle here. And she promptly managed to flub it up."

"Tess can be very persuasive when she wants something. And Mandy is sort of fresh game to the child, not knowing your boundaries yet, or just how much Tess likes to cross them at every opportunity."

"Standing there on the porch last night, watching them cross the lawn all fixed up with triumph on their faces, all I could see were the striking similarities between the pair."

"What a precious observation!"

Growling, Brett turned a page of newspaper, and spotted a photo of a seal jumping through a hoop. When it came to females like Mandy—and his own child—he felt a lot like a trained seal, doing what was expected of him for small rewards. Rather than a fish treat, in his case it was a small, sweet smile or a kiss or a hand squeeze.

All in all, he was settling for too little. He deserved his daughter's obedience and Mandy's cooperation, not to mention overall consideration for his feelings from both of them!

Della moved to sit on the arm of the sofa to his right. "You know full well that Mandy has no way of knowing where you're at with Tess. How you've altered her life, how important it is that she not wear that mass of corkscrews."

Brett looked to her with a flash of vulnerability. "Did you do anything to fix it?"

"Despite her wiggle-worm protests, I got her into the shower first thing this morning, lathered her hair and washed away every trace of curl. Her hair is still short, of course, but it's straight again."

"So where is she now? Upstairs drawing pictures of her bad daddy?"

"No, she's at Hailey Corday's house."

Brett paused. "Christopher and Erin Corday's daughter?"

"Yes."

"Jack recently treated the girl for an earache or something last week. They live blocks from here, though, don't they?"

"Not that far away. The girls struck up a friendship at school. I didn't think you'd mind. Beatrice knows Erin Corday quite well, as they work together at the library. And Frank knows Christopher from his bowling league."

"Couldn't they have played here?"

Della placed a hand on her heart. "I pitched the idea. But I don't have an awesome swing set." When he remained silent, Della went on. "It was bound to happen. Tess hit school and discovered that children venture more than a block away from home."

"I would have liked a little say in the matter."

"I tried to call you at the office but no one picked up. So there stood Erin on my stoop, telling me Hailey and Tess had made these plans yesterday in class. I didn't know what to do. In the end I figured a few hours' play wouldn't upset the course of the universe." She reached over from her perch on the sofa arm and patted his back. "You've always seemed to welcome my input in the past, so I'm going to be straight with you now. It's high time you loosened the strings on Tess so she can mingle with her own kind. Being around adults so much has made her almost diabolically clever. Perhaps being with her more naive peers will distract her in a good way, steer her on to more childlike pursuits.''

Brett sighed. "You're right. When we moved here, my main concern was sheltering her from the public, all the while hoping she never revealed too much.''

"No matter how mischievous that child gets, she's never once broken her word about your secrets. She knows how much that one condition means to you.''

Brett felt a wave of relief and remorse. "Of course, you're right on all counts. It'll do her good to spend some time in another girl's home. Maybe pick up some good habits,'' he added hopefully. "Like staying out of other people's bedrooms, knocking on closed doors, things like that.''

"Don't expect her to come home reprogrammed after one visit.''

"Well, let's hope the time is well spent.'' He glanced down at his newspaper only to hear his landlady take a hesitant breath. "What else, Della?''

"I didn't mean for things for go any further, believe me. But Erin called a little while ago. Now they wonder if Tess can spend the night. I told them I'd get back to them.''

"Tess doesn't even have a toothbrush along!''

"I could call with the okay. And you could drop off some of her things on the way to the Blue Parrot.''

"What's all this talk about the Blue Parrot?''

"It's bound to be a bit more fun than usual tonight, as Ivy rolled through here to pick Mandy up for a crack at the musical limelight.''

"Oh, I see,'' he crowed. "I'm supposed to rush over there and make amends with Mandy in that smoky fantasyland.''

She blissfully ignored his sarcasm. "See now. You aren't as socially dense as they say!''

"Have you any idea how annoying it is to listen to people with absolutely no talent singing their hearts out?"

"I run a boarding house," she said, enunciating slowly as if speaking to a half-wit. "With four bathrooms. A day doesn't go by that I don't hear a tinny rendition of some beloved song in a shower. If nothing else, I'm satisfied that anyone who is singing a peppy tune is happy. Besides, you spend plenty of time at the Blue Parrot, so you must get some fun out of it."

Della always had a way of cutting to the truth with a surgeon's precision. It was simple pride holding him back. He was Doc Hanson, Fairlane big shot, revered by at least eighty percent of the town. Generally, in a verbal tug of war, people ended up apologizing to him. But Mandy wouldn't do that. Not after he'd dashed off rather than confront the issues. She'd made her attempt and wouldn't make another. That much he knew about savvy city girls. If he wanted her back in that hot, expectant place where lovers danced, he'd have to make the first big move. But to a karaoke beat? In front of half the town?

"So, Doc, what do you say?"

He continued to fight his desires with an awkward protest. "Uh, Frank, there, is probably expecting me to play cards."

Della leaned over to nudge her husband, snoozing in an upright position one cushion over on the sofa. "Frank!"

Frank snorted and twisted his neck, then opened his eyes. "Huh?"

"You have your heart set on rummy tonight with the doc?"

"I'm watching TV." With that garbled reply, he thrust a limp arm in the direction of the droning television.

Della turned back to Brett. "Twenty years' experience as Mrs. Francis Scherer tells me there will be no cards dealt by Frank tonight."

"There's Beatrice to consider," Brett maintained.

"She's always up for a Saturday night video and some microwave popcorn."

"I think she's otherwise engaged."

"But it's her weekly routine. And I just spotted her in the dining room not long ago, scribbling in a notebook."

Della sang out in a coy way that instantly set Brett on edge. "Beatrice! Can you step in here for a minute?"

There was a lapse in time before the plump woman bounced into the doorway. "I'm rather busy. What is it?"

"Doc has something to ask you," Della said, gesturing to him.

"Yes, Brett?" Beatrice asked briskly.

"Well." He drummed his fingers on the wide armrest of the chair. "I was sort of wondering what Saturday night movie you had in mind?"

Beatrice positively glowed. "Haven't you heard?"

"Heard what?"

"I am working on a novel." She held up the pen in her hand.

"You?"

"Don't look so stunned. I am quite capable of writing things."

"I know that. You've done some great poems. I only meant that Mandy was the one with a book in mind."

"Well, we're in it together, Mandy and I."

Brett glanced back at Della to find her beaming. "Isn't that nice, Doc? The way Mandy has included Beatrice in her project?"

"Yes, Della. It was very thoughtful of her."

"I'm being an enormous help," Beatrice said rather defensively. "For a girl on a mission, Mandy seems terribly disorganized. But I've seen to the seed jobs, like creating characters, naming them. It turns out I'm quite good at it!"

Brett glumly cut to the bottom line. "So you're not watching a movie tonight."

"No, sorry. My muse is quite the insane taskmaster."

She fluttered pudgy fingers. ''As it is, I'll be up all hours jotting down outline ideas.''

Della leaned over to the chair, crowding Brett's space. ''*Now* can I interest you in a bit of smoke, drink and karaoke?''

Chapter Eleven

"So this is where the town hot spot sits, just down from the dental office." Amanda surveyed the Blue Parrot Lounge as Ivy pulled her Saturn off County Road 6 and into a gravel parking lot out front. It was a one-level structure of gray cedar boasting a glowing neon blue parrot in the front window. "No wonder the police patrol this road so diligently. It's where the action is!"

"I am so happy you didn't get a speeding ticket yesterday, hon," Ivy said. "If that cop had asked to see your driver's license and you'd produced that fake ID for Mandy Smythe, there would have been big trouble."

Amanda knew her smile was faint. "I know it. I shouldn't have let loose on the accelerator, but that Vette handled like a dream. Too bad its owner isn't as easy to handle."

Ivy dug a compact out of her purse and opened it to have a peek in its mirror. "These tensions between you aren't a bad test, really. I mean, Brett's finding out now if he can manage your kind of impetuosity before he gets in any deeper."

"So you do think there's a chance for us then?"

"You've always gotten exactly what you want, Amanda."

"True. Though I'm beginning to suspect my problem lies in wanting the wrong things."

"My experience exactly." Ivy applied fresh lipstick. "If it can happen to me, it can happen to you."

"Don't get misty just yet. I'm not about to go as radical as you have."

"It just happens here in Fairlane," Ivy cautioned her. "You slow down, start appreciating people not for their connections but for their human qualities."

Amanda borrowed the compact for a look at her own reflection. There was no argument that this past week she'd discovered a gentler slant to her features that shone through even now in full makeup. Spending hours in the clinic's file room had given her the opportunity to think. Always the type to run from her troubles, from her true self, she had needed courage to examine herself, the mistakes she'd made, the goals she'd chased, where she hoped to steer her future. It felt rather satisfying to hash things through. And she wasn't nearly finished with the project.

The women emerged from the car, Ivy dressed in white slacks and a red knit top threaded in gold, Amanda dressed in a black miniskirt and pale blue silk tank top with narrow straps. They'd shopped for shoes in town that morning during their walk and bought identical black sandals with chunky heels, which they wore tonight, as well as some gold jewelry.

As they rounded the corner of the building to enter, Amanda noted Rochelle's car parked in the side lot. When she remarked on it, Ivy was quick to reply that Rochelle was a regular, along with most everyone between the ages of twenty-one and thirty-five.

"She's got such a crush on Brett. It's a wonder she doesn't find someone else at a place like this," Amanda said.

"She has to be on the lookout first," Ivy retorted. She

pushed open the heavy wooden door to a dark smoky room thumping with an instrumental beat.

Amanda followed closely behind, taking in the bar to the left, the tables to the right and the large stage dominating the far wall. Small blue parrots were on display everywhere: wall murals, glowing centerpieces on the tables, wood carvings above the bar.

Ivy leaned close to speak above the din. "I'll get us a drink. What do you want?"

"A vodka martini, straight up with a twist."

"How about something simpler, like a gin and tonic on the rocks?"

"Think they can manage at least a wedge of lime with that?"

"I'll see what I can do."

Amanda stood near the wall, scanning the crowded tables. She caught sight of a group from the clinic seated together not ten feet away. Her heart hammered a bit faster as she took an inventory of the patrons. Nurses Rochelle and Kaitlyn, nurse's aide Sarah, and Doc Jack Graham. But no Brett. Ivy had whisked her out of the house before Amanda could quiz Della on any plans Brett might have for the evening. But she had hoped that he might show up here, so she could at the very least give him some static for stalking off on her.

It was the cheery blond Doc Jack who spotted her first and hailed her. She held up a hand as if to stall him. She didn't want to make a move without Ivy's approval. As it turned out, Ivy was more than happy to join their table. She was grinning as she handed Amanda a tall, cool glass.

"Don't tell me you're interested in Jack?" Amanda queried with new understanding.

"I just might be." Ivy nudged her along with an elbow. "Never considered him until lately, as he was tied up more often than not with Faith Barton. It was never very serious, but Faith taught at the school and I didn't want to damage our friendship over a man. But Faith has since moved to Kansas, making Jack a totally free man. Wouldn't hurt for you to sing the praises of young attractive schoolteachers, if the opportunity arises.''

''You do realize you'd have his grandma Charlotte in the deal.''

''I admit the lineage has driven off some fairly resilient contenders so far. But there are advantages. Charlotte would pound to the ground anyone who tried to hassle Mrs. Jack Graham and there would be an endless pipeline to the town's most tantalizing gossip.''

''All I can say is, he'd have to be really good in bed to make up for her.''

Ivy slanted Amanda an old familiar smile from their wildest times. ''He can audition for me anytime he likes.''

Together they burst into schoolgirl giggles.

The jolly crowd welcomed the pair. Rochelle even slid over a seat to open up two adjoining chairs. Amanda had to admit that even she seemed okay with their arrival. She suspected this might be due to the fact that she wasn't Brett's date for the evening, either.

''Welcome!'' Jack lifted his beer glass in toast. ''Everyone ends up here eventually.''

Amanda smiled. ''I just had to find out what people were talking about. According to Ivy, this place is jammed with *American Idol* hopefuls.''

Her remark brought a round of delighted laughter.

''Rochelle's husky voice is like liquid velvet,'' Jack said. ''The closest thing we have to Elvis.''

The feisty redhead gasped and slugged his arm. ''If you weren't my boss, I'd—I'd—''

''Snip his stethoscope?'' Kaitlyn Miner peeped from behind her bottle of wine cooler.

Jack reared in mocking affront as he became a figure of fun. ''I believe I'll have a talk with your husband, Kaitlyn.

You shouldn't be allowed out on your own with ideas like that!''

"My husband is coming later on," she announced. "To do his weekly gig of Beach Boy faves."

Groans greeted this news.

"So where is my learned partner tonight?" Jack asked Mandy.

She shrugged with forced gaiety. "I haven't spoken to him today."

Rochelle cleared her throat. "There's a rumor that you tore up the town with Tess yesterday after school, got her a big-city makeover."

"I didn't say it that way," Sarah Draper, the shy nurse's aide, protested. She turned to Amanda. "I'm sorry, Mandy. I overheard Doc Hanson on the phone with Della and got the impression that he was unhappy with the way Tess turned out. Please believe me, I meant you no harm by repeating it. I was merely complaining to the gang here because he was so grumpy all day."

Amanda, in the business of reporting just that sort of reliable gossip on a larger scale with the nation's most prominent celebrities, suddenly felt rather magnanimous about the mild betrayal. "No harm done, Sarah. What you say is absolutely right. Brett was annoyed with me for taking Tess to the salon. But in my own defense, I must say her hairstyle is darling and her little red toenails the cutest imaginable."

Tensions 'round the table subsided as quickly as they'd swelled.

"So, Mandy, how is your novel coming along?" Rochelle asked.

"Slow but sure. I've gotten Beatrice Flaherty involved and she's been a great help."

Rochelle expressed surprise, then offered a rather begrudging smile. "That's very kind of you. Beatrice is my cousin and I'm very fond of her. A project like this could give her a lot of joy.''

Jack nodded approvingly. ''She spent a lot of years nursing frail parents. Once they died, within months of one another, she couldn't bear to be alone, so she sold the family home and moved into the Scherers' boarding house. Never once in all the years did she ever take a risk of any kind, follow a dream.'' He glanced at Rochelle. ''This could indeed be her big chance.''

Amanda gulped her drink, almost choking on the lime wedge. Beatrice's joy? Her big break? She didn't want that kind of responsibility. But in small towns, apparently people never stopped looking out for one another. And through her own action, she'd sort of adopted Fairlane's spinster librarian!

A short while later a man hopped up on stage and announced that karaoke time was about to begin. With a round of applause, the boarding house's mailman, Mr. Stokes, grabbed the microphone and the melody for Billy Joel's ''Piano Man'' burst through the sound system as the lyrics popped up on a giant screen over Mr. Stokes's head.

Ivy signaled Amanda that it was time for another round, then went to get it. The next tune was a soulful one.

Jack leaned over the table to get Amanda's attention. ''Thanks for all you did this past week.''

''What do you mean?''

''Putting up with Charlotte, filing all those forms in that tiny room.''

''That tiny airless, windowless room?'' she teased.

Jack grinned. ''It'll all be different on Monday. You have both feet back on the ground and a new uniform all your own. Definitely prepared to represent us at the front desk.'' He extended his hand over the table and she shook it.

Ivy appeared moments later with two gin and tonics and slid into her chair beside Amanda. ''So, were you making a fool of yourself gushing about me?''

"Of course not."

"Well, why not?" Ivy took a sip of her drink, then stood again. "Guess I'm up next."

Rochelle smiled. "She always sings Cher tunes. The kick-ass ones."

Amanda nodded. "I can't tell you how many of our college friends would like to be here for this."

"I suppose the kindergarten class would enjoy it, too."

Ivy took the stage and the mike. "I am doing Cher, of course. But I'm going to slow it down tonight with a tune called, 'After All.' It's dedicated to two of my closest friends."

Amanda's first clue that something was happening was the change in Rochelle's expression. As she stared over Amanda's shoulder, her smile quickly began to fade.

A hand touched Amanda's shoulder. Slowly she turned on her chair to find Brett, dressed in a white polo and jeans, standing over her.

"Care to dance?" he asked tentatively. "I suspect that dedication was meant for us."

Silently, Amanda stood and allowed Brett to take her hand and guide her to the dance floor.

Gathering her close, he tipped his forehead into hers. "Hi, there."

"So you are talking to me again."

He lifted his chin. "Thanks for not letting on to the others that we have a problem."

"Oh, they already know. But not through me. The last thing I want to do is make things uncomfortable for you, Brett." She paused. "Well, let's just say that the last thing I want to do is tamper with your work situation."

Chuckling, he steered her slowly across the dance floor. "I saw you with Jack. Is he already cutting in on my territory?"

"Yes. But it's strictly business. He likes the way I handle Charlotte."

"You have been patient with her all week long."

Brett guided her along in a gentle sway. Amanda stayed silent, forcing herself to just stare at him. Long silences had always been a great way to prompt the celebrities she interviewed to talk.

"What?" he finally demanded.

"I'm just surprised that you're here, I guess, even though you did sort of unofficially invite me the other night."

"I'm a bit surprised myself. The clinic was busier than most Saturdays. And then I returned home to find that Della had allowed Tess to go a friend's house without my knowledge. It's been one of those rough days a guy usually would just like to see end."

"Work, I understand. But is there something wrong with Tess going to a friend's house?"

"Don't start in. Della already convinced me it's a good thing."

"It is. I never got to do it much at her age, either. And when I aged enough to realize what I had missed, I wasn't happy about it."

"Hey, she's even staying overnight. I stopped there on my way with her things. I'm still a father in training," he added. "Five years in and still learning as I go along."

"So have you come to realize that more likely than not I had good intentions with Tess yesterday?"

"I never doubted you had good intentions. I just have trouble with your impetuosity."

"That's part of my charm, running with my feelings. And Tess, being a little girl without a mommy, has really hit me where I live. I saw myself mirrored in her eyes as she pleaded for some attention, some female bonding. I was determined to go overboard pampering her, not only for her sake, but to prove I was worthy of your trust." She paused expectantly, hoping that he would understand.

His expression softened. "I still feel that you should have called ahead and checked things out with me."

"Oh, Brett…"

"And I'd like to believe you'd have been gracious enough to accept my answer of no."

"For Pete's sake!"

He pressed a finger to her lips. "Never mind. The issue isn't even negotiable. But I do realize that I overreacted and for that I'm sorry."

Plainly he wasn't prepared to draw her closer. It was disappointing.

He hesitated. "It's just that I want to make decisions about Tess's appearance. I figure if she gets used to that arrangement, she won't go off and do anything radical later, like hair colors and piercings."

She chuckled. "That is so lame, Doc. Considering you've had twenty-four hours to prepare something."

"It's the best I can do right now."

"So don't tell me the truth."

He held her closer and twirled them deeper into the crowd. "The bottom line is, I realize I need to allow Tess more space to grow and I intend to follow through."

"Tess is doing fine. You're the one who needs to grow," she protested. "My guess is that no one in this town is out to hurt you. So the walls you've built up around yourself seem so unnecessary."

He smiled. "Okay, Mandy. Let's have the whole thing out tonight. I'll tell you all my secrets after you tell me yours."

She tensed in his arms. "On second thought, I realize I'm being greedy. You're speaking to me again and that's reward enough."

His mouth crooked sexily. "Don't be so hasty. There are a lot of rewards that require very little talking."

By ten-thirty their table was jammed, chair locked against chair. Kaitlyn Miner's husband Justin had shown up as well as Ivy's landlord Oliver Pratt. Stories were being bandied about by all the clinic staff about nurses gallantly covering for a couple of prankster docs, and the docs were fighting back with tales of nurses hiding paperbacks every place. It was all exaggerated but in the best of fun.

Amanda couldn't help but note that Rochelle had grown extremely quiet since Brett's arrival but she felt helpless against the other woman's jealousy. Apparently, Brett felt her negative energy, as well, for he tried at length to get the nurse to laugh over office buffoonery.

Finally, when Jack Graham took the microphone to belt out a jazzy rendition of a Bob Seger classic, Amanda suggested that Brett ask Rochelle to dance. Rochelle froze briefly at the offer, but stiffly followed him out to the dance floor full of gyrating adults.

Ivy, seated at Amanda's right, expressed doubt over the act of kindness. "Rochelle has no right to complain about not having her chance with Brett. She's lived here all her life. She was one of the clinic's original staff members when Jack took over three years ago and therefore has been available to Brett since he arrived two years ago."

"We will have to have some kind of working relationship," Amanda reasoned. "Especially now that I'm being sprung from the file room to work out front. I figure it's all about communication—with everyone on staff."

"Well, even if you weren't having a thing, it's high time Rochelle laid off him."

"I only wish he and I could get away from here, to make things up properly." As the song wound down, Amanda stood. "I think I'll go to the ladies' room. Be right back."

Amanda wended her way back to the bar area and discovered the rest rooms in a corner just to the right of the entrance. She was reapplying her makeup several minutes later when the door popped open and a redhead charged inside. Amanda winced. It was Rochelle.

"You were really tearing it up on the floor," Amanda said pleasantly.

"You actually told him to dance with me, didn't you?"

Rochelle's enraged image appeared beside hers in the long mirror above the row of sinks. Her pale freckled face was full of angry red splotches.

"No—"

Rochelle smacked the vanity top. "Oh, knock it off. I'm not some pity case, Miss City Airhead."

Amanda flushed with anger. "You had a huge head start on me, Rochelle. If Brett wanted you, he had plenty of opportunity to show it."

"Oh, is that what you think? Well, we've had a good relationship for quite some time."

"He hasn't been really dating you, has he?"

"Not the way you probably mean. But a man doesn't have to take a woman to bed to prove he cares deeply for her."

"No, but it sure is fun."

Rochelle shook a clenched fist, which bore her high school class ring in an honored place on her left ring finger. "It's not fair the way you are distracting him. I am hardworking, stable. I can provide him a nice home and children." She shook her head ruefully. "Your ditzy type is liable to toss him aside once the *fun* wears off."

"You're wrong!" Despite Amanda's cry of denial, she was stricken by the thought that someone like Rochelle might be better for a practical man like Brett in the long run.

As if sensing her rival's uncertainty, Rochelle forged ahead. "Brett hasn't dated anyone regularly for heaven knows how long. He's found his comfort in hanging out with the work crowd. We dance often, without prodding from the likes of you. We're good together. We understand one another, in a deep way you can't begin to understand." Rochelle leveled a finger in her face. "Think about everything I've said. Maybe the best thing you can do for Brett during your little visit here is to stay out of the sack!"

With that she spun on her heel, flung open the door and charged out.

Amanda slowly returned her cosmetics to her purse as her mind whirled with clashing suppositions. If Brett was fond of Rochelle, he would have made love to her by now, in the privacy of her own home. Why, he had made love to *Amanda* at the boarding house, even though he felt it was inappropriate due to the gossip it might stir up. On the other hand, Rochelle and Brett did share their dedication to medicine. After a hard day at the office, he could share his troubles with her and she would understand.

But was professional understanding what Brett needed most? She'd never once heard Rochelle laugh in a light-hearted way or make light of any situation. Some considered laughter the best medicine, which was something Amanda could provide in high doses.

Amanda found this internal war most enlightening. She'd seriously begun to imagine a long-term future with Brett, wondering if she was worthy of the job.

It was the first time in her life she'd ever wondered if *she* measured up, rather than vice versa.

She emerged from the rest room to find Brett pacing in the dark alcove at the entrance. She collided with him as he strode forward.

"Everything all right?" he asked.

"Excuse me?"

"Rochelle just about mowed me over a minute ago."

"That's what you get for loitering near the ladies' room. Didn't they teach you caution in junior high?"

"Okay, don't tell me what went on."

"I think you already know what went on. And I'd appreciate it if you didn't get that infuriating twinkle in your eye at the very idea of two women in the heat of battle."

He sighed. "I'm beginning to see it's more serious with Rochelle than I ever knew."

"Finally!"

"Well, only because Ivy told me," he admitted. "She saw Rochelle note your absence at the table and take off with a full head of steam."

"Why haven't you cut the cord with Rochelle one way or the other?"

"Never felt the need. We've never had anything. I've never encouraged her beyond a friendly working relationship. You've gotta give me a break. She's never put any real moves on me directly."

"It's probably still partly your fault," Amanda asserted, feeling unexpected sympathy for the intense other woman. "You socialize with the work crowd all the time and have shown no interest in anyone else."

He grasped her shoulders and shot her an urgent look. "That's changed now with you. As far as I'm concerned, my intentions for Rochelle have always been the same. It's high time she accepted it. And I will speak to her. I promise."

"Fair enough, Brett."

"So we're cool?"

"Of course." She rubbed her temples as someone's tin voice belted out a popular song. "How I wish we could be alone. But," she hastily added, "I understand your situation back at the house, not wanting to confuse Tess."

To her surprise, Brett smiled, then held up a key ring.

"What's that?"

"The key to Ivy's apartment. She insists we relax there alone for a couple of hours."

"And what will she do in the meantime?"

He showed her his watch, which read eleven. "About midnight she does a long medley of rock tunes that require bumping and grinding. Then, if Oliver is here as he is tonight, they team up for some duets. About one o'clock, she'll be joining the clinic gang at Jack's house for pizza. And she's promised to drag Oliver along to that, too, so he won't intrude."

Amanda clasped her hands in delight. "I'll repay her somehow."

"She says you already did in college, the time in Denver when that ski instructor couldn't keep his pole to himself."

"She told you about that!"

"Just a sketchy replay. Though she doubts he ever took a slope on his rear end before."

"He was lucky he didn't have that pole between his legs when I gave him a shove."

Brett winced as he guided her to the door. "You women are really tough."

Chapter Twelve

Brett guided his Corvette down a deserted Main Street a short while later. Staring out the passenger window, Amanda remarked on the fact that only every other street-light was aglow.

"It's a budget cutback for the city," he explained. "The council—of which I am a member—voted for it unanimously. The extra light seemed unnecessary, as there is little action on this street after dark."

She reached over and squeezed his thigh. "Until now."

With a chuckle he shifted gears.

Brett circled the block housing Oliver Pratt's building, then parked in the rear alley, in Pratt's reserved space.

"You could have parked in Ivy's space," she chided. "As we are using her place."

"I could have. But last month when Oliver was in to the clinic to see Jack about some trivial ailment, he had the nerve to park in my space. The lot was full, due to a stomach bug passing through the grade school, and I had to park on the street and walk a full block with a repaired coffee urn and my medical bag."

"Oo-oh, revenge is sweet," she teased, easing out of the car.

They circled the building on foot, pausing at the door that led directly to the apartments upstairs. Amanda held

Brett's penlight near the doorknob as he tried to insert one key, then another into the lock. The second one worked, allowing them access to the small foyer and steep bank of stairs. Brett took the penlight back and held it high for Amanda's benefit.

"It's so nice to be off those crutches," she confided, taking the stairs with a quick step.

"Gee, somebody's in a hurry."

Holding tight to the banister, she half turned with a smirk. "Of course. You're going to seduce me and I can't wait to see how you do it."

"Slow down a little," he said gruffly.

"Why? You think I'm clumsy enough to twist my leg again?"

"Not at all. I only want to enjoy your legs in that postage-stamp miniskirt."

"Ha!" she cried. "You men are all alike, wondering if I'm wearing panties."

His voice grew husky. "Aren't you?"

"Just try and find out!" With that, she skipped up the last few stairs and popped through the fire door.

Moments later they used another key to gain access to Ivy's small apartment.

"Ivy mentioned that the wall switch near the door doesn't work," Brett cautioned. "There's another one near the kitchen doorway."

"I'll go," she volunteered.

"No, I have the light." Brett took no more than three steps before he grunted in pain.

"What's wrong?"

"I just hit my knee on something." He aimed the beam lower to discover that there was a weight set in the center of the room. Skirting it, he proceeded to the wall switch. Flicking it on brought two more lamps to life. Wandering back to Amanda, he placed an arm around her shoulders. "This whole place is a mess!"

"It's not so bad. Maybe a little cluttered."

"Was she like this back in college?"

"Who wasn't?"

"I wasn't."

She eased up close to him. "Well, you could use a little mussing up every now and then." When he grinned she reached up and ran a hand through his thick black hair. "There! Ruffled hair. Looks sexy."

He gently touched her face. "You look sexy all the time. Night and day. You drive me nuts."

She moved even closer to him for full body contact. Grasping his rear end, she pressed her body up against his and began moving. He released a slow groan of pleasure.

"Take your time, imagine how fun this will be without any clothes."

"Oh, yes. We won't hurry this time."

No sooner had he spoken than he abruptly released her. "Hang on. I'll be right back."

"Hey, what's the matter? You going to comb your hair?"

"Ha-ha. Ivy had the nerve to tell me she keeps condoms in her medicine cabinet. I acted all put out by the inference, but I do need one."

She gasped in teasing surprise. "I can't believe it. A man who doesn't carry a condom in his wallet?"

"You know I don't have a girlfriend!"

"That's what you think," she said with a wink.

When he returned, she was peeling off her silky tank top.

"Hold it. That's my job." He moved up to assist, pulling it over her head, tossing it aside. His gaze immediately fastened on her breasts, held fast in a strapless lace bra. Using his fingertips, he caressed the small globes of flesh, then shuddered as her nipples hardened under the textured fabric. In plain and utter fascination, he was soon bending over to nibble at her rigid buds through the lace, skimming his tongue over the coarse surface. Finally he unhooked the clasp and put his tongue on her bare skin.

A hot fever snaking through her now, Amanda anxiously moved her hands to his waist. Opening his belt and zipper, she hooked her thumbs in his briefs and pushed his clothing to the floor.

Kissing his way back up to her throat, he clamped a hand to her thigh and boldly slid it up her skirt. ''Ah, so you are wearing panties.''

''You sound pleased.''

''I am. The very idea that you would wiggle around the Blue Parrot without 'em, in a skirt this short, is unthinkable.''

''You're right. But there are times when I do indeed go without the skivvies. Especially when I'm wearing clingy formal wear.''

''Then we must go formal real soon. You'll be wearing nothing at all underneath and only I will know it. What fun…'' He used his free hand to brush aside her hair to fully expose her face. The other hand, still riding her hip, circled 'round and clutched the swell of her bottom and squeezed. Then watching her carefully, he pushed her firmly into his groin.

Amanda's response could not have disappointed him. She lost her breath as her belly hit his rigid erection. Grasping his penis, she stroked it with a quick motion, arousing him further.

His mouth fell on hers with hot, crushing passion. With a low groan he jabbed his tongue into her mouth, hungrily tasting the sensitive lining of her cheeks. All the while his fingers kneaded the swell of her bottom, eventually tugging at the tiny silken panties until they slipped down her legs.

She gasped against his mouth as his fingers slipped between the ridge of her bottom, probing the sensitive skin hidden there, moving to her feminine opening. The more she squirmed in pleasure, the deeper inside her he drove his fingers.

Tearing his lips from hers, he muttered, "You are an irresistible witch in that skirt."

"With a spell on you." She hooked her arms around his neck to get closer, feel the planes of his body. For a long moment they melded as one, caressing one another. By mutual agreement, she slid the condom on him.

Then abruptly, he hoisted her in the air. Instinctively she wrapped her slim legs around his waist. Moving to the nearest wall, he leaned against it and drove her down over him, thrusting himself inside her. Amanda gave a small cry of pleasure as his solid flesh invaded her soft, sensitive tunnel.

Together they rocked upright, Amanda gently bumping the wall over and over again. Closing her eyes, she lost herself in the sweet, burning friction, the steady mounting pressure. Eventually, ever so gently, they sank to the floor in release. There Amanda crawled on top of him and lay quietly, listening to his heartbeat slowing down.

The emotional depth of their union was staggering. She had never felt closer to another human being.

"I believe you could kill me within a month," he confided, stroking her back possessively.

"A month of this?" She lifted her chin from his chest. "Suppose it would be well worth the prison term."

BRETT AND AMANDA arrived back at the boarding house at nearly 2:00 a.m. Rather than just the usual night-lights in the foyer and on the stair landing aglow, lamps still burned in the living room. Investigating, they discovered Beatrice seated in a rocker-recliner and wrapped tight in a white terry robe, notebook and pen in her lap, head thrown back and snoring rhythmically.

"So it's true," Brett murmured smugly.

"What?"

"That Beatrice snores louder than Frank."

"Oh, Brett."

"But she's always maintained the mysterious snore-in-the-night couldn't possibly be her. Why is it that all women are in denial about snoring?"

Amanda gently removed the book and pen from Beatrice's lap and set them on the end table. "We need to hang on to some illusions."

"You wouldn't believe how unusual it is to find her here this way," he remarked with interest. "She's never stayed up later than eleven-thirty in the two years I've known her." He rubbed his chin thoughtfully. "I suppose she dozed off working on *your* book project."

"So you know about that."

"Yes. Like everyone else, I couldn't be happier with the proposition."

His affectionate smile almost melted Amanda on the spot. She was rarely recognized for good works, even when she had the best intentions. Brett—all the residents here, in fact—seemed to have no problem in seeing her good qualities, giving her the benefit of the doubt.

Now she knelt beside the chair and spoke gently. "Wake up, Beatrice."

The middle-aged woman's puffy face twitched and she cracked open her eyes. She focused on Amanda. "Sorry I dozed off. Were we working together? I dreamt we were."

"You were on your own tonight, I'm afraid. But I'm free tomorrow for a real musefest."

"Good, good. Just close my door as you leave."

"Bea," Brett interposed.

Her eyes flew open wide now. "What are you doing here, Doc?"

"This isn't your bedroom. You are in the living room. We just got home and merely want to help you upstairs."

With a yawn, Beatrice struggled to sit upright in the deep, cushioned rocker. A sound at the doorway startled them all.

"So it *is* you!"

Della stood in front of them with hands on hips, dressed in a peach tricot nightgown that was ready for the rag bag, gripping a brass candlestick as a weapon. "You're later than usual. Lucky I didn't call the cops before checking."

"As if." Brett rolled his eyes.

Della lifted her chin. "I might have, smart man."

"Sure, and give up the chance of making the front page of the *Fairlane Gazette*? I can see the headline. Landlady Kills Colonel Mustard In Living Room With Candlestick."

"You're mocking me, Doc, because Clue is my favorite game. And you think it's childish."

"You like it best because it's the only game you can win every time."

Della conceded as much with a nod. "So how was your evening at the Blue Parrot?"

"Just fine."

"I was right, wasn't I, Doc?" Della smiled.

Amanda frowned as he shifted nervously.

"What do you mean, Della?" Amanda asked.

"Only that I made him go on over there to make up with you. No sense sittin' around here pouting because his child's toenails are red. Even Tess had a social commitment."

Brett was traumatized. "Now, Della, don't trivialize parenting issues—"

"Well, you and Mandy must have worked things out because you've come home together. And that's what matters most, I guess."

Amanda grinned. "We gave everything a complete workout and we're friends again."

"Can we all go to bed now?" Beatrice whined, now on her feet.

Della humphed. "Oh, fine. You three hit the sack. I'm wide awake now after listening to you chatting down here. But go ahead, leave me alone."

"Make some warm milk," Brett suggested.

"Some prescription. See you in the morning for church." With a wave of disgust, Della headed down the hallway toward the kitchen.

Beatrice shook her head. "I suppose I can keep her company. For a little while." Ambling over to the liquor cabinet in the corner, she took the brandy bottle and disappeared.

"I would have made up with you on my own, you know," Brett murmured, winding an arm around Amanda's shoulders. "By tomorrow at the latest."

She winked. "At the latest. But to think that Della cared enough to push you is pretty nice."

"She did it for both of us."

Brett kept his arm around Amanda as they took the staircase. Then he dropped her off at her door. "What are you thinking about, with that far-off smile?"

She poked him in the chest. "More than your basic animal urges, hotshot."

He leaned against the door frame, looking suitably surprised. "Really."

"Yes. As good as we were together, I'm also enjoying the family atmosphere this whole house brings me."

He enveloped her in his arms. "You've brought this house a lot of joy, too. Not that we aren't a fun bunch in general. But your ideas, your laughter, your wacky spirit, have breathed new life into our old routine."

She wrinkled her nose. "I do wish you could come inside, just for a bit."

He removed the fingers climbing his shirt. "Not after all we went through to be discreet."

"We didn't go through that much, did we?"

"No? My shin must have a bruise the size of a pancake on it from hitting that barbell set." He took the key from her hand, slid it in her lock and opened her door. Wide.

"Now good night. I'll see you in the morning. For church."
With that he pushed her inside and out of reach.

Early the next morning, the boarders prepared for church.
Amanda was private about her religion and wasn't sure she
wanted to attend church the following morning with the
boarders. But at breakfast Brett explained that the service
was nondenominational, that a belief in God would put her
on common ground with those attending.

Upon reaching the church a block off Main Street,
Amanda was surprised to discover the grand, old, steepled
structure was named Common Ground. And the place was
packed with men in suits and women in pretty dresses.
Even Ivy was there, in a cotton blouse and denim skirt.

Afterward, standing in the shade of a large oak, Amanda
waited while Brett gave a patient named Julie Kessel some
free advice. Julie was giving Brett a first-hand look at the
ingrown toenail on pitiful display in her open-toed shoe.

"I wish I could recommend some miracle medicine,"
Brett said patiently. "But you'll just have to muster your
courage and come in to the clinic for a surgical visit. I
promise I'll be gentle," he added with a smile.

Visibly disappointed, Julie hobbled away.

"Good morning, kids," Ivy said brightly as she came up
to them. "Have you something for me?"

Amanda took one look at her outstretched hand and
shook it.

"No, I mean my key ring," Ivy whispered with a laugh.

Brett dug into his pocket for the ring and he slipped it
to her. "Sorry. In all the excitement, I forgot to leave it
under your mat."

"Yeah, well I had to trot down to Oliver's place for a
spare, after fending off some very nervy advances. Then I
had to allow him to think I lost my key ring at the Blue
Parrot. He gave me a lecture on carelessness, then vowed
to shake down the owner until he 'spit it up.'"

''You can handle that pretentious dope,'' Brett said. ''Tell him you found them on the staircase this morning.''

''Yes, I'll do that. He sleeps until noon on Sundays. He won't know the difference.''

''Thanks, Ivy,'' Amanda murmured. ''It was a nice favor, offered at just the right time.''

''So how was the rest of your evening?'' Brett inquired.

''Best as could be expected, being obligated to keep Oliver on a short leash and away from the building.''

Brett gave her a knowing grin. ''Amanda tells me you're interested in Jack.''

''Maybe. He was unavailable for so long, attached to Faith Barton, I never expected a chance at him.''

''You're sure a slow mover. Faith took off for Kansas a month ago.''

Ivy fingered her short black hair as a fly buzzed 'round. ''I didn't want to be his rebound chick. Or part of the flock standing in line at his back door with a casserole.''

''Probably because you can't make a casserole,'' Amanda teased.

''And Charlotte's needed time to settle down, too. She's been buzzing around him like our pesky fly here,'' Ivy said, swatting at the swooping pest. ''Making sure no woman has the chance to upset him.''

Brett nodded in understanding. ''Charlotte's better. She's on to hoping for just the right donor for great-grandchildren.''

Ivy rolled her eyes. ''I can hear his wedding vows now. 'Do you, Jack Graham, take this woman to be the mother of Charlotte's great-grandkids?'

The threesome erupted in laughter loud enough to turn heads.

Amanda looked around. ''I don't see Jack here this morning.''

Brett shrugged. ''He's on call today, so he's liable to be distracted.'' He looked at his watch and took Amanda's arm in his. "It's time to pick up Tess at the Cordays'. Hope she wasn't too rambunctious."

Ivy brightened. "I noticed that little friendship taking shape. They're a nice couple, Erin and Christopher. You'll like them, Mandy."

Within minutes Brett was pulling onto a blacktop driveway on a quiet residential street some blocks away from the Scherer boarding house, in a newer section of town. The Corday home was a more modern split-level style and their yard boasted trees and shrubs that hadn't had time for much of a growing spurt.

Amanda fleetingly wondered what it would be like to live on this street, sprinkling her own grass, leaning over the neighbor's fence to chat. What did people here talk about? Their flowers? Their children? The weather? Amanda's jet-set lifestyle allowed her so much freedom worldwide, access to just about anyone. And what entertainment it was to consort with the planet's hottest celebrities. There was always something going on, something to arouse excitement.

But did any of it hold true meaning in the long run? Or was it as surface as it seemed, a whirlwind of faux relationships like she had had with Trevor? Those hot celebrities generally had selfish motives in mind, courting her to either encourage a story or to kill one. She was beginning to wonder who, if anyone, truly liked her for herself. If she'd have a friend left if she broke off from her father for good, leaving behind his mantle of power and riches.

She'd have friends here in Fairlane, she suspected. And that might not be half bad. Ivy had done it, made the switch from the fast track to the slow lane. Was it right for Amanda? Would she get bored with this more limited routine?

A good-looking couple of Amanda's age emerged from behind the house, looking cheery and content, dressed in shorts and T-shirts. She couldn't help envisioning Brett and herself in their place. And wondering…

Introductions were made. Amanda played the good sport as they gave her an inspection and asked her some leading questions.

"Come into the house for some lemonade," Erin invited. "The girls are having some now."

They entered the house from the backyard's redwood deck. Christopher opened the sliding-glass door and little-girl chatter rose in the air.

One look at Brett had Tess bouncing off her kitchen chair. "Daddy!" She charged into his arms and gave him a huge squeeze around the middle. "We had the best time!"

He ruffled her dark hair. "Did you miss me at all?"

"Nope. Too busy."

The girls went back to their snack. Erin took hold of the plastic pitcher on the counter and poured four more glasses of lemonade.

"Did you see the swing set, Daddy?" Tess asked over the rim of her plastic mug. "It is super awesome. Maybe Frank and Della will want one."

Brett shifted uncomfortably. "I don't think so, honey."

"Well, you can make them!"

"No, the Scherers own the house. They make the rules."

"Then maybe we should have our own house!" With a solid nod, Tess turned her attention back to Hailey.

Brett's jaw dropped at the bold and ruthless assessment, but he said nothing.

Christopher gave them a tour of the house while they sipped their drinks. There was a spare third bedroom in shambles, with wallpapering equipment stacked in the center.

"This is to be our nursery," Erin explained. She pinkened then, holding up a hand. "Not that I'm pregnant yet. Don't want that rumor to get started. But we're trying to conceive and want the baby's room to be ready, perfect. When Hailey was born we were stuck in one of those old apartments near the highway. Night and day, all you heard was the roar of traffic, but no one had tolerance for our crying child. We were constantly having to keep her quiet in that single bedroom. Having this space for our family as it grows is especially important to us.''

Amanda nodded. She'd wondered what made people happy along this street and she'd pretty much gotten her answer. Making children, raising children, decorating personal space big enough to shout in, apparently brought untold happiness to young intelligent people who, like herself, only wanted to love and be loved. Miracle of miracles, she was beginning to believe she could figure out this love business yet. Identify the real thing and take advantage of it.

Brett and Amanda left some fifteen minutes later, without the child they'd come for. The Cordays were planning a picnic with Christopher's folks and welcomed a playmate for Hailey.

''Have you ever thought of owning your own home?'' Amanda asked him as they rolled down the street in the Vette.

Brett braked as a dog loped in front of the car, followed by a frazzled owner. ''Sure. It was my original plan. The stop at the Scherers was only meant to be temporary, until I could get settled in the family practice. But weeks there stretched into months somehow.''

''Della made it clear to Rochelle, on my first day here, that you were best off under her roof.''

Brett smiled. ''She and Frank have been like parents to me, though they're only in their forties. Guess what it came down to was the fact that I would always need a live-in housekeeper to care for Tess. As much as I miss owning my own domain, I know that no one could tend to Tess's needs better than the Scherers and the other boarders.'' His voice took on a husky edge. "It's just all worked out so well for us. I'm so grateful to all of them."

Amanda rarely felt shy or at a loss for words, but she hesitated before replying. "Maybe in the right circumstances, you might consider, well, buying a backyard for that swing set."

He glanced at her in sharp surprise, as if he had misheard. "The situation would have to be perfect. Everybody involved would have to be absolutely certain that was the only kind of swinging they cared to do. Ever again."

Amanda stared out the window with a sigh. His message clearly registered on the side of caution. But this was understandable. He was putting Tess first, as a good father should. She also sensed that he had at least a sketchy picture of her background. If not the players' names, certainly the names of the playgrounds.

But none of this would deter her from pushing deeper into their affair with the highest hopes. The idea of being entwined in true love and loyalty gave her a quiver of excitement that no frolic could ever match, on any playground.

Chapter Thirteen

Charlotte Evenson's gray eyes glittered like diamond chips as they surveyed Amanda from her bandage-free ankle to her new, more stylish uniform. She spoke with a knowing smirk. "So you've done it. Earned a seat of honor here in the hub."

They were standing together behind the clinic's check-in counter on Monday morning. Amanda took a moment to gaze back at the file room where she'd been trapped all of last week. "Hardly seems that momentous a journey, rolling my stool from in there to out here."

"Don't underestimate the trip, my girl," Charlotte bellowed. "By crossing that threshold, you have entered phase two of your training. Understand that coming in direct contact with our patients is no small matter. Clerks seated in the hub have a huge responsibility. We are the clinic's official greeters, the first call for help, the Mother Earth of Medicine."

Amanda was startled by the daunting job description. "Medical training isn't required, is it?"

"Not officially. Though after years in the game, I do see myself as an unsung member of the team. Competent without any sort of recognized license."

Never especially good with even a small cut or bruise,

Amanda felt her usual bravado failing her. "Maybe I don't have what it takes after all."

"Well, the docs say you do. They've made it abundantly clear." She heaved a tremendous sigh. "I got you through phase one, so there's nothing for it but for me to pull you through phase two, as well."

"Where does phase two begin exactly?"

Charlotte patted her stiff yellow hair cloud. She seemed genuinely bewildered. "Not sure. Never had to carry on past phase one before. Always managed to crack my novices during the first week with a variety of grunt work. Sometimes it took a day or two. Three at the most. Guess the Pearson girl hung on a whole week. But in the end she found a higher-paying, less-demanding position at Ludlum Attorneys-At-Law." Her aged face pinched craftily. "Don't know how those lawyers got hold of her glowing résumé so fast."

"Gee, I wonder." Amanda regarded Charlotte with the dubiety she deserved.

"But none of those tricks are up my sleeve now. Jack vowed to fire me if I didn't slow down a bit, get my blood pressure back under control. And I can tell he means it this time."

The phone rang then. With a practiced motion Charlotte whirled to scoop up the receiver and punched the blinking button on the console. "Fairlane Clinic. Hello, Tracy. Doc Graham? What do you wish to speak to him about? I figured it was the baby, but what about her? Crying all the time? It's probably out of pain, yes. *Painful gas.* You know nursing is a big responsibility. You drinking caffeine after Doc told you not to? How about eating tacos? Don't try and lie to me, young lady. You were seen at the Skyline Café shoveling in all sorts of junk. Never mind how I know. In any case, Doc can't come to the phone right now, he's with a patient. Take my word on Suzy's condition. I can hear the crying in the background and it sounds like gas pains. Sure, there's different kinds of cries. Short sharp screams mean, 'Gas, my mommy's eating junk.' Yes, rest assured I will tell him you called.''

Amanda gasped as Charlotte hung up the phone. ''That's how you handle things?''

Charlotte snapped her fingers. ''Nothin' to it.''

''How do you know so much about babies' cries?''

''Read an article about it last year in *Family Circle* magazine. But it doesn't matter where or when I got the scoop. All that matters is that I know the right thing at the right time.''

''Wow. Never in my life have I heard a receptionist do more than direct calls, take messages, make appointments.''

''That's impersonal big-city procedure to a tee.''

''Well, yes. But is there that much difference here in a small town?''

''Sure there is! It would be ridiculous to stand on ceremony around here, where there's only so much time for so many needs. If I allowed all calls to go through to the docs, they'd fall behind in their appointments. It's my duty and pleasure to assist callers like Tracy.''

Amanda knew her jaw was hanging open.

''You will have to work hard if you want to live up to that new jazzy uniform of yours. The docs have no concept of what I do for them each and every day. They see me as nothing more than an overworked clerk.'' She held up a fat palm as Amanda began to speak. ''Now don't get me wrong. I'm not saying the job is impossible to learn. I'm just saying that it takes time and dedication. That you will have to study my moves extra hard.''

''I happen to be reasonably intelligent and friendly,'' Amanda said.

''Even you gotta admit you didn't catch on to my filing system right off. But I agree that you do have a winning personality, which will take you a long way. And you make Doc Hanson so happy. He was grinning at me like some kind of dope last Monday all the while he and Jack were chewing me out for stashing you in the file room. I was smiling myself, all the while I was yelling back about the crummy job you were doing. But all of that is water under the bridge.''

''Gee, thanks.''

''You'll be fine. Throw yourself into the job heart and soul.''

''Watch and learn?''

''Precisely.''

The front door opened and a balding middle-aged man in a garage mechanic's uniform ambled in and over to the counter. ''Afternoon, ladies.''

''Hello, Timothy.''

His voice dropped a notch. ''I'm picking up something. From Doc Graham.''

Charlotte shuffled to a wide wooden cupboard, opened it and pawed through a plastic basket of brown envelopes. She pulled one out, broke the envelope's seal, appeared to verify its contents, then brought it to the counter. ''So you decided to try Viagra. I suppose this means that Vicki won't be available for the bowling league on Thursday nights anymore. I mean—'' she intimated in a stage-like hush ''—I recall that Thursday night was always your night for nookie. Before you hit the rough spot.''

Timothy gritted his teeth. ''I'm sure that's our own business.''

''I'd agree if we hadn't changed our bowling schedule from Tuesdays to Thursdays in the first place so you two could take dance lessons of the Latin rhythm flavor to rekindle the dying flames of your marriage. All I'm saying is, I suppose now you'll still be dancing on Tuesdays and having a bit of the nookie again on Thursdays, clogging up two whole nights.''

''I'll tell Vicki about your concerns,'' he said tightly.

"I'm sure something can be worked out with your bowling league."

"Would appreciate it. We're playing the Portland Roundabouts next week. They're especially tough and nobody picks up a spare like Vicki."

Looking lost for words, Timothy snatched the envelope, turned on his heel and marched out.

"There walks another healing soul on my watch," Charlotte declared with wistful modesty. "Vicki confided to the team about Timothy's performance problems. And who but I would be in a position to tell her that the clinic gives out samples of Viagra? 'Why not give it a test drive?' I said. 'All he needs is Jack's okay.' And mind you, I did all of this knowing it would most likely screw up bowling something awful."

Amanda gaped. "Amazing again."

"Thank you." The words suggested a brisk dismissal as Charlotte turned her back on her to sift through phone messages.

"So what, exactly, do you want me to do here?" Amanda pressed.

Charlotte looked around and scratched her cheek. "We could use some fresh coffee in the break room. The urn could actually do with a scrub."

"Charlotte…" Brett's deep voice rumbled behind them. As he appeared around the corner of the hallway, it was highly likely that he had been eavesdropping for at least a moment or two.

Amanda's heart skipped a beat as it always did at the sight of Brett in cool physician mode, with a crisp white lab coat over a white shirt and dark slacks, stethoscope hanging casually around his neck, black hair clipped short, handsome face arranged in supreme confidence.

"Oh! Morning, Doc." Charlotte suddenly looked like a child with her hand stuck in the cookie jar.

"Just thought I'd pop out to see how things are going."

Charlotte shrugged. "Well, I have to admit, Mandy's uniform is very nice. Maybe I've been an old fogey about hanging on to these old nylon numbers. Any chance of outfitting all of us the same way?"

With ill-concealed impatience, Brett cut to the chase. "Are you going to give Mandy responsibilities or not?"

"Of course I am. Just know," she muttered, "how important the coffee is to everyone."

"I washed the urn myself this morning."

"Oh."

"I will speak to Jack about more new uniforms, when I tell him how smoothly this transition is going out here."

"Fair enough."

"So what is Mandy's first order of business?"

"Well…"

"What do you do when you arrive?" Brett pressed.

"First thing, I go over the appointment book and jot down the names of the patients scheduled to come in."

"Then?" Brett prodded.

"I go and collect those files out of the file room."

Brett handed their protégé a pen and pad of paper. Amanda dutifully moved to the open book lying on the counter and began to jot down the names.

"You can't take forever doing this task," Charlotte warned. "The patients will be streaming in soon."

"Not a problem." Amanda smiled sweetly. "I know the files very well now."

"Then what happens?" Brett asked.

Charlotte sighed loudly. "She brings the files out here and arranges them in order of appointment."

"Do I separate them by doctor?"

"Hells bells, this isn't *ER*. Sometimes the patients don't even have a choice of doctor if something comes up." As Brett opened his mouth to speak again, Charlotte went on, standing beside her trainee. "So the files get stacked in this basket. When a patient arrives, you take their file, *open it,* check to see if their insurance information is up-to-date, ask for any co-pay listed.'' Charlotte walked over to a file rack hanging on the wall near the corridor leading to the exam rooms. ''A nurse will come out and check the rack and lead the patient back to a room.''

''And when the telephone rings…''

Charlotte glared at Brett. ''She isn't going near that telephone until I think she's ready. Now for the sake of time, I suggest you get your girlfriend sashaying back for those files!''

Alone with Brett in the file room, Amanda leaned against him. ''Shoot me now.''

He pressed a consolatory hand to her back. ''It isn't that bad.''

''How can you lie like that?''

''Charlotte will get used to you.''

''I should live that long.''

''I do admit she'll probably outlive us all.''

''I want you to know I'm not accustomed to being pushed around this way! People generally…look up to me.''

She watched him struggle for a comeback. ''Well, you really skunked her by learning her nutty file system.''

''Wowee.'' She tipped her face to his. ''You know, I have the feeling I could find a more pleasant job along Main Street.''

He tapped her nose. ''You could. But then you wouldn't get to spend the day close to me.''

''O-oh, you're one clever healer.'' Amanda glanced at the first name on her list. ''Geringer. He a patient of yours or Jack's?''

''Jack's.'' Brett watched her move to Jack's bank of files. ''Care to go out for lunch today, just the two of us?''

Amanda opened a drawer and thumbed through the file tabs. ''Sounds wonderful. But Beatrice is dropping by the clinic. We're going to work a little on the book.''

"But you were working on it last night, as well."

"Only for a few hours."

"Primetime hours. I normally count on Beatrice to be in the living room to vote on HBO's Sunday lineup along with Della and me. Frank and Colonel Geoff voted for the History Channel and won a tie breaker on the flip of a coin." Brett rolled his eyes. "How many times can a man enjoy black-and-white footage of soldiers invading Normandy?"

"I'm afraid I'm having too much fun with Beatrice to stop the creative flow now." The excuse popped out of Amanda's mouth before she could censor it. Upon reflection, she discovered she really meant it.

"All right. But with my luck you two will write a bestseller, go on tour, sell the movie rights and never be seen again."

She touched the collar of his lab coat. "Would that trouble you, Doc?"

"Well, sure. There is my HBO to consider."

Amanda gasped in mock outrage. "Aren't you in a joking mood today?"

Brett pulled her out of view to give her a quick kiss. "We're no joke and I know it," he said softly.

"Don't worry, I'll do my best to outwit, outlast and outplay Charlotte on the front lines."

"My sweet, brave girl." He kissed her again. Longer.

Charlotte eventually stuck her head in the door. "How cutesy. I'll just tell Professor Geringer all about it as he sits out front nursing his kidney stones, waiting to check in. *Without his file at the ready.*"

Meekly, Amanda held out the man's file. Charlotte marched over, grabbed it and left.

Beatrice hustled into the clinic about noon with a tote slung over her shoulder, wearing a floral shirtwaist, one of her dozen or so similar library frocks. The staff was just assembling in the waiting room to take off for lunch. To Amanda's chagrin, Rochelle Owens was the designated person to stay behind to handle any emergencies. She'd forgotten Rochelle and Beatrice were cousins, until Beatrice asked after Rochelle's parents, currently vacationing in Hawaii. The pair giggled over Rochelle's report on her mother's embarrassing first hula lesson, at which she'd accidentally wiggled out of her sarong, and her father's snorkeling adventure that turned wild when some fish that might have been a tuna started chasing him.

Amanda didn't want to see a softer side to the rock-hearted Rochelle. But plainly it existed, and it made the nurse seem more fragile, more human.

Rochelle did turn back to stone minutes later, however, as she addressed her. "Are you going to work at the Lego table where you and Brett like to lunch? Or in back? I want to be near the phones and intend to eat behind Charlotte's counter."

Amanda could see that Beatrice was rather upset by Rochelle's rudeness, so she made light of it. "Those darn building blocks are too big a distraction. We'll go back in the break room. C'mon, Beatrice."

As the pair seated themselves at a small wooden table, Beatrice opened her tote bag and unloaded a notebook bearing the working title *City Girl* on the cover, pens, and a sack containing two buns wrapped in cellophane and some homemade cookies.

Hungry, Amanda eagerly took a sandwich. "Looks like Della's work."

"She was so happy to hear about our brainstorming lunch, she whipped this up." Beatrice's voice dropped to a whisper. "I think part of it is that she knows you probably can't afford a lunch. And today Doc wouldn't have the chance to buy you one."

Amanda hated this part of the charade, pretending she couldn't afford things. But for the time being she was trapped in her own lies.

Beatrice opened their fat, dog-eared notebook. "So,

Mandy, have you given any thought to my character of Stanley, our city girl's sexy but quite inappropriate neighbor?"

"Yes. I suggest we call him Stefan however. The name Stanley is sort of old-fashioned."

"But he is fiftyish, with gray at the temples. I've always found the name of Stanley quite appealing. Went to the prom with a Stanley."

Amanda smiled patiently, thinking how short a time Beatrice would last in the brash newsroom of her father's *Manhattan Monitor* with her delicate sensibilities. "The thief is international, though, right? The name Stefan suggests a continental background—more so than Stanley, anyway."

Beatrice bit the tip of her pen, flipping to the character's information page. "Perhaps you're right. My Stanley did end up working in the hardware store. As fond as I still am of him, he doesn't conjure up the necessary exotic image." She studiously changed his name in her notes.

"If Stefan were closer to thirty, he could still easily manage second-story work."

"Yes!" Beatrice beamed, changing his age, crossing out his gray temples. "That might be a nice subplot. Stefan is still stealing jewels. Maybe he wants to steal our heroine's jewels."

"Or steal a jewel for her. One that her family lost during a bankruptcy."

"Brilliant!" Beatrice flipped back to her outline and scribbled.

Amanda realized with the jewel reference she was stealing a bit from Ivy's predicament with her jeweler family, but it was her understanding that novelists stole bits and pieces from real life all the time.

"So have you considered my offer, Mandy? We hash out all the details. Then I do the first draft and you polish it up afterward?"

"Sounds fair to me."

"Have you given our heroine's name further thought? We can't call her City Girl forever."

"Have you come up with any possible names?"

"I think Laverne sounds rather exotic. It's Rochelle's mother's name."

Amanda frowned at the mention of the nurse. "Rochelle already has problems with me. I'd rather not upset her by using that name. How about the name Leah instead? It's timeless."

"Very well." Beatrice scribbled it down. "I'm sorry to see that you and Rochelle aren't hitting it off."

"I didn't do anything to her!" Amanda said a bit more sharply than she meant to.

"I'm sure you didn't. It's Brett's feelings for you that makes her angry."

Amanda rose from her chair and went to the small refrigerator to get them drinks. Finding only diet cola, she brought back two bottles. "This all right?"

"Yes, thanks." Beatrice busily opened her bottle. "Everyone knows that Brett isn't a match for my cousin. In a way, I'm glad you came along. Maybe now she'll stop dreaming about him and look for someone else."

"Are you looking for yourself?" Amanda couldn't help asking.

"Me? I'm fifty-one and chubby. No, Rochelle is much younger and quite lovely when she smiles. She still has what it takes to make a dream relationship come true."

"You are beautiful, too, Beatrice."

Beatrice blushed. "I can see you are suited to writing fiction." But plainly, she was flattered.

"Brett!" Jack Graham barged into his partner's office Wednesday afternoon, his face lit up like a boy's. "It's all happening! Right now!"

Seated behind his desk, Brett gazed up from the medical journal he was studying. "We on fire?"

"Yes, man, we are." Jack beckoned for Brett to follow and shot off.

Brett followed Jack through the maze of corridors to the front office space, where Rochelle and Kaitlyn were crouched in the nook used to prepare patient preliminaries. Taking their fingers pressed to their lips as a signal for silence, he eased into the nook along with Jack. From their vantage point they had a clear view of the counter, as well as Charlotte and Mandy.

"I don't know about this. I just don't know."

"Charlotte, this is your own doing."

Charlotte whisked a nylon scarf over her head only to whisk it off again. "This is the first time I've ever gone to the beauty parlor on a weekday during business hours."

"I didn't tell you to make the appointment."

"Nor would I have listened to you if you had. It was my pesky grandson, hinting that my dye job of Tuesday night hasn't given my hair its usual golden tones." Charlotte pulled a hand mirror out of her purse. "Come back to the rest room with me and help me get a better look at the back of my head."

Mandy stood her ground. "I refuse to go through that again. You keep saying the mirror's too small and the lighting inferior."

"You've been no help at all. None of you office girls have."

"If you can't leave your post to fix the problem, so be it."

Charlotte thrust a finger at her. "Aha! So you admit I have a hair problem!"

"It might be a little uneven in places. I'm no judge."

"Appears so, with that funny hair color you use." Mandy gasped, but Charlotte didn't even seem to notice. "I should be gone a total of two hours at most. Still, that is a long time for a rookie to be on her own.'' She surveyed her protégé with a click of her tongue.

"Hey, I know,'' Mandy said brightly. "I simply won't do a thing while you're gone. I won't check in patients or answer the phone. I'll save it all for you. Until you return with the right color hair.''

Charlotte flashed her a deadly smile. "If you weren't the doc's squeeze, I'd be sorely tempted to drop you to the mat right here and now.''

Mandy smiled. "Then you'd be late for your appointment, because I'd put up a heck of a struggle.''

"All right then. Must admit you don't seem to have a case of nerves or anything. You should do nicely.'' Charlotte took her purse off the counter. "Just don't let the power go to your head.'' With a huff, she was out the door.

Brett wasn't surprised when the staff in the nook began to exchange quiet high-fives and soft cheers.

"We did it!''

"Charlotte actually left someone else at the helm.''

Jack nudged Brett with an elbow. "Mandy played her perfectly.''

"Let's hope she can deliver now,'' Rochelle said.

The foursome remained motionless as Jacob Sanderson walked in the door. Brett so badly wanted Mandy to make him proud. His pulse jumped as she sat at Charlotte's chair, reached for his file, on the top of the afternoon stack, and noted that Jacob was in for an allergy shot. They all sighed in relief as she efficiently buzzed the lab to let them know they had a patient waiting and directed Jacob to take a seat.

Four minutes or so passed and the telephone rang. They watched as she picked it up.

"Fairlane Clinic. Yes, Mrs. Bloom is still here. All right, I'll tell her.'' She deposited the receiver back on its cradle and peered into the waiting area where a few patients sat reading magazines. "Mrs. Bloom, that was the pharmacy,''

she called out in a very Charlotte-like bellow. "Your oint-
ment for that armpit rash is ready for pickup!"

With sagging mouths the foursome watched Mrs. Bloom
launch herself out of her chair and over to the desk. "Of
all the nerve! That sort of grandstand play was uncalled
for, Miss Smythe."

"But I—"

"Now everyone will figure out that I sprayed shoe de-
odorizer on myself in the dark by mistake!" With that she
stormed out.

Before Brett could think, react properly, his colleagues
were nearly rolling out of the nook with laughter. He could
only follow them to the counter. And watch a startled
Mandy take her hits.

Rochelle was the first to speak between gulps of laughter.
"Good grief, Mandy!" was all she could say before her
funny bone was struck again.

With hands on hips, Mandy scanned them all. "What is
the matter with that patient? With all of you?"

Jack cleared his throat. "Mandy, you are following in
Charlotte's footsteps a little closer than we expected. A
little too close."

"There is certain protocol that should be followed,"
Kaitlyn attempted to explain. "That Charlotte has always
ignored."

Brett saw his own doom coming the moment Mandy's
innocent eyes locked with his. He tried hard, ever so hard,
to keep a straight face. But in the end he couldn't. He began
to crack up, too. Laughter bubbled forth from his gut until
it ached.

"What am I doing wrong?" she shouted.

Attempting to control his mirth by biting his tongue,
Brett took her back to his private office to tell her.

"Of course I know it's silly—stupid, even—to shout out
personal business." She paced in agitation.

"Have you ever been in a clinic where it happens?"

"Well, no."

"I told you from the start that confidentiality is paramount."

"You said nothing leaves this clinic. Even Charlotte supported that statement. I just thought this hollering practice was some sort of small-town peculiarity." She glared at him. "The least you could have done was to have been totally honest about why you were trying to replace her. If I'd have known it was because her manners are offensive, I wouldn't have repeated her mistakes."

"That was our quandary. You deserved to have the whole picture, but given it we feared you'd chicken out."

She nodded knowingly. "Like the rookies before me. I heard from her own lips how she managed to scare off each and every one."

"With her awful reputation, you can see why we tapped you, an innocent newcomer. Without Charlotte's reputation to intimidate you, we figured you'd have a better chance of matching wits with her. And it worked!" Brett grinned.

"All this trickery. I wonder if any of it is fair to Charlotte. She is brassy, but she is also sincere."

"Don't ever worry about that old gal. Our larger goal has been to gradually ease someone into her receptionist seat, then in time, offer her an entirely different job with the billing department, make it out as a promotion, which in fact it will be. As it is, we farm out that work and would prefer to have it done in-house. It would be a better deal for her, with shorter hours, more pay and no contact with patients concerning their medical conditions. With you ready and capable to take over, we expect she will soon cooperate."

"It would have been nice to survive the test with my dignity."

"Oh, c'mon, we were just having some fun. And Mrs. Bloom's ailment wasn't highly personal or sensitive. I intend to have a word with her—"

"I'll do that myself. And set the blame where it be-longs!"

"You should try and laugh at yourself more, Mandy."

She tilted her chin. "I'm not accustomed to doing that."

"Give it a try anyway."

"Give me a break. You couldn't even chuckle over Ivy allowing Tess to paint you in polka-dot boxers."

Brett bit his lip. "I guess we both could learn to relax a bit more."

There was a knock on the door and Kaitlyn popped in. "Sorry to interrupt, but it's time for my break. We need you out front again, Mandy. If you don't mind."

She looked at Kaitlyn's sweet merry face, then Brett's, and gave in to her own laughter.

Kaitlyn held the door open for her. "Don't let Rochelle bother you. I think she's going to ride this for all it's worth."

Brett wasn't surprised when Mandy swiveled on her heel to level a significant stare at him. "Doc Hanson has been planning to have a word with her about a lot of things. Haven't you, Doc?"

"Yes." He spoke up to confirm, "Let her know I'd like to see her when she's free."

Brett would have rather had a cavity filled than have The Talk with Rochelle. But judging by her recent treatment of Mandy, it had become necessary to set her straight on their relationship.

The lanky redhead was quite cheery as she entered his office without knocking. "Wasn't that scene priceless?"

"Sit down a minute, Rochelle." Brett was leaning against the front of his desk, as he had been during his meeting with Mandy, but he was standing taller now.

Rochelle took a chair and leaned forward alertly. "What is it? Something the matter?"

"Well…" He sighed deeply.

"I think I get it. Mandy's singled me out for laughing at her."

Brett rubbed his chin. "Mandy herself has decided to see the humor in what happened. And I must say, Jack and I are mostly to blame for not telling her in the first place what parts of Charlotte's training might be wrong."

"But any fool—"

"Cut it short right there." His curt tone startled her into silence. "When you berate Mandy, you are not only berating a fellow employee, but also somebody I care deeply about."

She extended her lower lip in a pout. "Oh, I see."

"I wouldn't be making this so personal between us if you weren't suddenly pushing so hard."

"Why, I never!"

"Rochelle, you've always been pretty territorial where I'm concerned."

"We're good friends!"

"Yes. Friends but never lovers. There is a very distinct line there that I've always known I'd never cross. As friendly as I've been, I really believe I've never given you false encouragement."

She grew more agitated. "Have I ever complained? Demanded more?"

"Not to my face. But the way you confronted Mandy at the Blue Parrot leaves me no choice but to set the record straight once and for all."

His comment clearly startled her. "I did overreact that night. I shouldn't have said the things I said."

"If nothing else, it's given me a clearer view of your intentions. As it stood, I always hoped you were reasonably satisfied with our friendship. But now that I've found happiness with Mandy, we need clearer lines drawn between us. I can't have you punishing Mandy because I care about her. Beyond the obvious pain you'd be causing her, it would destroy our office dynamics, which you must admit, have been wonderful.''

"I do realize I've put much of myself into what you call office dynamics. But I love my job. The challenges of medicine mean the world to me—as they do to you.'' She hung her head. "Guess I've always thought we'd make a remarkable team.''

"On paper, it does look good,'' he admitted gently. "I respect and like you. But somehow, the chemistry never hit me.''

"If only you'd given us some effort, a fair chance!''

Annoyed with her stubbornness, his voice grew firmer. "The initial spark between a man and a woman should never need work. That comes later,'' he added with a smile, "when the relationship deepens and kids are crying and pots are boiling over.''

She rose, looking wistful. "I never thought you'd confront me this way, given your quiet nature. Thought I'd be able to sort of *nurse* my dream indefinitely.''

Brett pushed away from his desk. "It'll be good for all of us, especially you, to move on.'' His hand instinctively moved to touch her arm. In midair, however, he thought the better of it and raked his hair instead. She noticed and frowned.

"If that's all, we have patients.''

"Yes, that's all. Except that I hope you'll give some of the other non-medical guys in town a chance. Men are crazy about redheads you know.''

"Ha. You aren't.'' With an eye roll, she departed.

About an hour later, his internal line rang. It was Mandy.

"I would have called sooner, but it's been crazy out here. How did it go with Rochelle?''

"Nobody died.''

"She going to lay off me?''

"If she's smart,'' he replied.

"What exactly did you say?''

"Basically, that there never could be anything romantic between us."

"She accept it?" Mandy asked.

"I think so. Have plans for tonight?"

"Dinner at the boarding house."

"Great."

"Oh, boy."

"What?"

"Charlotte is back. With copper-colored hair."

Chapter Fourteen

"You should have seen Charlotte when she burst back into the office with her hair rinsed the color of a shiny new penny." Amanda was telling the boarders her afternoon's tale as they sat 'round the kitchen table enjoying dinner by Frank. The head of the boarding house liked cooking simple fare and treated boarders to a casserole once every week. Tonight's was a chicken-and-rice concoction bathed in mushroom soup.

"What on earth happened?" Frank asked.

"A new girl mixed the wrong balance of ingredients for the color and slathered it on Charlotte before one of the senior hairdressers had a chance to check her measurements. Then Charlotte sat under the dryer on low heat to let the color really sink in. It was way too late to do anything by the time one of the seniors got to her. And due to the strength of the chemicals, she's been advised to wait a few days before getting yet a third coloring."

"She almost pierced the sound barrier when she got a look in the mirror," Colonel Geoff reported.

Della slanted him a sly smile. "You at Lindy's Salon, Colonel?"

"Rubbish. I was at the barber shop next door and the walls are like paper. She was ranting on about their slipshod policies concerning interns, how *her* intern was most competent indeed."

"That would be our Mandy she was bragging about," Beatrice murmured.

"Maybe, but I sure did have my own struggles today." With good humor she told them of her blunder in revealing personal information Charlotte-style.

They chuckled with her rather than at her, which made the confession fun and therapeutic. Not only did the group understand her ignorance about small-town ways, but they went on to voice some of their most embarrassing moments. Amanda had never had a conversation like it. Her high-society friends lived with their guards up 'round the clock and were especially cutting when someone made a mistake.

"We were at Lindy's Salon, weren't we, Mandy?" Tess piped up. "The day we got all pretty."

Amanda cast Brett a quick, self-conscious glance. "Yes."

"It's okay, Daddy's not mad anymore."

"I know. I apologized to him for taking you there without permission and he has forgiven me." Amanda gazed 'round the table and thought the boarders looked extremely uncomfortable all of a sudden.

Della recovered first. "It's all in the past."

Just the same, Amanda sensed there was still a lingering tension over it and suddenly felt a bit left out of the circle. What was the problem with Tess going to the salon? She suspected they all knew full well. But how important could it be?

"It's not good for daddies to get mad too much," Tess went on. "Does your daddy get mad too much, Mandy?"

Already off balance, she reeled from the query. "He has been known to be a bit gruff."

"I wonder about him."

"Why?"

Tess shrugged with an impish smile.

"What's important to you, Tess, is that you appreciate having such a nice dad and home." Dabbing her mouth with her napkin, Amanda stood. "If we are going to see a movie tonight, Brett, I better get ready."

Brett glanced at his watch. "Yes, scoot. I don't like to miss the coming attractions."

"Thanks for a great meal." Amanda exited the dining room, only to pause in the hallway as Brett addressed his daughter. "I smell a rat, my child."

"Oh, Daddy, you always say that to me."

"And you know what it means."

"Yes. That I've been a busy girl."

"Have you been putting that nose where it doesn't belong?"

Tess giggled. "You know my nose is stuck to my face all the time."

"Have you been poking into Mandy's business?"

"Like how?"

"I don't know. Like, listening in on her phone calls, maybe?"

"Oh, no, Daddy. I never did that. Kindergarten makes my brain full."

A round of chuckles followed and Brett fell silent. Amanda took the stairs quietly, forcing herself to relax. Tess could know nothing of Lowell Pierpont, apart from what she herself had hinted at in her occasional self-pitying spouting. But the kid's sixth sense about feelings was formidable. She'd make a great spy for the government.

THURSDAY at the clinic was madness right from the start. First news of the day was that a toddler at the day-care center had fallen off a play set. Amanda took the call and relayed it to Jack, who grabbed Kaitlyn and rushed over to assess damage. Kaitlyn called to report that the child had broken his collarbone, and as the mother was a young, single parent, Jack was going to accompany them to Portland by ambulance. This meant that at least all the morning patients would be transferred to Brett.

Charlotte was late for the first time anyone on staff could

remember. She barreled through the entrance a full half an hour off, actually relieved to see her protégé stationed behind the counter for a change. "Sorry about the delay. But for the life of me I don't know how to style copper hair to its best advantage."

It was the first time in Amanda's life that she had regarded another woman's tizzy over her appearance as selfish and shallow.

By lunchtime things had grown even more hectic. When Beatrice appeared for their writing session, Amanda felt compelled to bow out with harried excuses. "I only wish I could take a break," she finished feebly.

Beatrice absorbed the chaotic scene and shifted on her oxfords, as if anxious to leave. "I understand. I'll just head back to the library."

"Why don't I meet you over there after office hours?" Amanda suggested on inspiration. "I'm sure someone will drop me off. We'll really dig in to those first two chapters, polish them up with facts and details."

Beatrice brightened. "All right. It'll give us a chance to do some research right there on site. I'll pull the sources I think we'll need."

Brett was waiting for a salesman from a pharmaceutical company, so it was Rochelle who dropped Amanda off at the library after work. The short ride was silent and uncomfortable.

Amanda didn't speak until the town's grand old library loomed ahead. "You going to brake at the curb or will I have to jump out and roll?"

The redhead slanted her a sour look. "That would be rather amusing."

"Do you know what displaced aggression is, Rochelle?"

"I know exactly why I'm mad—and at whom! Did you have to tell Brett about our chat in the Blue Parrot? Or don't women keep things to themselves where you come from?"

Amanda stared right back at her. "Blame your own bad

timing. You chewed me out in a public rest room, then almost mowed him down on the way out. He demanded answers and I wasn't going to lie to protect you."

"I did handle that stupidly, I suppose."

"Wouldn't it be better to move on, look for someone else?"

Rochelle jerked to a stop in front of the library's red stone building. "Yes, dammit! But I had my heart set on him!"

Amanda opened the car door. "I'm really sorry about that. But I didn't steal him away from you."

"I know it. I *know*. Now get out of my car. I drove you over here only for Beatrice's sake. I don't have to like it." Amanda didn't even have the passenger door securely shut before the nurse sped off.

Beatrice was waiting for her near the door at the top of the stone steps. "C'mon," she coaxed. "The place is supposed to be closed and I don't want anyone to try and barge in with us."

Amanda hustled inside but not without a teasing grin. "Is that a problem, people trying to barge into a library?"

Beatrice remained serious. "Certainly."

"I mean, it's not like a movie theater or a hot nightclub."

"You'd be surprised. Many people find great joy among the stacks." Beatrice led her down a wide marble hallway, their heels echoing in the stillness. "It's a place for solitude or socialization. A place to lose yourself in the written dreams of far-off places." She hung a left at the first doorway. Inside was a circulation desk, a bank of computers, shelves loaded with books and magazines.

Some very impressive round tables were arranged in the center of it all. One table in particular held Beatrice's belongings, laptop and notebooks, and an array of magazines and books. "I thought we could stick exclusively to research. My supervisor wouldn't want us to linger too long after closing."

Amanda smiled at Beatrice's devotion to duty. What supervisor would begrudge this dedicated head librarian time in the library? She made no protest, however. This was Beatrice's turf. She could make the rules. As Beatrice picked up where she'd obviously left off in her research, Amanda spotted a coffee urn and accessories on a counter and volunteered to get them refreshments. She filled an insulated pitcher with some steaming brew and set it on a tray with two mugs, napkins and some artificial cream.

The project took its first tedious turn as Beatrice began to pore over books about London, where their story was to open with Stefan the thief, and magazines about high fashion for ideas on how to dress their city-girl heroine. Amanda knew much about both subjects and would have preferred to just plug the information into the story as Beatrice demanded it. But she didn't want to appear too knowledgeable, as that might lead to probing questions about her identity. So she passed the time thumbing through magazines, sipping cups of coffee.

It was by sheer accident about an hour later that Amanda spotted herself in a copy of *Cosmopolitan*. The setting was Paris, the event a fashion show. The media sometimes liked to highlight nonprofessional model celebrities like herself on the runway—especially when the celebrities were in full-stunt mode, seeking attention. This particular show had gotten out of hand, since the fashion on display was provocative. A sudden burst of rain had drenched the proceedings, plastering the models' flimsy outfits to their skin. They'd taken the party further by jumping into a public fountain and having to be dragged out by security guards.

Confronted with evidence of her old antics, lying flat on the table in full color, Amanda was jolted with lightning force. She didn't want to be that person in the picture ever again. For the first time she truly cared how people might react to her behavior. Especially Brett.

With that in mind, she did the first thing that came to mind. With a flick of her wrist she tipped her freshly filled coffee cup over. Liquid poured quickly over the layout, adequately marring the revealing two-page spread.

With cries of dismay, both women threw paper napkins over the magazine to stop an overflow to the other paper on the table.

"I am so sorry." Amanda rose to her feet beside Beatrice. "I'm afraid this magazine is ruined."

"Yes. What happened?"

"I went sort of catatonic there, I guess. You know what a nightmare the clinic was today." In an effort to remain calm, she closed the soggy magazine and took it in her hands. "Is there someplace I can get rid of this?"

Beatrice handled the situation with serene professionalism. "Take it to that basket right over by the desk. The night crew will pick it up tonight."

Amanda tried to conceal her relief. "Please let me pay for it."

"That won't be necessary. We make allowances for such things. You aren't the first person to damage a magazine. It's the recipe and coupon clippers I try to police. And it isn't worth much. We—" Beatrice halted herself, patting Amanda's arm. "Don't give it a second thought. It won't be missed."

Amanda swiftly tossed it away. "I think we've done enough for today, don't you?"

"Yes," Beatrice agreed.

Amanda glanced at her watch and blurted out a lie of convenience. She felt as though her other life was pressing in on her, and she had to get away from Beatrice. "Ivy invited me over tonight. If you don't mind, I'll just wander over to her apartment, unless you need help with your materials."

"Run along." Beatrice waved a plump hand in dismissal. "I'll just make my way home like I always do."

Heart hammering, Amanda headed for the library's front doors. That had been close. Really close.

IVY, DRESSED IN GRUNGY yellow sweats, ushered Amanda inside her apartment. "This is a surprise."

"I know. I needed a place to decompress. And you are my only real friend in town."

"That isn't true."

"I know it. But you're the only one who knows my history, in whom I can confide."

Ivy warily watched her friend over the tops of some funky red-rimmed eyeglasses. "What happened?"

"It's nothing to worry about, I promise." Amanda moved deeper into the apartment, trying not to look at the wall where Brett had made love to her less than a week ago. It broke her concentration. And gave her distracting ideas.

Ivy tore off her glasses and tossed them on the maple table holding a sheaf of papers, childlike attempts at the alphabet. "Okay, give."

Amanda swiveled on her heel. "I was at the library with Beatrice and came across a fashion show photo spread in *Cosmo* of me and Madison Fuller."

"Oh, damn."

"Don't worry, I handled it fine. Must say, it really jarred me, though. Made me realize I no longer feel like that exhibitionist!"

"How did you handle it?"

"Spilled coffee over the pages."

"Smooth, real smooth."

"It gave me the excuse to toss the mag in the trash. And Beatrice didn't seem the least bit suspicious."

"I can't go on until I know what you and Beatrice were doing with *Cosmo* in the first place."

"Research for our city-girl heroine, of course!"

Ivy laughed approvingly. "I bet she's never even paged through one before. If nothing else, you are doing that woman a world of good, expanding her horizons to impossible lengths."

"Let's face it, Ivy, we could expand her horizons a whole lot more if we liked."

"Oh, yeah, maybe with memories. But as things stand, we are a couple of heiresses down on our fortunes, naughty girls in reform with nary an extra cent."

"I still have money."

Ivy lifted a brow. "Some hundred-dollar bills. That's nothing if the Pierpont coffers are suddenly closed to you."

Amanda winced. "Funny you should mention that. I mean, with my big decision and all."

"Okay, exactly what are you getting at?"

"I've decided that I am going to risk the old comforts for some new principles."

Ivy eyed her with some uncertainty. "You mean, you're finally going to make an honest woman of yourself?"

"Yes. This close call with Beatrice made me realize that the truth could come out sooner rather than later. And I want to be the one to tell Brett before he finds out another way. Oh, Ivy, staring down at that magazine's silly layout, my first thought was, 'What will Brett think? Would it shame him?'" Ivy's brows rose in surprise but Amanda didn't let that slow her down. "I've finally got it. The love thing. I know what love is. I know I love him—and that little scamp Tess—with all my heart. I want to stay on here and make a life with them."

"A broken engagement, a steam-fried father, a legacy in the balance." Ivy exhaled hard. "That kind of triple-header confession could be enough to send Doc Handsome to the clinic's sedative cabinet."

"I'm going to be sensitive, pick the proper time to lay out the pieces."

"In broad daylight, with clothes on and a stiff drink at the ready," Ivy advised her.

"Certainly. I wouldn't try and tell him while we're making love. I believe in tasking."

"I can just imagine how your father will react to this turnabout. He'll swoop in here without need of a jet. But I wonder how Trevor Sinclair will take the news that even big daddy can't cram that engagement ring back on your finger? How Trevor will handle Brett?''

''What can he possibly say after I caught him telling his parents he was marrying me for the love of Lowell?''

''I don't know. But it's gonna be a circus you could sell tickets to.''

BRETT WAS RELAXING on the front porch swing that evening when he caught a glimpse of Beatrice scooting up the sidewalk with her signature book bag slung over her shoulder. As she wheeled onto the Scherers' cracked concrete walk, he gave her his full attention. It never ceased to amaze him that despite her plump form and advance toward middle age, she was amazingly swift and balanced on her feet. Another thing that caught his eye was the fact that Mandy wasn't along.

''How is the writing project going?'' he asked by way of greeting.

''Fine. I suppose.''

''Rochelle did drop Mandy off at the library, didn't she?''

''Yes.'' Beatrice pressed her rosy lips together.

''What's the matter, Bea?'' he asked gently.

''May I sit beside you?''

Brett straightened and patted the bench swing. ''Of course.''

Beatrice slid down beside him, set her tote between her knees and dug around, producing a magazine. ''The library has two copies of each and every periodical, you know.''

Brett was mildly amused. ''Can't say I knew that.''

''Neither did Mandy. I didn't tell her.'' She laid a copy of *Cosmopolitan* on her lap and nervously flicked through its pages.

Brett grew more alert. ''What are you doing?''

Finally she found what she was looking for. A two-page spread entitled ''Debs Take Dip In Parisian Landmark.''

"It's her, you know. The debutante on the left. With her—everything showing."

Brett gripped the magazine in his hands and took a good hard look at it and the caption. "Irrepressible heiresses Amanda Pierpont and Madison Fuller, in town for fashion show, cool off sizzling selves." He went on to read the companion article about the pair's trip to Europe, their friendships with celebrities. "How did you ever make this connection?" he asked.

"This magazine is only a spare copy. Mandy was reading the one set out for the public when suddenly she got clumsy and spilled coffee all over these exact pages. I didn't think much of it at first. She insisted on tossing the soggy copy away and that seemed reasonable, like the accident itself. After she left I replayed the event in my mind and decided to have a look at our spare. For your sake!"

"I appreciate it. But aren't you jumping to a big conclusion, linking our Mandy to this deb?"

"Mandy is a nickname for Amanda. And Smythe is a rather common alias. Not a very inventive cover-up, but probably good enough to avoid immediate discovery."

Brett thought for a minute, back to motel owner Fritz Geller's claim that Mandy had arrived in town as a blonde. "Have you any sort of markers in you bag, like Tess uses on her artwork?"

Beatrice produced a marker set. "I've been color coding my notes."

Brett plucked a brown one from the package and added a trace of brown to Amanda Pierpont's hair. The similarity was now unmistakable.

"It is her. I told you!"

Her urgency puzzled him. "Well, I knew she was hiding something. And suspected she came from money." His mouth went crooked with desire. "She sure isn't hiding anything here though is she?"

"Men! All you think about is...is exposure!"

His eyes continued to twinkle. "Not all the time. And

it's kind of fun, really, to unmask her this way. She's admitted she's here to think through some confusion. Maybe she's changed her name to evade the press. You know how I hate the press myself."

Beatrice sighed impatiently. "Have you ever heard of the Pierponts, Doc?"

"No." Suspicion finally took root in his mind. "You?"

"As a librarian, I see all sorts of published material about the famous. Amanda Pierpont is the daughter of Lowell Pierpont, publisher of the *Manhattan Monitor*."

"The newspaper?"

"Amanda herself," she confided rather reluctantly, "*is* the press. Their celebrity gossip columnist, I'm afraid."

The news slammed Brett hard. He was off the swing like a shot, pacing and muttering unmentionables under his breath.

Beatrice's lower lip quivered. "I am so sorry to cause this upset. But it's you who has made all of us suspicious of strangers, more inquisitive than the norm. A family unto ourselves."

Brett brusquely waved off her explanations and apologies. "It's time to gather our little family for a meeting."

It took only a matter of minutes to assemble all the residents of the boarding house—except Mandy—in the living room. Colonel Geoff and Frank were already there playing cards at the small table facing the bay window. Della came in from the backyard, where she had been weeding one of her small colorful flower gardens. As luck would have it, Tess was safely out of commission, resting peacefully in bed, still recovering from a rigorous game of kickball at kindergarten. She wasn't accustomed to fast physical games with other children and tackling them with her usual gusto had left her drained.

With a stiff back and gritted teeth, Brett gave the residents an idea of what had gone on at the library. Beatrice rounded the room with the open magazine, modestly allowing the men only a brief glimpse of the temptingly drenched Amanda Pierpont.

"Are we sure it's her?" Della asked.

Brett grimaced. "There's little doubt. Especially now that I've noted the small birthmark on the Pierpont woman's shoulder in the photo."

Frank smirked at the implication, only to meet Brett's glare. "Got to admit she is a sweet thing, Doc, no matter who she is."

"But we understand your dilemma," Colonel Geoff put in. "Being a news hound, she might very well unmask Tess."

"Might? She is a glorified tattletale who must be here with that express purpose in mind!" His roar set them all back in their chairs, but he didn't care. The whole life he'd built for himself during the past two years was about to melt under a fresh glare of spotlight.

Della remained calm. "Where is she now?"

"Ivy's house," Beatrice supplied. "After the magazine incident, she couldn't wait to escape me."

"Has she any idea that you might have been on to her?"

"No, Della. Quite sincerely, I didn't have any serious misgivings until after she left."

"To think I fell for her every word!" Brett raved, waving his arms.

"This seems like such an unfair trial," Della protested. "The defendant not present, everything so slanted against her. Wouldn't it be more fair to give her the benefit of the doubt until you are sure of all the facts?"

Brett frowned. "What more do you need?"

"I don't know. It's just that I've lived long enough to know things can be complicated." She thrust a finger at Brett. "Find out her side of the story before you hang her out to dry."

Brett sank into an armchair. "I wouldn't know where to begin. I think I'm in love with her."

"Ah, a very good beginning."

"Oh, sure. I tell her I love her and ask her if she is here to betray me."

Della frowned. "That approach does need a little work."

"Is it possible that she is as devious as she seems?" He rubbed his face. "I certainly was a poor judge of character when I got involved with Tess's mother. Sarita was exciting like Mandy, then turned calculating and selfish once we married. I'm so easily fooled. No wonder I'm still single."

Della remained stubborn. "I still say clear the air fast."

"No. I'm too overwhelmed right now to handle it properly. Everything I thought I knew about her is up in the air."

"It would be sad to lose the affection of such a tempting lady," Colonel Geoff observed. "But whatever else, you don't want a telltale story to come out of this."

Brett nodded. "I've gone to a lot of trouble to make a quiet, ordinary life for Tess. I don't want it spoiled with any fanfare."

"That is the bottom line." Frank agreed. He turned to Della. "But how to handle a headstrong woman does take some finesse. Bulldozing her might make matters worse, fast. A little slow and careful manipulation is in order."

"Oh, Frank," Della scoffed, "how do you know?"

"I am married to a headstrong woman. Brett would be wise to tread carefully."

"But time may be of the essence," Beatrice said, squarely in Della's corner. "If this whole trip is a lie, she won't be staying on as she claimed. She'll collect her story and be off."

"So at the very least you must seduce her into staying," Della suggested, "so we can redirect her purpose—change her mind!"

Brett nodded. "You have the right idea. I need to pull myself together. Pretend nothing is wrong. Hope that I stumble on the best persuasive method to stop her."

"Whenever you make your move, I hope you first appeal to her heart."

"On the condition that she has one."

Brett couldn't resist waiting on the porch swing for Amanda Pierpont's return. He didn't have a plan. He just wanted to assess her with his newfound knowledge. She didn't look a bit different strolling up the walk in the moonlight, swinging her purse like a carefree teenager.

If anything, she looked happier, sexier. In fact she had a most appealing glow about her. As if she was carrying the most marvelous secret and longed to shout it to the world.

The sight of him concealed in the shadows of the darkened house had her skipping over the last few cracked concrete squares and up the porch steps. Before he could stop her she was hopping into his lap, causing the swing to sweep back on its old heavy chains.

"Somebody oiled the chains," she murmured in his ear.

"Me."

"When?"

"Before." *Hours ago, when I still looked forward to cozy little rides of the future. Before I knew about you.*

She kissed him crushingly, eagerly. "Well, I have a little surprise for you, too."

"Oh?" He braced himself. Here it comes.

"What we have…" She trailed off in unusual shyness. "I don't know how to tell you how much it means to me."

"That's the surprise?"

"Give me a chance!"

"Mandy—"

She pressed a finger to his lips. "Don't trip me up or I'll lose my nerve. Brett, I know now that I am in love with you. It's no small thing, either. Normally, I wouldn't have slowed down long enough to appreciate a responsible and caring man like you. It had to be divine intervention that helped knock me off that bike, forced me to take a look at things.

He tried to smile back at her, but couldn't. This confession was nice, but not thorough enough. "Is there anything else I should know?"

She continued to smile, apparently too wrapped up in her own joy to see his distress. "That's all for now." With another kiss, she was off.

By Friday afternoon, a mere twenty-four hours after her hair color fiasco, Charlotte had decided her copper penny shade was a triumph after all. A street cleaner had whistled to her from his machine and she had a date with the UPS man. She wasted no time putting the salon on notice that they would have to figure out exactly how their new girl made the coloring mistake in the first place, so they could keep it on file for future tints.

"Mandy, dear," she said silkily, breezing in the door from lunch.

Dear? Amanda, stationed behind the check-in counter, looked up from the appointment book in front of her with some suspicion. "What is it?"

"Are you busy tomorrow?"

"Saturday? I don't know. Met Ivy last week for a walk and some ice cream. Thought maybe we could do that again."

"Well, you noticed Teddy earlier on, didn't you?"

"You mean, Theodore? The skinny, bald delivery guy?"

Charlotte's eyes narrowed. "The thin, dignified UPS gentleman."

"You weren't so complimentary of old Theodore last week when he didn't come promptly to pick up that specimen for the Portland lab."

"Tut, tut, that wasn't his fault."

"It was last week. You called him an inept boob behind his back."

Charlotte's voice hardened. "Just the same, we just had a sandwich and he has asked me to the pops concert tomorrow in Fairlane Park. I do hope to accept."

"You have my blessing." With what she hoped was a

glorious smile, Amanda took some files off the counter and headed for the file room.

Charlotte was right on her heels. "It's my new hair, you see. Somehow, it makes me more desirable to the opposite sex. It seems the exotic color gives me a goddess quality."

Amanda yanked open a file drawer. "Theodore say that?"

"No, the street cleaner said that. But no matter. I would like you to do me a favor. I generally go along with Doc Hanson to the grade school at September's end when he immunizes the children. That would be tomorrow."

"Why don't they come here?"

"It's more orderly and fast over there with the teachers keeping their students in line. And no one has to pay for an office call."

"I see. So what's the favor?"

"I was wondering if you could go to the school in my place."

Amanda thought back quite squeamishly on some of the shots and invasive procedures she had seen during her brief stint here. "What exactly will I be expected to do?"

Charlotte pressed her lips together in obvious impatience. "Isn't it obvious? You'd be there to keep score. We have records of all the children, what shots they need, when they need them. The odd kid is allergic and that's noted, too."

"To keep an accurate record, I will probably have to watch the proceedings." Amanda cringed. "The idea of all those cries and screams."

"So put a tongue depressor between your teeth to control your cries and screams."

"Very amusing. You know I mean the kids."

"Doc Hanson is bound to appreciate your help. If I have to go I'll be all grumpy. Naturally he likes a cheery face along, for the sake of the children." Charlotte laid a heavy hand on her shoulder. "Can I count on you?"

"Sure, I guess."

Amanda used her break time to track down Brett in his

office and tell him the good news about their immunization date. He barely looked up from the open file on his desk.

"Is that really part of your job description, Mandy?"

She was startled by his lukewarm response. "Well, no. But I do like the kids and Charlotte promised to be a bear if you make her tag along."

He smiled faintly then. "It's fine. See you then."

"See me then?" She moved to his desk and reached over it to touch his cheek. If she didn't know better, she'd have believed he winced at the contact. "Don't we still have a lot of living to do today?"

"Not together I'm afraid." Brett's voice was unusually formal. "Tess and Hailey want to see the new Disney movie at the Plaza tonight, so I'm booked with that."

"Can't I go along?"

"It's only the dads this time. Sorry."

He didn't look particularly sorry. Just like he hadn't looked particularly sorry this morning when he pled a disorganized start and asked Frank to drop her here at the clinic. These events linked suddenly and made her wonder. "Is something the matter, Brett?"

"Not really."

His response was level, but his suntanned features were noticeably strained. She studied him, her mind backtracking over yesterday. Naturally, she landed on their talk on the porch swing. "Are you annoyed about my confession last night?

"No."

"Yes, you are."

"Okay! It wasn't what I expected from you just then."

"Sorry if I seemed to be pushing too hard."

"It's not— This isn't a good place to discuss it." He launched out of his chair and paced by the window overlooking the rear parking lot.

She followed, putting a hand on his lab coat sleeve. "How about we discuss it after the movie? I haven't seen a Disney film in years."

"No, Mandy. I want a little space to get my head together."

"All because I love you?"

"Truly loving someone means opening up about everything. And we haven't reached that level yet."

"I can't change how I feel."

"We'll just have to see if your feelings are right—for us."

His rebuke tore at her heart. "Maybe too many women in this town have told you they love you," she said hotly. "Maybe that's when you push them away!"

"Don't be silly. I haven't gotten really close to anyone else since I arrived. What we've had together has been wild, special."

"But not special enough."

"Stop pushing me."

"Fine. Take some time. Get your head together."

"Now you sound sarcastic."

"Just disappointed." *And wondering if I'll ever find real love.* Eyes downcast, she left.

Chapter Fifteen

By the end of Amanda's Friday shift at the clinic, she'd heard enough talk to realize that Saturday's pops concert was important not only to Charlotte, but to the entire town. Apparently a famous orchestra was making its yearly trek from Boston to perform.

When she entered the boarding house kitchen around nine the next morning she discovered the residents already in the spirit of the day. Della and Beatrice were busily assembling chicken salad at the counter. Colonel Geoff was washing out a large cooler at the sink. Frank was measuring ingredients for lemonade into a giant jug at the table. For her part, Tess was kneeling on a chair at the table near Frank, running her finger through his spills of sugar, pushing the fine sweet crystals into her mouth.

Colonel Geoff was the first to spot her. "Ah, good morning, Mandy."

She was disappointed not to find Brett in the mix but kept her voice bright. "Looks like there's a lot of concert spirit right here under our roof."

A cheery Della turned, waving a big plastic spoon. "Means more to us than most. Colonel Geoff's brother is the conductor who makes it all happen."

"So, has anyone seen Brett?"

Della was surprised by the query. "Thought you knew. He took off for the clinic."

"Without me? He said things would start at the school about ten."

"He hasn't abandoned you," Della assured her. "He merely wants to keep the immunization process timely. The concert starts at noon and the parents of all those children will want to be free 'round then to head for the park."

Frank smiled at her. "Asked if one of us could drop you by the school around ten. I'll be happy to do that."

"Oh. Thank you very much."

"In the meantime, we can use some help with this salad," Della interposed. "Frank chopped celery last night and the pieces are the size of radishes."

Her husband bridled. "They're not that big, Del."

Della moved to the fridge and fished out the sack of evidence. "We'll give Mandy a chance to eat something, then put her to work."

Tess held up a gooey finger. "You want some sugar, Mandy?"

The child's innocent offer brought unexpected laughter bubbling up her throat. "I think I'll have some orange juice instead."

Ruffling Tess's glossy black hair, Amanda allowed herself to join in the gaiety.

The school was located a half block from the church, within easy walking distance of the boarding house. Just the same, Frank ignored her offer to walk. Realizing he was determined, Amanda hopped into the station wagon with him.

By the time he pulled up along the boulevard fronting the old brick building, cars were packed into the modest parking lot. Brett's red Corvette was visible near the entrance.

Amanda put her hand on the passenger door handle. "Thanks a lot, Frank. Hope I didn't put you out too much."

He looked surprised. "Don't even mention it. We do things for one another without a second thought. You know that. You're a part of it now."

Amanda was deeply touched by his ease and familiarity. She brushed his hand on the steering wheel. "I've gotten a lot more than I've given. Never before have I felt so accepted."

Her husky response made Frank fidget behind the wheel. "And never before have you ever chopped celery!"

"I suppose that seems strange to all of you."

"Makes us a little curious."

"Hope I didn't do it wrong."

"Guess there's no wrong way of doing it," he said diplomatically, "just different ways. You made it a whole lot harder on yourself using that steak knife with the serrated edge."

"Oh. I'll remember that for next time." With a shrug she swung open the door and eased onto the boulevard.

"People handle their feelings in different ways, too," he hastened to add. "The Doc for instance..."

Amanda arched a delicate brow. "Yes, Frank?"

"He's like me. I mean, we have sincere feelings but sometimes have a problem expressing them."

Shoving the door closed, Amanda leaned in through the open window. "Is this why you were so anxious to drive me over here?" she asked gently. "To tell me that?"

"Sort of." He traced a finger around the steering wheel. "Things have been a little tense between the two of you. And, well, you seemed so genuinely sad this morning that he took off alone. I'd hate to see any trouble between you get out of hand."

Amanda caught his gaze and held it tight with her own. "Is there some trouble that Brett should be talking over with me, Frank?"

"That isn't for me to say."

"I've asked him if anything is wrong."

"It's gonna take some patience. He's been hurt you see, by the wife who died. It makes him slow to trust. And excuse me for saying so, but you move along at such a breakneck pace. Since the moment you arrived in fact, ramming the motel bicycle into that car. And all for a look at him." He smiled wistfully. "In your favor, that had to be a real ego booster, even for a high-class doc."

"I want you to know, Frank, I have my sights clearly aimed on Doc. I care for him in a way that's all new and wonderful to me. I wouldn't want to ever lose that feeling."

He took this news with pleasure. "And I just want you to know that Della and I have a lot of faith in you. Believe that you'd never hurt Doc on purpose. Not ever."

"Of course I wouldn't!"

"Then it's all right. Everything will be all right." With a final salute, Frank rolled away from the curb.

Amanda turned Frank's conversation over in her mind a couple of times as she took the school's steps, only to have all rational thought leave her head as she entered the cool, musty building. There were forty children at the very least, lined up by age along the hallway with a side order of adults. As she walked the length of the corridor toward the room bearing a Nurse's Office sign, she decided there wasn't one happy face in the bunch. Under the circumstances, she understood.

Brett was stationed in the office along with a stocky, middle-aged man with a pretty awful comb-over, dressed in a gray suit. In full professional mode, Brett was assured and pleasant. "Ah, Mandy. I want you to meet Mr. Duncan, the school principal."

Mr. Duncan shook her extended hand then beat a hasty retreat.

Brett's smile faded slightly. He gestured to the setup that was not unlike one of the clinic's own exam rooms with exam table, worktable, desk and chairs. On the table was

Brett's medical bag along with a giant case of syringes and medicine. On the desk was a tall stack of file folders.

"The kids are lined up in alphabetical order according to grade," Brett explained. "Open up the file, call the name and show me their immunization record sheet. Then have the parent sign on the line at the bottom of the page."

So the production line began. Read, sign, swab, jab.

After thirty minutes Brett called for a small break, taking Amanda down the hallway to the cafeteria. Dropping coins in a soda machine, he bought her some Mountain Dew.

She tried to turn away. "No, thanks."

He pressed the cold can into her hand. "Look, you need a pick-me-up. You're white as a sheet."

New hope sparked inside her. "Glad you care."

"I care mostly for the kids. Your trepidation is bound to be affecting them."

"Sorry. Watching those needles piercing those poor little arms is especially gruesome."

"There, you're doing it again!" He pointed at her. "That flare of nostrils, that crunch of eyes. The moan is the worst part though."

"Hey, don't forget, I'm here as a favor." She took a swig of soda to busy her shaky hands. The drink was surprisingly fruity and good.

He sighed, looking slightly penitent. "Point taken. No one else jumped up to volunteer their help today. The pops concert is too big an event for people to miss."

"So why do this on concert day?"

"It isn't supposed to be concert day. The orchestra usually comes the Saturday after Labor Day. But they had a scheduling conflict and changed dates. As for the immunizations, they've always been done the last Saturday in September and it was decided it would be too confusing to tamper with the date. So here we are." He gave the sort of shrug that made him look tough and sweet all at once. Charmed, Amanda gave him a quick hug.

"Okay," he said gruffly, "let's get back in there and finish."

The stroke of noon passed and while the line of students hadn't evaporated, it was fairly small. Several minutes later, as Brett lectured an eighth-grade girl about biting her nails raw, his beeper went off. He glanced down to read the message on the small box clipped to his belt and waved the relieved girl on her way.

Reaching for the telephone on the desk, he punched in a number. "Hello, Kiley. More cramps? How far apart?"

Amanda watched Brett's face as he spoke to the young pregnant mother who'd had more false alarms this month than the fire station. Suddenly his expression changed from strained tolerance to near panic.

"Oh! Where's— I see. Okay. Just lie still. We're coming." He hung up the phone and snagged Amanda's arm. She had the sinking feeling his use of the plural pronoun included her. "Help me pack up my medical bag." Then he thrust a finger at the gangly freckle-faced kid next in line. "Go down to the office, Jerry, and get Mr. Duncan. Run!"

"But we aren't supposed to run in the halls. Duncey Duncan will kill me."

His mother cuffed his shoulder. "Hurry up. We'll protect you." The mother then turned to Brett. "Kiley in labor, Doc?"

"Yes, Jen." He swiftly stowed things into his bag.

"Poor kid, barely nineteen."

"So, Jen, care to do me a tremendous favor?"

"Name it."

"Get over to the park and round up Rochelle. Tell her I need her help pronto."

The principal showed up to disperse the line. Jen took off with her son to locate Rochelle. And Brett took Amanda by the arm and led her to his Corvette.

Brett shot out County 6 past the Blue Parrot, to a small development of nondescript gray duplexes.

"What's happening here, exactly?" she asked.

He glanced at her sharply. "Didn't I say?"

"You never say enough about anything," she retorted, folding her arms across her chest. "I mean, why do you think she's really in labor this time versus the other times? Her due date isn't for nearly a week."

"For starters, her mucus plug dropped out a week ago, which is one signal the birth is imminent." He glanced over, and from his expression Amanda knew she was cringing. "You asked."

"I know. Go on."

"Kiley's contractions are about four minutes apart. Or so she thinks. Her husband's gone fishing for the day so she's all alone."

"She must be scared."

"Considering she's barely old enough to vote, I'd say petrified."

"So this could be another false alarm."

Brett's profile hardened. "Could be. But don't count on it."

Her voice shook a little. "Oh, but I am going to count on it."

He took his eyes off the road to flash her a bolstering smile. "Take it easy. I'll walk in there and simply determine whether her labor is genuine, if she needs to go to the county hospital. We'll either take that ride in Rochelle's car or an ambulance."

"And you need me for..."

"Backup."

"I am not a nurse."

"You're all I have, though. A very important aide. So please, show the confidence of one!"

"I only wish I was more prepared."

"Just stay alert and follow my orders. Rochelle will be hot on our heels I'm sure."

"Have you ever thought of buying yourself a more comfortable car to transport patients in?"

"No. This Vette is my only vice."

"You wish."

Moments later Brett took a sharp turn into the Tyson driveway and leaped out of the car with his medical bag. Amanda scurried after him.

They burst inside the duplex only to hear soft cries coming from the upper level. Brett took the stairs two at a time to find Kiley, dressed in an old terry robe, stretched out on the kitchen floor lying in a pool of her own broken water.

Amanda was well acquainted with nineteen-year-old, pregnant Kiley through her office post. Still she was dumbstruck by her current condition, belly swollen so far out of proportion, twisted in a pose that stripped away her dignity. "It's really happening, isn't it?"

"Yes!" Brett knelt down beside his patient and grasped her trembling hand.

"Want me to call 9-1-1?"

"Yes."

"Where's the phone?"

Brett fumbled for the cordless one on the floor beside Kiley and handed it up to her. "Take this in the other room. The street is Filborn. The house number is 2276. Unit one."

Amanda quickly made the call and returned to the kitchen. "They're coming."

"Good. Now go into the bathroom and bring back big clean towels and a cold, damp washcloth."

When Amanda returned, he instructed her to spread the towels underneath Kiley as he gently lifted her off the floor. Then he swiftly got organized, snapped on surgical gloves and snatched a flashlight from his medical bag. He dropped to the floor, pushed Kiley's knees up and opened her thighs to check her cervix. Glancing up at Amanda, he shook his head. "They won't be in time."

Amanda and Kiley released twin cries of dismay.

"I want my mom. Please!"

Amanda half crouched by Kiley's head, deciding that with her yellow hair and face plastered in sweat, she was too young to vote after all. "Where is Mom? The pops concert?"

"She hates that music." Kiley puffed the words out. "Went to Portland."

Brett patted Kiley's knee. "You should have called me sooner. You didn't need to go this far alone."

"I called so much. For nothing. You had to be...sick."

Brett tsked in gentle reprimand. "Sick of you? How ridiculous. I've been waiting for this day for a long time."

The sweetness of his assurance made Amanda's heart melt.

His tone grew more professional as he laid out the facts. "Your cervix is eight centimeters. And contractions..." He glanced at his watch as Kiley braced in agony. "Are now a minute apart, lasting for...about forty-five seconds," he reported behind her howl of pain.

Amanda watched the proceedings, at a complete and utter loss.

Rising from his knees, he pulled Amanda near an ancient gold refrigerator. "Listen carefully. I need you to hold her hand through her contractions, dab her face with the cloth. I'll begin to lead her through her breathing and I want you to try and catch on, take over the job."

She tried to keep her face neutral, even though her heart was pounding with stark fear. "Okay."

"And try not to look so damn scared."

"Okay."

The next twenty minutes seemed like hundreds to Amanda. Brett kept her busy seeing to Kiley's comfort, demanding things from his medical bag. He took Kiley's pulse, checked her heart and checked for fetal tones.

"Doc, you said I'd get something for pain," the girl huffed.

"Sorry, Kiley, I don't have anything to give you. But you took the natural childbirth classes. We just have to go through the motions."

Amanda watched Brett coach Kiley through her contractions. She managed to catch on and with some confidence took over the prompts. Through it all, Brett exerted his trademark professional calm. But Amanda knew him well enough to read stress in his expression. Under these primitive circumstances, with the contractions growing in intensity, he had to be overly concerned about both mother and baby.

"Kiley, your cervix is completely dilated and effaced," he finally announced. "Remember, we talked about this at the office just last week."

Kiley's eyes strayed up to the hovering Amanda, who was holding her hand tight. "We both remember how that goes, Doc," Amanda lied.

"You need to push the baby through the birth canal."

Kiley grimaced. "It hurts so much."

Amanda nodded down at the girl's tear-stained face, struggling to keep her composure. "It can't be harder than the time you won that canoe race, can it? Remember how you told me that everyone was giving up but you kept on going? Kept on pushing that oar into the water? Then it was over. All over."

Brett met Amanda's eye. "She needs to push when I say. The baby is big. So she needs to push hard. But only when I say."

Upon Brett's curt direction, Amanda encouraged Kiley to push, screwing up her own face, making grunting sounds for the first time in her life. If her old friends could only see her now, she thought fleetingly. To her own surprise, she realized she wouldn't care what they'd think—about this or anything else ever again.

"Stop!" Brett checked his patient's progress. "I can see the baby's head. Now get ready, Kiley. When I say push once more, go for it. This should be the last time. Push… Big push now!" he shouted. "Okay, stop. It's coming."

Suddenly, Brett was staring down at a long, chunky newborn in his hands. "A girl," he announced huskily. "Have you ever got your work cut out for you."

Brett set about clearing the baby's airway, examining her.

"She look healthy?" Kiley asked, lifting her head.

"She looks perfect." Brett winked at his patient then addressed his assistant. "Look in my bag for some clamps."

Amanda scooted over to the medical bag and riffled through it. "What do they look like?"

"If nothing looks like a clamp, I don't have any." He looked around the kitchen. "We need something to tie around the umbilical cord. Mandy. Get on your knees."

Amanda reeled back. "What for?"

"To take the shoelaces out of my shoes. Come on. Quickly now."

Feeling utterly foolish, Amanda obeyed.

Brett set the baby on her mother's belly and took the laces. He tied each lace a short distance apart near the navel. "Now, get the scissors from my bag. And a pair of gloves." When Amanda returned with the items, he told her to put on the gloves.

"W-why?"

"To clip the cord." His steady gaze held challenge and unmistakable admiration. "It's an honor."

"Yes, Mandy," Kiley coaxed weakly. "You do it."

Amanda put on the gloves and looked down at the transparent cord with a purplish tinge. She was about to slice through real human tissue. But it was an honor and she couldn't refuse. Taking a deep breath, she laid the scissors into it and snipped.

"There! Another girl cut loose to make men crazy." Beaming, Brett gently wrapped the baby in a towel and handed her to Amanda. Her vision misted as the full impact of what they'd done—what she'd done—hit home.

The paramedics arrived shortly thereafter as Brett was pushing on Kiley's abdomen to deliver the placenta. He allowed the trio to move in to take over mother and child. He stripped off his gloves and tossed them in the trash. Amanda did the same, then fell into his arms.

He pulled back and looked at her, wonder in his eyes. "You were nothing short of amazing."

"You don't have to sound so amazed by it."

"Can you blame me? Just this morning you paled at the sight of a needle."

"Now that it's over I wouldn't have missed it for the world." She grinned up at him dazedly. "Suddenly I have a much better understanding of how you must feel every day."

He chuckled. "I don't feel this high over my work all that often. Bringing life into this world is a unique pleasure and a privilege. The most satisfying part of my job."

She began to laugh and cry all at once. "Guess I don't know how I feel right now."

"Try proud."

Rochelle arrived moments later as the paramedics were easing the weary mother and baby onto a stretcher.

Catching a dirty look from Brett, the nurse chose to keep Amanda between them. Before Brett had a chance to speak, Kiley came rolling by. "You coming with me, Doc?"

He gave her a quick, encouraging smile. "Naturally."

"In the ambulance?"

"Naturally!" He touched her damp temple then stood back so the paramedics could ease the stretcher down the short bank of stairs to the foyer. At which point he turned to his tardy nurse in fury. "What happened to you?"

Rochelle swallowed hard. "I'm sorry. I misunderstood, thought you wanted me at the school for the shots."

"Why the hell would I want that? What did Jen tell you?"

"She told me Kiley contacted you—as she had so many times before with Dr. Stanley Hickock. I knew she was alone this weekend. Figured she just had some abdomen pains again and panicked. Thought you'd go calm her down and come back to the school. You gotta admit, Brett, her due date isn't for a few days and first-time mothers are often late."

Brett hesitated, then begrudgingly stabbed a finger at Amanda. "Scared witless of a simple immunization, she took your place here today, Rochelle. And under the circumstances, did a damn fine job." With that he skimmed down the short staircase and out the door.

Rochelle stood her ground with her nemesis. "Okay, let me have it."

"Maybe later. Right now, I gotta sit down." Amanda sank onto the nearby sofa.

"I suppose you're pretty pleased with yourself."

"Do I look like it?"

Rochelle studied her. "No, guess you don't. You look like the survivor of a disaster."

Amanda sniffed. "That is exactly what I am. How can you possibly tend people this way all the time?"

"Because I love it." With a more confident smile, Rochelle paced a bit, then sank beside her on the sofa. "Suppose, considering how decent you're being, I do owe you some thanks. If Brett had been left alone to cope, he might very well have been angry enough to fire me right on the spot."

"He just might have," Amanda agreed. "I'm beginning to believe he can be quite ruthless—without explanation."

Rochelle reached over and patted her knee. "All things considered, I feel I owe you a favor in return."

"Yeah?" Rochelle's chummy tone made Amanda sit up and take notice.

"He knows."

"Excuse me?"

"Brett knows exactly who you are. Amanda Pierpont, wild and wacky newspaper heiress."

"Oh, really."

"Really. And he doesn't like it one bit."

As AMANDA AND ROCHELLE went about tidying up Kiley's kitchen, the nurse explained how Beatrice had checked out the magazine layout Amanda had spilled coffee on, realized Mandy was the Pierpont heiress and quickly reported her findings to Brett, who promptly went ballistic.

Rochelle dropped some towels directly into a garbage bag. "Beatrice told me all this cousin-to-cousin, confided that there had even been an emergency family meeting about it at the boarding house."

Amanda was on her hands and knees scrubbing a linoleum floor for the first time in her life, awkwardly slopping water 'round the floor with a sponge. "She never let on she was the least bit suspicious. I wonder why she made such a big deal about it?"

"I wondered, also, and asked. That was when she realized she'd let too much slip. Even though she and I are the ones who are truly related, it's the bunch over at the Scherer place that holds her deepest loyalties."

Amanda pondered the situation. "This certainly explains why Frank was acting funny today. Whatever's going on, he and Della have decided I deserve the benefit of the doubt."

"Why are you here at all, Mandy? If you don't mind my asking."

"Problems with my own family," she admitted. "My

own family of one, Lowell Pierpont. He made me so angry, I needed to escape, think. To do that I had to go under-cover.''

''So you had a fight with your father and chose this burg to hide out in.'' She was stupefied. ''It's tough to believe you couldn't solve your problems back in luxury. Tough to believe you have any real problems!''

Amanda felt equal measures of patience and pity. ''I am grateful that I came to realize I needed distance from it all to gain a clear perspective.'' Realizing she was still doubt-ful, she added, ''People can be enormously happy with the simple things. You're surrounded by living proof.''

Chapter Sixteen

Brett didn't return to the boarding house until well after dinner. He discovered Mandy seated at the kitchen table paging through a magazine when he entered through the back door.

"Hey, there, Doc Handsome."

"Hello." He had come in the back in the hope of avoiding interaction with their in-house heiress. All he wanted was a hot shower and to lie on his bed and listen to public radio. His eyes darted 'round the room looking for backup. There was none. "Where is everyone?"

In a rather cheery voice Amanda gave him a rundown. "Frank followed Colonel Geoff out the door 'round seven to join him on one of his constitutionals. Rochelle insisted Beatrice join her at the Blue Parrot Lounge tonight for some fun. Della took Tess and her friend Hailey back to the park."

"To watch the fireworks I suppose. It's a tradition on concert day."

"Hungry?"

"No, I picked up a hamburger at the hospital."

"So how is Kiley doing?"

"Very well. Thanks again for all your help."

"You're welcome."

He set his medical bag on the counter and gestured to

her magazine. "I suppose you're still trying to decompress."

"Nothing like a good magazine to soothe. At least most of the time. Some people get far too excited about them."

The implication was clear. She knew that he knew her secret. He was too strung out for this now. If only he'd come in the front door. Seeing no way around it, he walked to the cupboard to get a glass. "The revealing magazines tend to make people excited. Especially those magazines that are too revealing for a girl's own good."

"What bothered you most, Brett? My scanty outfit or my roots?"

He smacked the plastic glass down on the counter. "Hard to choose. I don't care for cheesecake shots and I don't care for rich players."

She sighed. "I'm truly sorry I didn't tell you sooner. Didn't mean for you to find out about me that way."

"So you intended to tell me sometime?"

"Of course. I've been working through some personal issues first."

"Personal is right! But it's my business we're talking about here."

"I don't follow."

He smiled thinly. "Amanda Pierpont, celebrity reporter. Tracking down a poor, innocent child!"

She stared blankly. "What the hell do you mean?"

"Oh, c'mon. What other reason brought you here if not to report on Tessa Frye, onetime movie star of *Wizards and Wands*?"

"What has that kid got to do with us?" Then sudden realization fell upon her. "Your Tess is Tessa Frye?"

Brett's blue eyes darkened in fury. "Don't play innocent with me after all you've done."

"Like what?"

"You slink into town under false colors, crash into a car to get my sympathy. Then go on to wage a campaign to worm information out of all of us. When nothing shakes loose, you get my child a haircut reminiscent of her Hollywood days, hoping that might force the issue.'' He nodded self-righteously. ''It all became so clear when I realized who you were.''

Amanda was stunned by his conclusions. ''I vaguely remember the *Wizards* plotline about a child sorceress in a family of good witches. And I recall a news item on the toddler actress losing her mother in a car accident. But I didn't pay much attention at the time. I never actually saw the movie and children were never my beat.''

''But her face was everywhere. There were dolls, games, puzzles.''

''None of which interest me.''

''Well, I have every right to be cautious about reporters. They made my life miserable for a while. When my wife Sarita was killed in the single car crash in the Hollywood Hills, rumors suggested that she was seeing a huge star, got dumped and went crazy. Even the police couldn't verify what really happened. The vultures kept digging, though, even hounding Tess. The story finally cooled down, but the invasion left me furious. I refused a movie sequel offer for Tess and skipped town to start over away from the spotlight.''

The very idea that Brett would believe she—or any responsible reporter—would be petty enough to chase down Tess was unreal. Anger swelled inside her. ''Oh, Brett!'' She hopped to her feet and charged him, poking at his chest. ''What you're suggesting would be disgraceful, reckless reporting.''

Her offensive move plainly took him off guard. ''Well, how am I supposed to know what Amanda Pierpont would do? You have a history of reckless behavior.''

''But reckless only to myself. I have made mistakes. But I've been trying so hard to mend my ways, to be a more thoughtful human being.'' She clapped her hands to her face. ''All this time I thought we were getting somewhere, that I'd finally discovered what real love means. Why, I even told you I loved you! No wonder you didn't reply in turn. You don't even *trust* me!''

''I do want to trust you.'' He grabbed her by the shoulders and gave her a shake. ''Give me a chance, a convincing excuse for your purpose here.''

She gazed up into his desperate eyes, realizing he was frazzled and dirt-tired by the day's events. But his heartless conclusions about her were unforgivable. ''No, you figured out your own nasty reasons. You don't deserve the real ones.''

''How can we go on if you won't tell me?''

''Go on?'' she cried in disbelief. ''You accuse me of wanting to betray Tess and expect us to just *go on?* More and more I'm beginning to wonder, is there any sign of intelligent male life anywhere on earth? Even one?'' She dashed out with a sob and a slam of the screen door.

Brett charged into the living room only to discover Della and Tess hovering near the doorway. He froze in shock. Della was repentant. ''We came back early. Hailey had a stomach upset. I tried to take Tess upstairs, but we heard voices and you know how stubborn she is.''

Tess glared at him. ''Is Mandy mad at me?''

He knew his surprise showed. ''No, no, honey.''

''I heard my name yelled out.''

''We were talking about you in a nice way, Tess.''

''Did you make her cry, Daddy?''

He shoved his hands into his pants' pockets. ''Well…not on purpose.''

The child stomped her tennis shoe. ''You made her cry. I heard. Now she won't be my friend.'' With an anguished expression much like her friend's, Tess dashed out of the room and up the stairs.

TESS DECIDED TO WAIT UP for Mandy. It was the kind of secret wait-up deal that nobody else would like, making herself at home in Mandy's bedroom after midnight.

Tess had just put on some very pretty pink lipstick from Mandy's cosmetic bag when that funny phone began to hum. Standing on tiptoe, Tess found it in its regular top drawer hiding place.

"Hello?"

"Finally! I've been calling and calling. Where've you been?"

"Kindergarten."

"Put my daughter on the line right now."

"She isn't here. I'm baby-sitting her room."

"Wherever you live, it must be pretty late. You should be asleep."

"But I have to wait for Mandy. I have to tell her I love her."

"You sound funny. What's wrong?"

"Everything."

"What has she done? My daughter. What has she done?"

"Daddy made her cry."

"Oh?"

"She cried and ran away."

"I see. The same old tricks."

"Don't you care that your little girl is crying?"

"Well—"

"Daddies are s'posed to dry those tears."

"I suppose they are. Wonder where she's gone this time."

"She probably went to Ivy's house."

"So you've decided to tell me a name for a change."

"Oh, I can tell you Ivy's name. Just not my name. See?"

"Yes, dear. What's Ivy's last name?"

"Waterman. In school I have to call her Miss Waterman. No, Ivy."

"Hmm. I haven't heard that name in quite a while. Should be able to track her down. Good night, dear."

"Good night."

Tess returned the phone to the drawer and stifled a yawn. Crawling onto the center of the bed, she fell asleep.

Sometime later Tess sensed someone in the room. She fluttered to life. "Mandy?"

"No, honey, it's Daddy."

She rubbed fists in her eyes. "You come to dry my tears?"

He sat on the edge of the bed. "What are you doing here?"

"Waiting for Mandy to come home."

"This is no place for you. It's one in the morning."

"She needs me! And she has a mean daddy, you know."

Her dad frowned. "More to the point, how do *you* know?"

"He calls all the time on her little buzzy-bee phone."

"And *you* speak to him?"

"You never asked me if I talk on her phone, only if I listen to her talk."

"Oh, Tess."

"I think Mandy runned away from home. And Lowell wants her back."

"So that's it." Her dad shook his head. "Her trip here is all about the princess herself. And not my princess."

"What did you say, Daddy?"

Brett gathered Tess close. "You are my princess, I said. And I want you to stay away from this room from now on." He stood, cradling Tess in his arms. "So what else do you and Lowell talk about?"

"Don't worry, I wouldn't tell him my name or where we live. Because he is a stranger."

He chuckled. "Good to know you do obey some rules."

"But I told him about Ivy tonight. He really liked that."

Brett carried Tess toward the door, pausing to shut off

the light. "Then I guess all we can do is let nature take its course and see where Mandy lands."

Tess curled her arms around his neck. "I think she should land right on top of you, Daddy."

He laughed. It was a funny laugh. "That would be an event."

AMANDA OPENED Ivy's apartment door early Monday morning to find landlord photographer Oliver Pratt on the other side carrying a tray loaded with breakfast goodies.

"Morning, sweetie." He whisked in uninvited, as he had half a dozen times since Amanda's arrival Saturday night. "Must say, Ivy's pink nightshirt does wonders for the both of us. I just may park in your camp for good one of these days."

"You're just sucking up because you've discovered I'm rich as sin," she retorted, slamming the door shut after him.

"Just as easy to love a rich girl," he crooned. With brisk steps he went about setting out breakfast on Ivy's table. Stifling a yawn he went on. "I'm tired as sin and it's all your fault. Been on the Internet half the night downloading information about the two of you. Gee, you girls know how to have fun. With a capital F."

Ivy appeared then, in a yellow nightshirt similar to the one on loan to Amanda. "I see the fly on the wall is back." She bristled as Oliver flashed her a knowing look. "I'm warning you now, I wouldn't care for my background to hit the streets."

"You're fairly safe. I had to surf some turbulent seas to connect the two of you. People here will be focused on Amanda and her background. Beyond that, you know they're satisfied with local gossip. Who pinched who at the pops concert. Which shop has the cheapest lampshades."

Ivy grew alert. "Which shop does have the cheapest lampshades?"

"Do you really care, Miss Got Rocks?"

"Like Amanda, I am estranged from my wealthy family, and I'm living on my teacher's salary. So don't get any ideas about even raising my rent."

His lips puckered in disappointment. "So this means I won't be choosing between the two of you. It's Amanda Pierpont for certain who will be getting this larger lemon muffin." He moved to the table, picked up a knife and began to slather the giant yellow pastry with what looked like whipped butter.

"I made coffee," Amanda announced, then shuffled barefoot to the kitchen to get it.

The threesome sat at the table to eat. While the girls each nibbled on a single muffin, Oliver quickly gnawed through two, as well as some orange slices.

"So, Amanda, what are your plans?" he asked.

Amanda sipped her coffee. "I haven't decided for sure. Thought I'd lie low here for a few more days, until the news of my identity has time to saturate. There is no doubt that news will leak out beyond the boarding house circle now that I've left there."

"So you aren't going back at all then?"

"Ivy's offered to go back to pack my things." She offered Oliver a dazzling smile. "You did mean it when you said Ivy could have a guest after all?"

The small, effusive man pretended to think. "Only on the condition that you'll be my good friend, too. It'll be so much fun to talk about places like the Bois de Boulogne and the Museum of London with someone who's really been."

"It's a deal. As long as you keep your shutter down— at all times."

Oliver looked grumpy but shook the hand she offered.

The next morning before Ivy left for school, the telephone rang. Ivy reached over to the countertop to snatch up the cordless. She had no sooner said hello than a boom spilled into the room. Rolling her eyes, she handed the phone to Amanda. "It's for you."

"I thought it might be. Hello, Charlotte. What do you want?"

"Ha! Take a guess. I want your sorry butt here at work."

"Haven't you heard the news?"

"That you're some kind of fancy heiress reporter? That you and Doc Hanson had a fight over your secret? Hell's bells, when I look at you, all I see is a green recruit. *My* green recruit."

"I assumed I'd been discharged."

"By whom?"

"Well…"

"The docs are both in-house and have said nothing of the kind."

"Then maybe my resignation is in order."

"But you made a commitment when you signed on with the clinic."

"You've been handling it yourself for years."

"But there's my blood pressure to think about. And I got a new boyfriend. *And* it looks like we're going to have bowling practice afternoons now because somebody's going to town on Viagra. My girl, life changes happen."

"People change their minds about jobs, too."

"Why, I thought you'd be the first one here this morning to brag about delivering that baby. Figured you'd be offering to take patients in for consultation."

"Very funny."

"Gee, I can't stop laughing. Now you do what's right and come to work."

A dial tone buzzed in Amanda's ear. She exhaled nervously. "I guess I'm going to work."

"You are," Ivy agreed heartily. "I don't want that dowager over here pounding down my door. Get dressed and I'll drive you."

Amanda entered the clinic just after nine o'clock, wearing Ivy's beige slacks and a melon-colored knit top. There were a couple of patients in the waiting room and Charlotte was stationed behind the counter. Charlotte's eyes sharpened at the sight of her. Amanda thought she detected a hint of pride. It gave her a dose of courage.

"Good morning, ah…" Her mouth hung open. "Now what do you want to be called?

"Mandy," she decided. "Classmates called me that when I was young and I've come to like it here."

"Well, Mandy, Doc Hanson brought your uniform along with him today. It's in the break room."

Charlotte crooked a finger and proceeded to lead her down a corridor, deeper into the office space. Mandy could have easily navigated the trip herself but realized she would have to be amiable if she hoped to survive her first day as heiress/reporter cum clerk.

The break room door was rarely closed, but it was this morning. Charlotte whisked it open to reveal most of the staff in wait. "Surprise!" they chorused.

Amanda blinked in wonder. "What's going on?"

Charlotte tugged her over to a square table. On it sat a toy medical bag, a baby doll, and a plastic baby bottle labeled Smelling Salts. With ceremony, Charlotte laid the baby doll in Amanda's arms. "On behalf of the entire staff, I'd like to congratulate you on a fine delivery this weekend. It has come to our attention that you held up like a trooper, save for some squeamish squeaks and the occasional grossed-out cringe." She looked 'round. "Where is Doc Hanson? Jack, go get him."

Moments later, Doc Graham brought back his partner. Brett took in the ceremony with a faint smile. "Charlotte's been to the toy store again, I see."

Rochelle broke free from the crowd with a small brown sack, which she placed in Brett's hand. With awkward hands he opened it to reveal a package of shoelaces. With a rumble of laughter he put a hand to his heart. "Gee, kids, just what I need most."

Another round of applause followed.

"Seriously, everyone," Jack said above the din. "I'd like to acknowledge a job well done for quite some weeks. Kiley was jittery during most of her pregnancy. It's in Brett's real favor that he took her each and every call seriously, compassionately."

"Guess he just knows how to handle women," Kaitlyn suggested to the merriment of everyone.

For several minutes the staff fired personal questions at Amanda. She answered them as best she could, stalling only about her plans. The ladies all made it plain that they hoped she would remain here in Fairlane for a while. Amanda shot Brett a glance, which he happened to catch straight-on. Startled at being caught, she turned away. Not that she expected him to say anything in front of the others. His professional dignity was so important to him, and he wouldn't want to risk embarrassment over some retort she might fire off.

"I'd say it's time for work," Brett announced, turning on his heel.

As the others filed out, Charlotte moved to a small cloakroom and brought back Amanda's crisp, white uniform trimmed in pastel green. "Don't dillydally by taking this to the bathroom, puffing up your hair. Just jump into it right here and join me out front." Charlotte marched off, only to pause at the door. "By the way, Pierpont, I personally think you have a lot of guts. As much as me, maybe. I've never said that to another soul in my life." With her nose in the air, she left.

The office was abuzz with activity all day long. The clinic did a brisk walk-in business of patients with bogus aches and concerns. In truth, great numbers of Fairlane citizens just wanted to have a look at or a word with the dishy Amanda Pierpont. A disgruntled Charlotte recorded every visit, determined to charge every person who took up the staff's time.

By 5:00 p.m. the last of them was turned out. Charlotte flipped the appointment book shut. ''Whew! We made a bundle today. Maybe tomorrow we'll put you in a wet T-shirt or something.''

Amanda gasped. ''You are gross.''

Charlotte stood up and stretched. ''Go tell it on the mountain. See who cares.'' Just then the steel entrance door creaked again. ''Well, who the hell is the cat dragging in now?''

Amanda gasped again. ''Dad!''

''Down from the mountain,'' Lowell Pierpont rumbled. ''So just what in blazes are you trying to do to me?''

Chapter Seventeen

"Here we go again," Amanda lamented. "It's all about Lowell Pierpont."

There weren't many staff members left in the clinic, but Charlotte had quickly gathered the stragglers into the small nook used for weight and blood pressure readings. Amanda was tempted to shoo them out the door, but what good would it do? They'd only stand by a window and listen anyway. And she wasn't going to budge from the clinic herself. This was her hub, where she faced real challenges with success.

She was grateful she had stayed when Lowell began to work on her. "Can't we get out of here for a talk?"

"No. So how did you find me?"

"Dropped by Ivy's place. She steered me here."

"I mean, how did you find me in Fairlane?"

"Oh. My new little friend spilled the beans. About a lot of things."

"Who?"

"Some kid."

"My kid, I'm afraid," a deep voice interposed.

Amanda whirled to find Brett standing nearby, looking cool and reserved and in command in his crisp lab coat. "Tess?"

"That's right. She's been camping out in your room a

lot. Answering your phone." Brett shook his head. "Sorry."

She smiled wryly. "It's okay. I know she was only looking for some motherly comfort. I always was, too."

"Well, she's one smart kid," Lowell rumbled. "Actually had the nerve to challenge my fatherly skills. Can you imagine?"

"Dad, you're saying a five-year-old taught you something?"

"I was just as stunned as you are. But sometimes it's the simple messages that mean the most. When she told me that I should care enough to dry my little girl's tears, it got me to thinking. I never did do that. Ever."

Amanda waved at him. "Oh, you aren't a complete washout. You always made sure there was enough hired help to do it."

He flinched. "Are you being sarcastic, Amanda?"

"Yes, Dad."

"It was wrong of you run away like you did."

"I gave you the chance to talk over my concerns but you were just too busy—as always. The story of our life."

His voice was uncharacteristically kind. "Well, if you want to continue that talk, I'm listening now."

"Okay. I came to tell you I know how you set me up with Trevor."

"Who's Trevor?" Brett asked.

Father and daughter glared at him and then at one another.

"I played matchmaker out in the open. You were grateful!"

"Until I found out about your cold, calculating methods. How you dug through the newspaper personnel files for *your* idea of a suitable husband. You found the perfect person for you and struck a deal with him. Marry me and you'd drop the whole company in his lap."

"That's what you think?"

"That's what he told his own parents the night of our engagement party."

"You're engaged?" Brett demanded.

"Yes, she is!"

"No, I'm not!"

They both glared at Brett and then at one another.

"Now, Dad," she said more sternly. "The least you can do is come clean about your actions."

"I intend to." He dipped into his suit jacket pocket for his cell phone and punched in a number. "Get in here. Now."

Amanda's heart jumped. It couldn't be…but it was. Moments later, the door flew open and in walked Trevor Sinclair, her former fiancé, his blond hair sliced in executive style, dressed in a thousand-dollar suit no doubt put on his company allowance.

"Amanda!" Trevor charged for the counter. Brett looked ready to stop him but Lowell did the honors. His arm block to Trevor's midsection nearly took the younger man's breath completely away. In fact, Trevor spoke with an audible huff. "I should be furious with you, running off that way."

"I ran off because you don't love me."

"Of course I love you!"

"Amanda, bring Trevor up to speed."

"I overheard you speaking to your parents after our party. Remember? Your mother was actually crying over our engagement, trying to sell you on some old girlfriend back home."

Trevor whitened. "I had no idea you were there. You should have said something."

"Like what? 'Sorry, Mr. and Mrs. Sinclair, that you think I'm a giddy fool?' And what about your claim that you never loved me the way regular people love each other, the way your own parents love each other?"

"Did you actually say that, Trevor?" Lowell demanded.

"I may have done so," he admitted, staring up at the ceiling.

"Why up until minutes ago, you were raring to carry on with the engagement," Lowell scolded. "Where is the truth here?"

"There are different kinds of love—"

"Dammit, young man!"

"All right, sir. Amanda's got it fairly straight. What she heard me tell my folks was the real deal. I'm a jerk who likes your daughter and loves his job. I could have made her happy, and to tell you the truth, if left in the dark about my feelings, I don't think Amanda would have ever realized a deeper love relationship existed anywhere. With all due respect, you never showed her one and I'm sure her world-class acquaintances haven't, either."

"He is right about that," Amanda conceded. "I'm not the least bit sorry I made a run for it. I had much to learn—still have much to learn—about handling relationships."

Trevor flashed her a dazzling smile. "I did say I was very fond of you, Amanda. And I meant it."

"I believe that much, Trevor, despite Dad's tough-guy matchmaking."

"I didn't pair you up coldheartedly." Lowell glared at Trevor. "Tell her I didn't."

Trevor nodded slowly. "I may have exaggerated Lowell's strategy, just to appease my parents. He didn't actually riffle his files to find a prototype husband. I courted him, suggested in many small ways I would make a fine son-in-law."

Lowell frowned. "You're not looking very gallant here, Trevor, willing to marry a girl you don't truly love, allowing your parents to believe I railroaded you into it."

Trevor pursed his lips. "Seems an unfair judgment, when you, sir, play the manipulation game every day. Encourage employees like me to do the same."

"But to dabble around with my own daughter!"

"But you've never set that limit for anyone to see. Never once have you proclaimed any real interest in your daughter as a person."

Lowell absorbed the blow. "Oh, hell, it's my own fault for immersing myself in work, never opening my heart. I probably did send the wrong signals. But I see it more clearly now. Daddies are supposed to dry their little girl's tears. From now on I intend to do just that!"

"Well said, Mr. Pierpont."

Lowell glanced sharply at Brett. "Who exactly are you?"

"I am the man who really loves your daughter. The man who showed her how it's done."

Amanda still refused to acknowledge him. "As it happens, I have come to discover what real love is. Even if it wasn't returned in a way I deserved, I finally get it. So whatever happens in the future, I will be equipped to make wiser choices."

Lowell's eyes lit up. "So does this mean you're ready to come home? Why, I'll even support your gossip column if you like. Expand it."

"You can't leave," Brett objected.

"Oh, I can," Amanda asserted heartily. "But I won't. As it happens, I like it here in Fairlane. It's my kinda town."

Lowell blustered and reddened. "Nonsense. What kind of column could you possibly write here?"

"As you can see I've taken on a different sort of job entirely."

"Ivy explained it's only been a cover to hide your wealth."

With a grin, Amanda picked up the toy medical bag presented to her that morning. "I'm so good I actually have my own equipment." Then, sobering, she went on. "But even if I do come to find this job intolerable for any reason, I intend to work somewhere else right here."

"But like your old man you're a writer. Ink runs through your veins."

"That need is taken care of, too. I am writing a book on the side with a friend. Which is another reason I can't possibly leave right now."

"If you're doing this to punish me—"

"Of course I'm not!"

Taking no more, Charlotte barreled out of the nook with Rochelle and Jack on her heels. "Hang on right here. Miss Debutante doesn't have the brass tacks to punish people, so don't talk her down. And she isn't going anywhere across the street or across the country because she is my girl now. Walked through hellfire to land the best job in the universe."

"How dare you, woman? More to the point, who are you?"

Amanda laughed. "Dad, this is Charlotte, your match for guts and brains."

Lowell stared intently at the copper-haired woman, nearly fifteen years his senior.

Charlotte held out a palm. "Hold your ground right there, Mr. Pierpont. I know my new hair tint drives the men wild. It was a fluke, a gift from God. You mustn't give in to your desires. We'd destroy each other with our passion."

"Grandma!" Jack exclaimed, acutely embarrassed.

Lowell cleared his throat, obviously rather shaken by the female steamroller. "All right, Amanda. I can see I'm trumped. Believe it or not, I want your happiness as much as my own."

Amanda joyfully scooted around the counter into her father's arms.

"There now." His thumbs wiped away her tears. "Am I doing it right?"

"We'll have to ask Tess. You have to meet her, Dad."

He hesitated. "I have a flight out later today."

"Please come back to the house," Brett said.

Amanda twisted toward Brett. "Hey, I'm still mad at you."

"But you'll get over it. Because people in love do that."

"So now you love me?"

"I started loving you the moment I picked you up off the boulevard," he announced with force. "The condition has proven incurable."

She could think of no convincing retort for that.

Lowell warned a sulky Trevor that there would be some changes in their arrangement and sent him off to the Portland airport to catch their scheduled flight. He in turn accompanied Amanda and Brett to the boarding house. Over turkey roast, the clan regaled him with tales of their Mandy's adventures in town, up to Saturday's home delivery. There was real pride in Lowell's eyes and Amanda had never felt so close to him.

As for Tess, she was thrilled to meet her man-of-the-buzzy-bee-phone and gave him the ultimate compliment, the job of cutting her meat. After dinner, she took charge of Lowell, giving him a tour of the house, coaching him on just what girls expect from their daddies, showing him the sewing room in which he would spend the night.

As midnight approached, Lowell finished the brandy he was sharing with Frank and took his daughter aside by the staircase.

"Going up, Dad?"

He nodded, then hesitated. "Were you like that child?"

"Yes."

"I'm so sorry I missed it all."

"Me, too. Best to put it in the past, to dive into the present."

"The present. Returning home without you."

She touched his shirt collar. "I'm not lost for good. I'll return for visits."

"And bring Brett and Tess?"

"We'll see."

Lowell hugged her close. "If he's the one, don't blow it."

She sighed hard. "Yes, Dad."

"And just for the record."

"Yes, Dad?"

"I had that special kind of love for your mother. It was sweet and wonderful. I'm afraid I died inside when she died, deliberately made work my focus to shut out the pain. I was too stupid to realize that I was supposed to carry on with you, keep the family love going."

"It isn't too late."

"It's very big of you to say that. Good night now." With a pat to her head, he took the stairs.

It wasn't until an hour later when the house was quiet that Brett coaxed Amanda out to the porch swing. He wasted no time winding an arm around her shoulders. "Oh, how I've missed you."

"We were only apart a day."

"More like thirty-six hours. Hmm, to think you were engaged behind my back."

She smacked his chest. "I broke it off before I left."

He took her hand and kissed it. "I only wish you'd leveled with me completely from the beginning."

"I needed time to sort out my feelings. If Dad had come rushing in too soon, who knows what I would have done."

"Gone back to that preppy jerk?"

"Trevor's not so bad. And yes, I may have gone back to him. You see, I did have a fear of being cut off from my legacy, losing my father's—albeit imperfect—affection. My whole life was wrapped up in being a socialite. I didn't know if I could survive without the Pierpont name and money."

"So can you forgive me for my rash assumptions about your purpose in town?"

"Boy, can you bring up my temper." She shook her

head in awe. "But once I calmed down, I put myself in your place, even pretended I was Tess's parent. Then it all became clear. Of course you would be on guard against snoops. One slipup could spoil Tess's privacy. Her whole life."

"I've lived in fear so long I guess I went a little crazy," Brett admitted. "But the scars from my years with Sarita, battling her bid for fame, may never heal."

"How on earth did a stable man like you get involved with her?"

"In short, she changed from the girl I fell for. We were high school sweethearts. Hollywood High. She grew up in a modest home. Her parents were servants to the stars. After all the stunts they'd witnessed from employers, they were thrilled that Sarita had found someone like me, with a calling outside showbiz. And Sarita seemed satisfied to be marrying a doctor who would treat the stars for medical ailments.

"After my residency I settled into a Hollywood clinic, began making respectable money. We were invited to some parties by patients, met famous people. We both enjoyed that, I admit. Tess was born and life was satisfying. Then one day Sarita ran into someone at a party who thought Tess should audition for a movie role. In *Wizards and Wands*. Nothing was ever the same again. Tessa was cast in that movie and it was a huge hit. Bit by bit Sarita was drawn into that Hollywood madness. She got Tess an agent, a manager. Eventually her life shifted to the fast lane with Tess as her ticket. By the time of her accident, I was fed up with the whole Hollywood scene, with treating spoiled people. And Tess was acting up in a way that wasn't acceptable. Longing for normalcy I decided to pull up stakes for good and head for Fairlane to work with my old pal Jack. The only thing I brought along from that old life was my Corvette. It's inconvenient at times, but I love it."

"You've been right to try and protect Tess, Brett, even

from the likes of me. Our relationship was new. I expected too much. I know that now. It was just that you'd given me my first real taste of love. I wanted to speed our relationship at any cost. It just crushed me in the end, to think you'd ever suspect I'd hurt Tess.''

''I realize now that it won't hurt to loosen the strings on Tess a bit. I have been too protective. And I should learn to trust the people I like best a little more. My heart assured me that you could never harm us but my psyche wasn't as swift.'' He tightened his arm around her. ''So, are we all good again?''

''We're all good.''

''I do love you so very much.'' He leaned over her and kissed her tenderly. As his hunger increased, so did his pressure. He would have taken things a step further if he hadn't felt a new kind of pressure on the swing. He broke free to discover it was Tess, a pink cloud in a frilly little nightie.

''Told you, Daddy. Told you she should land on top of you.''

Amanda smothered a laugh. ''Why?''

The pixie insinuated herself between them. '''Cause then you can't get away anymore, Mandy. You like to run away too much.''

''I promise to never run away again.''

With a beautiful smile, Tess patted her knee. Then she turned to Brett. ''Are we getting married pretty soon?''

''I hope so! For me it's just a matter of reserving the church.''

A joyful Amanda squeezed Brett's hand. ''You in a hurry, silly girl?''

''Yes. Then Daddy can buy us a house like Hailey's. And we can wear those undies on our heads.''

''What!'' Brett nearly fell off the swing.

''I have some lacy lingerie that your daughter likes to wear on her head.''

"Like Della does for church."

"Huh?"

Amanda patted his hand. "She thinks the lace looks like a veil. It's a long story."

"I don't think I want to know."

"Right," Amanda agreed. "It's really mommy territory. Like nail polish and buzzy-bee telephones."

"I would like a phone," Tess decided. "Maybe Lowell will get me one. He'll be my grandpa."

Brett set her down on the porch. "That's it. Go back to bed."

"I haven't been to bed yet."

"Then go now. Scoot."

Tess popped back inside the house. Brett took Amanda back in his arms. "Now, where were we?" He began to kiss her again. This time for a good sixty seconds. Beatrice was the next to interrupt them as she moseyed up the walk.

"Oh! Excuse me!"

Brett leaned back again. "You don't look sorry in a convincing way."

Beatrice didn't argue the point. "I find your father very attractive, Mandy. And his life at the newspaper most intriguing. Do you suppose he might find my writing talent intriguing?"

"There's a good chance," Amanda said politely.

"Oh, my, oh, gracious."

Brett lolled his head at Amanda. "Families."

She sighed. "Can't escape 'em."

"Or maybe we can."

Popping to his feet he pulled Amanda along with him. "Bea, will you check on Tess?"

"Of course."

He gave Amanda's hand a tug. "We're going for a drive in my little red Corvette."

Beatrice was taken aback. "Going far?"

Dipping down, he brushed Amanda's lips. "Just far enough."

Coming soon from

HARLEQUIN®

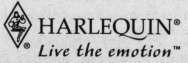

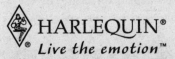

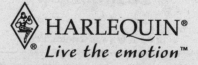

HARLEQUIN®

AMERICAN *Romance*®

proudly presents a captivating new
miniseries by bestselling author

Cathy Gillen Thacker

THE BRIDES OF HOLLY SPRINGS

Weddings are serious business in the picturesque town of
Holly Springs! The sumptuous Wedding Inn—the only place
to go for the splashiest nuptials in this neck of the woods—
is owned and operated by matriarch Helen Hart. This no-
nonsense Steel Magnolia has also single-handedly raised
five studly sons and one feisty daughter, so now all that's
left is whipping up weddings for her beloved offspring….

Don't miss the first four installments:

THE VIRGIN'S SECRET MARRIAGE
December 2003

THE SECRET WEDDING WISH
April 2004

THE SECRET SEDUCTION
June 2004

PLAIN JANE'S SECRET LIFE
August 2004

Available at your favorite retail outlet.

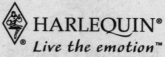

HARLEQUIN®
Live the emotion™

Visit us at www.eHarlequin.com

HARHS